CHERRY DARK

R.L. WILBURN

CASTLE BRIDGE MEDIA
DENVER, COLORADO, USA

CASTLE BRIDGE MEDIA
Denver, Colorado

Cover art by Cover photos by Leontyev Oleg/Shutterstock,
Josh Hild/Unsplash, and Kenny Nguyễn/Unsplash.
These photos have been modified.

This book is a work of fiction. Names, characters, business, events, and incidents are the products of the authors' imaginations. Any resemblance to actual persons, living or dead or actual events is purely coincidental.

CHERRY DARK
© 2024 Rich Wilburn
All rights reserved.

ISBN: 979-8-9895934-4-6

*For my wife Becky, who has brought me back to life
more times and in more ways than I can count...*

One

BALANCE.

It's a simple word. Two syllables. A word so commonplace and ordinary most people don't automatically assign any consequence or significance to it. But in my experience, people attach *immense* importance to it. So much so they spend their entire lives struggling to find it. Career and family. Work and play. Indulgence and abstinence. Joy and pain. Light and dark.

Good and evil.

Yeah, apparently life is all about balance. Who'd have guessed that death is, too?

Not surprisingly – given where I was sitting at that moment – balance seemed even more important to me than usual. It was, in fact, foremost on my mind. Well, that, and the runners at second and third with only one out.

The top of the abandoned Millennium Hotel is one of the best places in St. Louis to watch a Cardinals game. And by 'top', I don't mean through the windows of the old revolving restaurant on the twenty-eighth floor. I mean the *roof*. From there you can look straight down onto the diamond from high above the left-center bleachers. The scoreboard blocked your view of deep center field on a few plays, but you sure couldn't bitch about the ticket prices. The trick up there was to keep that all-important 'balance' I mentioned before and not go sliding down the sloped roof and over the edge, to be immediately followed by a three-hundred-foot plummet straight to the concrete pavement below.

Not that the fall would have killed me – that ship sailed a *long* time ago. But if you manage to miss that little grass courtyard in back and land in the truck-dock area – well, let me tell you, that hurts like a *bitch*. The first and only time I'd done it, I couldn't get myself turned around in the air and ended up landing on my right arm and hip. Shattered more bones than I cared to count. I had to drag myself into the deep shadows nearby and lay there on the ground for hours while they knitted themselves back together. I still ache from that fall when there's rain on the horizon.

I like to think I handle myself with a *bit* more panache nowadays. I've nearly perfected my superhero landing – that move where Iron Man plummets from on high and slams down onto the pavement – one knee and one fist on the ground, the other leg out to the side, chin up to face down your enemies. I just about had that down pat. It just sucks that there's never anybody around I can show it to.

But I wasn't ready to make like Tony Stark just yet. Not with one out in the top of the ninth, a one-run lead, and our number one closer looking shaky as shit. The uncertainty in his dark brown eyes when he turned away from the batter, staring up plaintively at the summer stars shining clear and bright in the cloudless night sky overhead, was unmistakable. You *never* want to blow a save – especially at home. Forty-four thousand people screaming for your blood is nowhere any ballplayer wants to be.

"Come on, Billy…" I muttered under my breath, as though he could actually hear me. "Just take it one pitch at a time. You got this."

I was so focused on his next delivery – a wicked twelve-six curveball that left Martinez blinking at a called strike two – that I forgot where I was for a moment and leaped to my feet, pumping my fist overhead. The roof was still damp from the rain that had pushed through earlier and my boots slid out from under me. I landed flat on my ass and started the long slide towards the edge. I managed to grab onto a vent pipe and steady myself. If my heart had still been beating, it would no doubt have been hammering out of my chest. But the near miss did take my attention away from the game long enough for me to remember why I was way the hell up there in the first place: the lights of a darkened eighth-floor hotel room two blocks north of the stadium had just come on. Through the blinds I could see the wide, dark shape of Chester Hamlish shambling towards the television. I shot one last, longing look towards the pitcher's mound, blew the boys a kiss for luck, and got to work.

Backing up to the southernmost edge of the hotel roof, I charged forward at full speed, kicking hard off the edge and covering the hundred feet across and four or five stories down to the lower roof of the next building over. I cleared the parapet wall there with room to spare, hit the ground running, raced across to the far side, and launched myself into the open air beyond once again. This time I sailed high over Walnut Street and landed hard on top of the little restaurant on the north side.

As soon as I hit the roof, I froze, waiting to see if anyone responded to the shockingly loud boom that had accompanied my landing. Sure enough, the door to the roof access stairwell blasted open, and a heavyset man in a dirty white apron stood silhouetted in the bright square of light for a long moment, his eyes passing straight over where I knelt just a few yards away. The camouflage glamour held, though, and he eventually went back inside, shaking his head and muttering curses in Italian under his breath. With the moon close to full and my 'talents' growing stronger by the hour, I could usually avoid being seen by mortal eyes when I wanted – so long as I didn't go out of my way to draw attention to myself. If anybody noticed me in passing, they would retain no more than a fragmentary memory of it a few moments later. The living only see what they *expect* to see – and a grave wight on the prowl doesn't typically fit the bill.

I smirked as the door slammed shut, turning my head to glance up at Chester's hotel window. I was far too low now to see directly into the room, but I could hear him just fine. See, the glamour isn't the only predatory reflex that becomes hyperacute as the full moon draws near, particularly if I haven't fed yet during the lunar cycle. And tonight – with the moon still a week away from full and sitting low and dim on the southwest horizon – I had seen individual beads of sweat running down the pitcher's cheek as he turned the ball over in his hand from a hotel roof a quarter mile away. I could smell garlic and oregano on the steamy summer breeze that blew in on a line from the Hill halfway across the City. And from four floors below, through a thick glass window and over the sounds of downtown traffic and a crowd of thousands just down the street, I could hear Chester Hamlish flipping through pay-per-view channels, searching for just the right "after dark" entertainment for his last night on earth.

I glanced back towards the stadium as a roar went up from the crowd. *Strike three.* No fireworks yet, so the game wasn't over. But I smiled tightly and turned my attention back to the dim light filtering through curtains above.

The TV was off again – apparently Chester hadn't found what he was looking for. Not that there was any chance he would ever find something to cater to his particular perversions on hotel cable. According to Uncle Mike, Chester's tastes tended towards boys of around eleven or twelve years of age, preferably tall and lanky and blonde. My prey had arrived in town for an insurance convention late last night, and Mike had kept constant tabs on him from the moment he got off the plane at Lambert until just a few hours ago. That's when he turned the babysitting duties over to me.

SLMPD had collared Chester six years ago for the murder of two South City boys whose bodies were found stuffed in a drainage culvert down by the river. Had him dead-to-rights, too, Mike said. But the scumbag hired a top-flight mercenary of an attorney, and somebody had royally jacked up the paperwork on the search warrant for Chester's apartment. So even when CSU discovered trophies he had collected from his most recent victims in his freezer, the evidence they gathered had been thrown out as inadmissible – fruit of the poisonous tree. How a judge decides a jury isn't allowed to hear that the accused had the pinky fingers of two twelve-year-old murder victims on ice in his apartment is beyond me. Especially when Mike said there were at least three other unsolved murders in the City over the previous two years, all of them cut the exact same way. What Chester had done with the trophies from his other three kills defies the imagination, but they were never found. Chester headed west to Topeka the day he was cut loose and just faded into the scenery out there. At least as far as anybody could tell.

I heard him pick up the phone, listened closely. *An escort service.* Must be feeling nostalgic being back in St. Louis again after all these years. Like the pay-per-view menu, nobody in this town would offer up what Chester was really looking for tonight, so he ordered up the next best thing, I guess – a younger girl: short hair, thin, and flat-chested.

I quickly choked down the revulsion and began to execute the plan. Glancing down to make sure the alley below was deserted, I stepped over the edge and landed gently in the shadows between the two buildings. From what I'd heard of his side of the conversation and what little I could make out of the female voice on the other end of the line, the agency had given Chester an ETA of about twenty minutes for his chosen companion to arrive – a tender little morsel named Kiki was headed his way. But that would be more than enough time for me to take care of business and be long gone before anybody even knew I was there. Anybody but my old pal Chet, of course.

Raising the cowl of my heavy black cloak, I passed through the revolving front door of the hotel and swept quickly past the concierge desk to the double bank of elevators and was soon shooting up towards the eighth floor. As I waited, I carefully adjusted the folds of the hood to let Chester get a little better peep at the merchandise. The heavy black fabric concealed my hair and build well enough – I was definitely a tad bit curvier than Chester's tastes would allow – but I still had to convince him to open the goddamned door. The sharp chin, full lips, and high cheekbones I had inherited from my late mother would stand out in stark contrast to the shadows surrounding my face, but the tight black shirt, long pants, and knee boots did a pretty good job of concealing the rest. The elbow-length black gloves might seem an overly-dramatic flair – especially in the hundred-degree swelter of a St. Louis summer night – but this late in the lunar cycle, it was just too dangerous to risk letting my bare hands accidentally brush against an innocent person. Not with the hunger raging like this. By now my fingers would be bone-cracking cold, and an unexpected, uncontrolled touch against the bare skin of a stranger – however brief – could draw enough living essence from their body to knock them flat out on the floor. Worse yet, I could never be completely sure what the hunger would do next, once there was blood in the water.

To get in close, I would need to conceal my eyes most of all. The irises were an inhuman shade of cotton-candy pink, and people tend to notice shit like that. I'd tried covering them up with colored contact lenses before, but something about my unique 'post-mortem' biology apparently didn't get along with things that were stuck in my eyes. For the record, having to *literally* rip my corneas off to get contact lenses out is not an experience I would recommend to anyone, dead or alive.

But regardless, the hunger had to be satisfied soon. Unfulfilled a week from now, with the full moon casting its pale, ghostly glow over the City, my eyes would have bled down almost to a pure milky white. And then there would *be* no controlling the need. Guilty or innocent, old or young, priest or pickpocket – it wouldn't matter in the least. The madness would overtake me, and I would become a mindless revenant, lashing out at the first warm body I encountered.

It had happened before. I swore it would *never* happen again.

No, tonight I had a date with Chester Hamlish that would set both of us to rights – Chester once and for all, and myself for another month, at least until the moon waxed towards full once again.

The elevator chimed as the doors opened on the eighth floor. I stepped out onto the brightly patterned carpet, striding quickly down the hall towards Chester's room, black cape billowing dramatically behind. His was the second to last door on the left, on the side towards the stadium. I paused at the door for a moment, carefully arranging my garments again before knocking quietly.

It took Chester a minute to haul his considerable bulk up off the bed and trundle heavily toward the door. I felt his eyes staring at me through the peephole, caught a momentary whiff of cheap whiskey wafting out from under the door. But eventually the knob rattled, and the door swung inward. The man of the hour himself stood in the opening, dressed in plaid boxer shorts and a thin, sleeveless t-shirt stretched tight across his broad belly. Since I *wanted* him to see me, he could, but I could tell by the glazed, distant look in his eyes that he was feeling the vague disorientation that came from standing within spitting distance of a walking, talking black hole for the soul. He finally focused and looked me up and down, clearly not at all pleased with what he saw. I guess the cloak didn't hide my curves quite well enough after all, and I just didn't have what he wanted.

"Who the hell are you?" he demanded, his voice slurring slightly.

I did my best to radiate pure animal heat – no mean feat for somebody who usually hovered a degree or two below room temperature. "My name is Cherry," I purred. "Kiki got hung up in ballgame traffic, so the agency asked me to come by to keep you company until she gets here." I lowered my hood and reached out a gloved hand to stroke his stubbly cheek. "And here I am."

His dull, piggish eyes seemed to swim for a moment from the touch, but it passed quickly. "Didn't ask for no goddamned goth chick. Ain't paying extra for you."

I smiled, wrinkling my nose playfully. "Oh, sweetie, you can just consider me… a free gift with purchase. The agency's little way of making sure our customers stay *completely* satisfied."

He hesitated for a moment more before finally shrugging and stepping aside to let me in. I sashayed to the foot of the bed and turned, twirling my cloak theatrically. He clumsily hung the 'Do Not Disturb' sign on the outer handle and bolted the door shut tight behind him before crossing over to the mini-bar fridge.

"You want a drink?" he asked, bending down to grab a beer out of the door rack.

"No, thank you," I said, untying my cloak and letting it fall salaciously to the floor. "Don't want to spoil my dinner."

"Suit yourself." He popped the top on the can and took a long swig. Charmer that he was, he cut loose with a long, foul-smelling belch. *Ugh… peppers and onions. Terrific….*

He eyed me lecherously. "So now what?"

I grinned wickedly, moving in close, and took him by the shoulders. Gently turning around until his back was to the bed, I grabbed the bottom hem of his t-shirt and, with an effort, managed to pull it off over his head. "Now *we* get down to business," I whispered.

He smiled crookedly, apparently starting to enjoy the show. I looked him up and down. I *think* I managed a look that said I liked what I saw, but it damned sure wasn't easy.

As I began to tug at the fingers of my right glove, a sudden, rapid series of explosions rattled the hotel window and sent bright flashes of crimson light rippling across the blinds -fireworks signaling the end of the game. *That's a winner!*

I smiled genuinely for the first time. "Looks like everybody's getting lucky tonight."

"Yeah," he said with a lewd grin. Real conversationalist, Mister Hamlish. But he frowned suddenly and leaned forward to stare deep into my eyes, apparently noticing their color for the very first time. "Hey, are those real, or–"

I freed my hand from the glove and smiled. "Yes, sir. They're real, all right. But they aren't *always* this color. Watch this…."

With a lighting quick strike that was probably too fast for Chester to see coming, my right hand flashed out, the palm sinking into the thick, graying hair that covered his chest above his heart. A rending screech like metal meeting dry ice ripped forth from where our skin pressed together, and a momentary look of shock filled Chester's eyes before they rolled back into his head. His knees buckled and I shoved him back, letting his heavy bulk collapse onto the bed behind him. I had to repress a gag as I was forced to kneel on the bed and lean my body over his to stay close.

Chester's life force roared out of his body like water from a fire hose, and I had to push hard to keep my hand pressed tight against his sweat-slick skin. The energy poured out of him in a raging torrent, filling my own body with power and warmth, and ripping through my mind with a euphoric force stronger than any narcotic I'd ever heard of.

But along with it came the terrible price – the *real* 'gift-with-purchase' that accompanied every feeding: *memories*. In the space of thirty seconds, I saw the murder of the two South City boys. I saw the deaths of three others he was suspected of but couldn't be linked to. I saw the two he had taken in Kansas since then, the ones whose bodies hadn't been found yet. I saw how brutally they died. I saw where they were buried. And to my horror, I saw what he did with the trophies.

No wonder they never found the rest of the missing fingers. Hell, the cops were lucky they found the two they did. Apparently, they'd gotten to Chester before he got hungry.

Finally – as quickly as it began – the flood of living essence stopped like someone had closed off a valve. I gasped and staggered back, collapsing against the dresser as I sank to the carpeted floor. I sat there, head spinning and stomach churning, for three or four minutes before I managed to struggle to my feet. As I stared down at the empty, lifeless husk that had been pedophile, serial killer, and part-time cannibal Chester Hamlish, I watched wisps of thin white vapor curling up from his chest. The skin there was frozen solid in the shape of my small hand, but in a few moments, it would thaw completely, leaving absolutely no trace behind. The medical examiner would find no cause of death – no stroke, no trauma, no signs of foul play of any kind. His death would be written off to natural causes – some electrical issue with his heart most likely. But two things were certain: nobody would mourn his loss, and the world was a better place without him.

Turning away from the body, I caught a glimpse of my own reflection in the mirror behind the television. I leaned in close, marveling as always at the change. My eyes now shone a bright ruby red, and my cheeks were actually pink with a faint, fading blush. My heart was as motionless as ever, the panting breaths I took more old habit than anything resembling an actual physical need. But in that moment, I was as close to human as I had been since the day I died.

I quickly pulled my right glove back on. Bloated with Chester Hamlish's life force, I was no longer a threat to nearby civilians, but there was no sense in leaving prints behind either. With the hunger fed and my ability to hide in plain sight pretty much gone, I would almost certainly be seen leaving the hotel by anybody who was remotely paying attention, to say nothing about the security cameras. I retrieved my cloak from the floor, tied it at my throat again, and raised the cowl, drawing the edges in even closer around my face than before. Turning back for a beat, I resisted the strong, sudden urge to spit in Hamlish's direction.

Just as I reached for the door handle, there was a quiet knock on the other side. Startled, I stumbled back a step before moving forward again to peer through the peephole. In the hall outside stood a petite, rail-thin girl with a square jaw and dishwater blonde hair cropped short in a tomboyish pixie cut. I guess whatever escort service she worked for really *did* believe in customer service: Miss Kiki was a good five minutes early.

Swearing violently under my breath, I glanced around the room in a rising panic, searching for another way out. The hunger whispered softly in my ear, *Take her, too....* But she had done nothing to deserve my attentions. Part of me wanted desperately to warn her away – to tell her to leave the life before she eventually *did* cross paths with a piece of human filth like Chester Hamlish.

In the end, I did neither. I crossed quickly to the window, but like every other hotel I'd ever seen, it wouldn't open far enough to let anybody squeeze all the way out. I briefly considered hiding in the shower or under the bed, but if the girl called for help instead of running for it, I was screwed. They'd lock down the hotel and I'd never make it out before they found me. And I doubted even Uncle Mike could haul my ass out of a fire that hot.

The second knock on the door seemed to clear my head and the only solution available suddenly became crystal clear. I grabbed the heavy desk chair tucked into the corner, rocked back, and heaved it as hard as I could toward the window. It smashed straight through – at least my physical strength didn't diminish with a feeding – and disappeared into the darkness outside. I backed up almost to the front door where Kiki was now knocking even harder and shot off towards the window at a full sprint. I timed the jump just right, clearing the jagged opening cleanly and plummeting seventy-some feet to the sidewalk below. I landed pretty well – *Iron Man, eat your heart out* – even managing to buckle the sidewalk in a nifty little indented circle around my body.

Unfortunately, the sidewalk wasn't the only thing that cracked. I guess I punched the ground a bit too hard, because both of the bones in my right forearm had snapped on impact, their jagged white ends jutting out through their thin covering of muscle, skin, and silk.

Holy Mother of GOD, does that sting…

I stared, stunned for an instant as a red haze of pain clouded my vision. But there was no time to stop and lick my wounds. In a matter of minutes, forty thousand people were going to come pouring out of the stadium, parking lots and garages nearby, jamming the sidewalks and filling the streets from curb-to-curb with swerving, honking mayhem. I rose quickly and raced east towards the river, cradling the injured arm tight against my side beneath the cloak.

Two

NORMALLY, LACLEDE'S LANDING ON THE banks of the Mississippi River would be as good a place as any to get lost in a crowd. The dark alleys and deep shadows of the 19th-Century district offered plenty of places to hole up for a while until the mess at the hotel sorted itself out. But though the neon lights and rough cobblestone streets beckoned, the gruesome compound fracture I was nursing at the moment would have to be dealt with first. I decided to skirt south of the Landing, passing the Old Cathedral and crossing the darkened Arch grounds at an angle. I kept to the cover of the trees as much as possible until I reached the grand staircase and hurried down to the river's edge.

I glanced around warily once I was out in the open, but the area was all but deserted at this hour. So, I just hustled along the base of the flood wall until I reached the massive support column that formed the westernmost edge of the Eads Bridge. At the height of the springtime floods, I might have had to wade out into the water to reach it, but it had been a dry summer, and the river level was unusually low.

Well, this oughta be fun…

Standing flat-footed, I jumped straight up in the air as high as I could, barely getting the fingers of my good arm around the lowest point of the great steel arch above. I hauled myself up into the shadows of the intricate iron latticework, finding a small interior ledge and finally settling down with a relieved sigh.

Once the immediate fear of discovery had passed, the searing pain in my arm demanded all of my attention. I carefully unwrapped it, wincing as the sharp ends of the bones snagged on the silk-lined fabric of the cloak. Getting the glove off was out of the question. It was brutal to look at – no denying that – but at least it wasn't bleeding. One of the few advantages of having a heart that didn't beat, I guess: no pesky bloodstains to launder away.

I couldn't put this off for much longer – with a full charge in my system, the healing process had already begun, and I wasn't loving the idea of having to carve on the flesh if the wound closed with the bones still sticking out. Standing up again, I reached up with the grotesquely crooked arm and grabbed on tightly to a girder overhead. I could hear and feel a Metrolink train rattling the tracks above as it approached from the East Side, so I waited until it was directly overhead before making my move.

As soon as the blunt nose of the lead car passed, I stepped straight off the edge of the column, letting the full weight of my body dangle from the broken arm. As the slack was taken up and the bones were yanked back into place, a ragged, involuntary scream ripped from my throat. As planned, the noise of the train drowned out the sound for any nosy passersby, but in my ears, it seemed to echo along the entire length of the bridge for an eternity.

I let myself hang there for a long moment, gathering my strength before swinging back onto the ledge again. A gentle probing of the area showed the bones had returned almost exactly to their proper places, and I settled back into the shadows again to wait for the pain to subside.

In the tight, claustrophobic space under the bridge, even the weak, intermittent breeze that had been stirring the air over the City all night was blocked, and for the first time I realized just exactly how hot it was. July had been a real scorcher, and though I didn't experience summer the same way I had when I was alive – no sweating or suffering in unseasonably heavy clothing for this girl anymore – I could still feel the intense, oppressive heat on my skin. And though every nerve ending in my body was sizzling with the life energy I had taken from Chester Hamlish and my arm was aching terribly, I felt a profound weariness spreading out from my chest and my eyelids seemed irresistibly heavy.

I leaned back against the wall behind me and closed my eyes, content to wait there until the arm closed up before venturing out again. I fought it for as long as I could, but the allure of a deep, restorative sleep soon wrapped itself around me. My head fell back against the sturdy old stone of the pier, and I gave myself over to the all-encompassing darkness that beckoned so tantalizingly from the other side….

#   #   #

I jolted awake from the nightmare, almost slipping off my perch and plummeting into the black water rolling swiftly by below. I could still feel the false echo of a hammering in my chest. But when the cobwebs were swept away and my vision finally cleared, there was no real movement in my breast except the ragged, shallow breathing that – in truth – served no real purpose. I leaned out to glance up at the sky overhead. It was still full dark out, but dawn was coming. I could smell it in the air.

I pulled off my gloves and gave the injured arm a quick once-over. Other than a pale pink scar and an ache like an abscessed tooth, everything seemed pretty much back to normal. I reached into my pants pocket and pulled out the burner phone stashed there, flipping it open to check the time: *four-thirty a.m.– time to move.*

It wasn't that the rising sun would burn me to a crisp or anything. I'm a lot of things, but a vampire isn't one of them – if such things even exist. Daylight wouldn't harm me. But my eyes were those of a nocturnal predator – designed for darkness – and it would be murder getting back to my apartment once the sun was up, even with the side-shielded Ray-Ban knockoffs I had stashed inside my cloak.

I retrieved the pack of menthols I had in the pocket next to my sunglasses and, tucking one between my lips, reached for the Zippo in my front pants pocket. I snapped it open with a flick of my wrist and lit the cigarette, taking a long, deep drag and holding it for a beat before blowing the smoke up into the web of interlaced steel girders above.

I couldn't really enjoy the electric tingle of the tobacco on my tongue – drugs in general had absolutely no effect on me anymore. Nicotine, caffeine, marijuana – fuck, even *alcohol* had no way to touch me now. Dead is dead.

But I could feel the slightest touch of the menthol chill, and smoking lent an air of humanity to my demeanor – something I found I needed more and more as the years went by and my tenuous connection to the teenage girl I used to be became ever more strained.

I turned my attention back to the phone, dialing Uncle Mike's number from memory. He answered on the second ring.

"Fourth District Homicide, Sergeant Benjamin."

"Hey, Mikey."

There was a loud sigh on the other end of the line. *"Charlotte. Are you okay?"*

"Doing a damn sight better than our buddy Chester, that's for sure."

"Yeah, I'm on-scene here now. I take it this is your handiwork?"

"Recognized the brushstrokes, huh?"

Mike chuckled. *"You do have a signature style. Exit strategy left a little to be desired.*

The ME is going to take a lot harder look at this one with the window blown out like that."

I took another long draw on the cigarette. "Well, just subtly float the theory that Hamlish did that himself. Besides, I didn't have much of a choice. I got surprised by the creep's escort service on my way out the door and had to improvise. It was either that or climb under the bed and wait for the uniforms to arrive."

"I'd say you did just fine. So," he asked quietly, *"we were right?"*

I shook my head in disgust. "Yeah, you had your man – no doubt about it. Not only on the two South City kids, but on the other three you figured him for, too. He did them all."

"You see where he put them?"

"Yup. I'll send you the pins on your phone. Shouldn't take too long to find them." I winced as more of Chester's memories bobbed to the surface. "Oh, and Mike? You better get in touch with the cops out in Topeka, too."

"Aw, fuck me...."

"Yup. He took two more out there. You can lay those at the feet of his dirtbag attorney the next time you cross paths with him downtown. But I've got the info KBI will need to return the bodies to the families. Maybe they'll at least get a little closure now."

Mike sighed softly. *"You're doing the Lord's work, Charlotte."*

I tapped tobacco ash into the rushing waters below, scoffed quietly. "Yeah, well, I'm doing *somebody's* work. Jury's still out on which side of the street I'm working, though."

"Your dad would be damned proud."

I grimaced, spat into the water below. "That's bullshit and you know it, Mike. Dad would have spent every waking hour hunting me down."

"You're wrong, Charlotte. I knew him a lot longer than you did. Spent more hours on patrol with him than you spent with him your entire life. He knew the way things were. The way they still are. And he'd have fought beside you all the way to take these monsters off the streets."

"I want to believe that Mikey, I really do. Just not sure if I can."

"Well, go on home now. We'll take things from here. Security cameras got nothing,

and the girl outside Hamlish's door didn't see a thing. No witnesses on the street, either, as far as we can tell. Looks like you're in the wind."

"Home is where I'm headed, then. Wrap this up as quick as you can, will ya? I'll keep my head down for a bit, but cash is running short, and I can't afford to keep missing shifts at the club right now."

"You're not still working that dive across the river, are you?"

"No choice – not a lot of job opportunities out there for someone with no identity, no education, and no social security number. The job pays cash, and the manager and I have an arrangement as to what I will and will not do."

"Those places are dangerous, Charlotte."

I laughed bitterly. "No more dangerous than me. Besides, Mikey," I said, flipping the stub of my cigarette into the river, "even dead girls gotta make a living…"

#   #   #

I did as I promised: I laid low. I managed to hold out for almost a whole week, by which time Chester's story had all but disappeared from the local news cycle. But even with the hunger fed, I still felt a sort of background noise of predatory energy rising in my body with each passing hour. And when the night before the full moon finally arrived, I found myself pacing the floor of my ramshackle apartment like a tiger in a cage, clawing futilely at the constant, searing itch inside my skull. I had to get out, so I called the manager of the club and asked him to put me on the schedule for the next night. All he had left was a lousy overnight shift, but it beat the hell out of staying home and climbing the walls.

The show club where I made my so-called living – The Daily Grind – was a few miles across the river on the Illinois side. All of the so-called "gentlemen's clubs" in the area were over there, since Missouri had too many restrictions in place to let those sorts of places operate freely, at least if they actually wanted to make a buck. But the run-down little towns that hosted the half-dozen or so clubs that dotted the East Side were only too happy to collect the flood of cash that bachelor and birthday parties, over-the-road truckers, college kids, and bored suburban husbands gleefully dumped into the local economy.

The state's stubborn refusal to issue driver's licenses to dead people also meant I was wholly dependent on public transportation, and the walk from the Washington Park Metrolink station to the club was a little over a mile. The neighborhood was rough – to put it mildly – but no real threat to me. Some nights, one of the other girls from the club, Kennedy, would pick me up and shuttle me across the interstate to where the long row of strip clubs stood. We worked a lot of the same shifts, and the Metro station was on her way.

So, when I stepped off the train a few minutes before midnight, I wasn't the least bit surprised to see Kennedy's battered blue Ford Fusion idling loudly in the handicap spot nearest the platform. She laid on the horn for an obnoxiously long time to get my attention, even after she clearly saw me heading her way. The stars were still shining in the purple midsummer sky overhead, but to the north the horizon was alive with distant flashes of lightning and thunder rumbled ominously. The walk to the club would almost certainly have been a wet one, and I felt an unaccustomed rush of affection for the grinning young woman, even as she continued to wear out the damned horn.

I sauntered up to the passenger side door, laughing as I leaned into the open window. "Goddammit, woman, knock that shit off!"

Kennedy giggled, finally letting silence settle over the brightly lit parking lot. "Get in the car, bitch. I don't want my seats getting wet when that rain gets here." Her voice was warm and gentle, with just the right huskiness to it, perfect for squeezing lovestruck customers for an extra couple of bucks.

I opened the door and slid in beside her, and she quickly rolled up the window, just as the first fat drops began pattering on the cracked windshield. "Kennedy, how many times do I have to say this? It isn't safe for you to be waiting around out here. These lots are sketchy as fuck in the *daytime*. I don't need you getting yanked out of your car and murdered – or worse – on my account."

She rolled her eyes, jammed the car in reverse and quickly backed out of the spot. "And I don't need *you* playing Little Red Riding Hood and skipping your narrow ass all the way across that highway alone at night, either. Too many wolves in these woods." As we rounded the corner of the lot, she waved at the security guard on the platform and blew him an exaggerated kiss. "Besides, my boy Rusty there is a regular. He keeps more of an eye on me than he ever does the people getting on and off those trains."

I chuckled knowingly and pursed my lips against the car window as we sped past Rusty's post. He grinned like an idiot and adjusted his hat to better shed the rain which was really starting to come down now. Not the sharpest knife in the drawer, young Rusty, but a nice enough guy, I guess.

Kennedy lit a cigarette as she guided the car out onto the road, offered me one. I shook my head. "I saw Vic add your name to the schedule last night," she said. "I figured I better swing by and pick you up before you went and did something stupid."

As we crossed the overpass and turned onto the frontage road that led to the club,

Kennedy got me up to speed with a non-stop flood of all the "juicy" club gossip I had missed over the last week. I just grinned and shook my head. I wish I could say I hate working at the club. That'd be the proper, feminist point-of-view for a young – so to speak – progressive woman of the world like me. But over the years, I'd actually come to love it in a perverse sort of way. I mean, yes, it *was* coarse and demeaning, and sometimes I just found the inherent *lie* of the whole thing repulsive. But it beats the living *hell* out of being alone.

Not to wax poetic or anything, but the world of a grave wight is a damned lonely place. I tend to stick out in a crowd, and my appearance invariably weirds the normies out. So just like a lot of my customers, I went to the club seeking some kind of human contact, whether it was with the other working girls or the customers themselves, craving the chance to connect with another human being in whatever way possible. Even if it was only for the length of a song.

Well, that and a *shitload* of untaxed cash.

Dying young had left all my parts in all the right places and, lucky for me, I had been an early bloomer. I still had the bright red hair and porcelain skin I'd been born with, and I gradually built my dancing persona around the red eyes and somewhat Gothic wardrobe I favored most nights. Her name was 'Cherry Bomb' – just a stupid play on my real name, Charlotte Baum, of course – and Cherry drove all the boys wild. Most of the girls too, come to think of it.

And most importantly, the character kept the awkward questions to a minimum. The bizarrely colored eyes were written off to an ever-changing series of contact lenses, and the outfit came off as just catering to a kink. I usually kept my hands to myself – just like the customers were asked to do – and, fully fed, there was very little chance I would hurt someone accidentally. And as the cycle rolled on, the hunger could even become a useful tool. A brush of my bare hand against a customer's cheek left them with an electric jolt and a dizzy, lightheaded feeling that fed powerfully into Cherry Bomb's mystique and sold a lot of extra watered-down drinks at the bar. And I got a tiny charge out of it myself, a minute pulse of life force that helped me keep my shit together until some real prey came along.

As always, the parking lot of The Daily Grind was bright as midday, and Kennedy parked out front, shunning the more secure employee lot behind the building as usual since we were already running late. I flipped up the cowl of my cloak to shield my eyes from the harsh glare and my hair from the now steady drizzle as Kennedy and I stepped out of the car.

The lot seemed unusually full, especially for a Tuesday night. I saw at least two booze buses parked along the fence, and a couple of limos lined up by the exit. I shot a glance at Kennedy, who grinned and rubbed her hands together gleefully under the bright yellow raincoat she had thrown over her shoulders.

As we hustled under the awning that covered the main entrance to the club, the head bouncer, Jerry, reached over and held the outer door open. "Evening, Miss Cherry, Miss Kennedy," he drawled in that oddly thick southern accent some Missouri natives have. He was an older guy, late-fifties maybe, with deeply tanned skin, a barrel chest, and slicked-back brown hair that was going grey at the temples. Some of the younger punks occasionally tried to push him around because he didn't look very dangerous. But Jerry was a "one-warning" kind of guy – after that, most of the serious troublemakers either got carried back to their cars by their friends or, occasionally, patched up by the paramedics.

I grinned at him. I liked Jerry a lot – unlike some of the guys who worked the door and inside the club, he genuinely cared about the girls he was supposed to look out for. I patted his shoulder as I passed, careful not to pull any soul strings. "Looks like a packed house tonight, Jerry. Full moon must have the pervs out in force."

He chuckled. "Well, any of them starts to actin' the fool, you jus' holler, Miss Cherry."

"I will. Thanks, Jer." I tapped on the cashier's window and waved to the woman seated inside as we passed, then pulled open the interior door that led to the main showroom. At that moment, I was suddenly grateful for the diminished senses that followed a good feeding. Cardi B pounded from the club speakers at a decibel level that shook my internal organs, and the air was thick with cigarette smoke, stale beer, cheap cologne, and vanilla musk. And above it all – jarringly – was the powerful smell of fresh roasted coffee.

See, that was the club's little twist – the thing that made it stand out from the rest: topless baristas. And as weird as that sounds, you wouldn't *believe* the amount of money they took in. Hell, just look what Starbucks is getting for a fucking iced coffee these days. Imagine what they could charge if the girl behind the counter was half naked. Double *that* and you've got

The Daily Grind. The owner, Vic, already had an architect drawing up plans to add a drive-thru to the place, just as soon as he figured out how to card people in cars before letting them get in line. A little privacy fencing would keep the gawkers at bay, but the Village would never grant the permits if he couldn't keep the kids out.

The crowd was big and boisterous, and there were girls dancing on all four stages at once – not a common occurrence on a weekday night. There seemed to be at least three cliques of customers drifting from stage to stage like tour groups, along with a smattering of regulars and couples filling the tables and keeping the scantily clad waitresses hopping.

Kennedy headed straight to the dressing room, but I was stopped dead in my tracks by a sight I honestly never thought I'd see – one which, by mutual agreement, I was never, ever, *ever* supposed to see: my unofficially adoptive uncle, Detective Sergeant Mike Benjamin, sitting at the end of the bar in *my* club. Mike was dressed in his regular plainclothes garb, nursing a venti Americano, but any idiot would make him for a cop in a heartbeat. I strode up to the bar a few empty chairs away, refusing to even make eye contact with him.

"Mike," I hissed, as the fury rose in my chest. "What in the bleeding blue *FUCK* are you doing here?" My hands gripped the edge of the bar so tightly I could hear the wood creak and pop under my fingers.

"Charlotte," he said quietly. "We need to talk. "

"*Not* here," I snapped, glancing around. "Take it outside. *Now!*"

He rose, tossing a twenty on the bar. As he passed, I noticed a strange ashen grey pallor had pushed aside the usual rich, dark umber color of his skin.

"I'll meet you out front in ten minutes," I snarled, still acting as though I couldn't see him.

He headed for the front door, and I walked straight back to the dressing room. I asked Kennedy to pass the word to the manager and Momma Wanda, the club's house mom, that I was stepping out and that I'd be back in a few minutes. She started to open her mouth, but something in my demeanor took her aback a bit. She swallowed her questions and just nodded.

I blasted out the front door of the club and into the parking lot, just as a black Chevy Tahoe swung away from the fence on the far side and cut diagonally across the lot towards me. Jerry immediately started moving my way, but I gave him the high sign and he reluctantly settled back to his post at the door. The truck – quite obviously an unmarked police vehicle – crunched across the gravel lot, rolling to a stop beside me.

The passenger-side window slid down, and Mike peered grimly at me from the driver's seat. "Get in," he said without preamble.

"Fuck you, Mikey. I'm working tonight. My rent was due last week, and I can't–"

"Charlotte," he said, his voice dangerously quiet. "Get your ass in the truck."

I wanted to dig my six-inch heels in and fight, but something in his voice sent icy claws skittering up my back. I yanked open the passenger door and slid into the seat. Mike hit the gas and pulled quickly out of the parking lot, throwing gravel as he swung out onto the frontage road.

As he drove, he reached into the center console and pulled out one of those little loop-handled suckers, the kind they used to give out at the bank when I was little. Cherry, of course. – my favorite. It was a peace offering – he knew full well that suckers were one of the few things I could actually eat – so long as I didn't try to chew them up. As usual, it worked. My anger subsided a bit, and I snatched it from his hand, unwrapped it, and popped it in my mouth.

"What the hell is going on, Mikey? You show up at my club, use my real name in public – are you *trying* to get us both in trouble?"

"You know I wouldn't have come unless it was absolutely necessary."

"Then what?" A dark thought crossed my mind. "This isn't about Hamlish, is it?"

He scoffed derisively. "If only it was that simple."

I frowned, watching him closely. "Mike, just tell me what's wrong. You're spooking me here."

His face darkened and he nodded grimly, kept his eyes on the road. "We found a body tonight in a warehouse off Fourteenth Street."

I stared out the window, pulled the sucker out of my mouth for a moment. "Yeah, so what? We average one about every other day now, don't we? And that's just in the City itself."

"Yes, we do. And despite our best efforts, damned near sixty percent of them still go unsolved."

"And that's where I come in, remember?" I said, trying to ease his mind. I knew the bad publicity the Department had suffered over the last few years was a real sore spot for Mike. "You find the bad guy, I go in, I make sure they're guilty, and put them out of our misery. Easy-peasy, right?"

He shot me an anxious glance. "Yeah."

I always knew some part of Mike still struggled with our little arrangement. Hell, he'd probably wrestled with his conscience over it every day since I showed up on his front door a few months after I'd gone missing – with ruby-red eyes, ice cold skin, and suffering from the incurable lack of a heartbeat.

Mike reached under the armrest of the truck and came out with an unmarked manila folder. He stared at it for a beat with an odd look on his face before slowly handing it over.

I sat up straight, flipping the folder open on my lap. With my eyes, I didn't need to turn on the map light to see clearly in the darkened interior of his cruiser. There were a dozen or so glossy color photos in there, none of them all that disturbing in and of themselves. At least not for somebody like me, who'd seen more than their fair share of dead bodies. No blood, no guts, no obvious trauma. The victim was a pretty woman who looked to be in her mid-thirties, dressed in a simple green dress with a demure pattern of pale-yellow flowers, laid out spread-eagle on a dusty concrete floor.

But one aspect of the crime scene immediately caught my eye, and if my heart *had* still been beating, it might have just stopped cold. Beneath the victim, someone had painted a complex geometric pattern – not exactly a pentagram, but a very close cousin. There were cryptic symbols painted on the walls all around and, judging from the red-black coloration, they appeared to have been painted in some kind of blood – human or otherwise. The symbols were all too familiar, though, and my stomach twisted into a cold, hard knot.

They were the same markings that had been scrawled on the floor and walls of the room where I had first awakened as a revenant more than a quarter of a century ago.

I realized Mike was watching me closely, standing by in case I started to flake. But I clamped down hard on my emotions and focused. "Who's the victim?"

"Karen Wagner, thirty-three, mother of four. Disappeared from a grocery store parking lot in Richmond Heights night before last."

"From the way you're grinding your teeth, I assume you recognize the markings, too?" "Yeah, I did. I checked your case file and they're an exact match."

"Anybody else make the connection?"

He shook his head. "Not yet. But I'm probably the last guy still serving who ever saw those markings up close. And your file was cold-cased twenty years ago."

That was a sore spot for *me*: my sister Annaliese's body had never been found. "How did this one die?"

"That's the funny thing, Charlotte. There's not a mark on her. To be honest, it looks an awful lot like –"

"Like one of mine," I finished for him, my eyes fixed on the woman's cold, vacant stare. "Except I don't prey on Suzy Homemakers."

He nodded again. "She's been dead less than twenty-four hours. Got an anonymous call late yesterday afternoon, and when the uniforms arrived on scene, they found that."

"Wait," I said, shaking my head. "Somebody actually called this *in*?"

"Yup. And they called it in to *me*. As in, to *my* desk, to *my* personal extension. And that's not even the fucked-up part."

I stared at him hard. "What?"

He sighed heavily. "Right before they hung up, the voice said, 'Say hello to Charlotte for me....'"

Three

WE SPENT THE REST OF the drive over in silence as Mike guided the Tahoe across the Musial bridge and into the North City neighborhood where I lived. Neither of us was willing to speculate any further as to what in the name of *hell* was going on without something more definitive to go on. But the ride wasn't all that quiet for me – my brain felt like it was on fire. Powerful memories had begun a slow, rolling boil in the back of my mind. Painful memories. Disgusting memories. And there was very little I could do to control them or hold them at bay. They were memories of the six weeks I had spent locked in the basement of a nondescript little house in South County. Memories of assault and torture and the vilest abuses the human imagination can conjure.

And the worst part of all: the memories weren't even *mine*.

\#   \#   \#

Reginald Donald Hargrove wasn't much as far as serial killers go. He wasn't charming and good-looking like Ted Bundy. He wasn't a clever chameleon like John Wayne Gacy. Hell, he didn't even have the sheer numbers of Gary Ridgeway, the Green River Killer. His greatest ambition was no loftier than just to have a mindless, submissive slave who would readily participate in whatever deviant and depraved behavior his wretched little viper's nest of a brain could concoct. More of a Dahmer sort, with a penchant for redheads. And less cannibalism.

He'd taken girls before me. Beat them. Drugged and assaulted them. Tortured them. And in the end, he always ended up with the same thing: a battered, broken toy that he was no longer able to play with. Some of them died on their own. Some of them he had to get rid of. But eventually, he would have to try again. Seven times to be exact – all teenage girls, all redheads, and all of them taken off the streets at night by force.

But by the time my sister Annaliese and I encountered him on that humid summer night over twenty-five years ago, he had just laid hands on what he thought was surely the answer to all his problems: a fairly new drug just hitting the streets in the US in the mid- to late-90s: Rohypnol. Nowadays, most people know it as "roofies" or the "date rape drug". It renders the victim helpless to defend themselves, with no self-awareness or memory of events that occur while they are under its influence.

For Reginald, this must have seemed like a gift from heaven, the answer to his most fervent and degenerate prayers. Just drop a little into the food or water he offered me each day, and I would be his for the taking – whenever and however he wanted. And best of all, since I had no memory whatsoever of any of the time I spent with him, my mind and body would last much longer than those poor girls who had eventually buckled under the abuse.

I lasted the better part of six whole weeks. God only knows how much longer it might have gone on if Reginald hadn't gone and fucked the whole thing up. But one night as he sat around watching reality television with a bottle of cheap vodka, he inadvertently ended up so hammered he could barely make his way down the stairs for that night's recreational activities. Worse, the alcohol had rendered him unable to 'perform', so he decided to just hang out with me until he sobered up enough to get on with business. In his inebriated state, he had been overcome by a wave of generosity and decided I should share in the celebration of his triumph, the realization of all his life's goals. He decided to offer me a drink.

One drink turned into two, turned into several, as Reginald became more and more amused with himself and with my increasingly disoriented behavior. What he found out the hard way is that alcohol and Rohypnol is often a lethal combination. Sometime during the evening, old Reg passed out, and when he awoke next to me on the concrete floor of his basement a few hours later, I was already stone dead. The idiot had tried mouth-to-mouth and CPR and even used bare wires ripped from the base of an old table lamp to try to shock life back into my corpse. But I was gone.

Reginald was devastated. For whatever reason, he'd taken a real shine to me. I was the perfect toy he'd dreamed of his whole life, and now he'd gone and broken me, too. My death sent him even further over the edge. Unfortunately – or *fortunately*, depending on your opinion of my current state of being – he knew a few people who had gone over an edge of their own a long time ago. People who, like him, had dabbled in the darker areas of the occult in their early years. He called a guy who called a guy whose people showed up the next morning to help old Reg out.

Reginald had never met the man before – he only knew of him by reputation. He was some kind of "foreigner" – Reg wasn't exactly sure what kind – and supposedly spoke with a thick accent. He went by the name of Mirsad, and he was in possession of a very special book – a fragment of a book, really – that would show Reg exactly how to fix his broken toy. But Mirsad wanted something in return. Something far more valuable than money.

He wanted my sister.

For all his myriad faults, it seems Reg didn't have a taste for little girls. I guess you could say that much for him. Taking Annaliese that night had been an unfortunate mistake – he didn't even know she was in the backseat of my car when he smashed me in the temple with a set of brass knuckles and drove off with both of us into the night. He hadn't laid a finger on her, just kept her locked up in a soundproofed room he'd prepared for his noisier former guests. Why he didn't just kill her I have never quite understood. Shockingly – given everything he had done to me – the idea of messing with little kids apparently freaked him out. But this Mirsad character clearly did not share his aversion to children. His people dumped the book in Reginald's lap, took my drugged-up sister in return, and disappeared into the night. Mike and I spent years trying to track that son of a bitch down – we never got any closer than an Interpol hit on the name Mirsad out of Spain in early 2009 that turned up jack shit. The guy might as well have been a ghost.

But Reginald did his part and followed the instructions on the tattered pages to the best of his ability. He had gotten fresh blood from a neighborhood stray. He painted the symbols on the walls and floor with great care. He lit the candles and said the words. And then he waited.

And waited.

And waited.

And every day, he would come downstairs and peer through the little window he had cut in the door of my chamber. And every day he saw the same thing – my increasingly ripe body lying cold and still on the basement floor.

See, Reginald's problem was he didn't understand the power he was wielding – like a child who finds a loaded gun in their parents' nightstand drawer. And he didn't understand that it took the full moon to infuse the circles of power with the stuff of life – whatever the hell that was. And when the full moon finally arrived on the 16th of September, it had been just another long night of waiting for Reg. Sometime after midnight, he wandered down the stairs once again, drunk as all hell, and leaned down to look though the little cutout in the door. To his surprise, my body was gone.

He quickly unbolted the door and eagerly dashed inside, where he found me sitting in the corner behind the door – head down, knees up, folded arms covering my face. He knelt beside me and cautiously – almost tenderly – pulled my arms aside. Reaching down, he lifted my chin with a single finger. My eyes were still closed.

But Reginald wouldn't be kept waiting much longer. When my eyes snapped open a half-second later, he stared in abject horror at the pure, featureless white expanses that filled the places where my dull, drug-addled brown eyes had been before. And then, without warning, my mouth fell open in a perfect 'O' and an unearthly banshee howl ripped forth from my throat. My hands lashed out, fingers curved like talons, and dug into the skin on either side of his face. It took only two or three seconds – just a fraction of the time it took with Chester Hamlish. In full-on revenant mode, the hunger drew so strongly that it drained the victim in an instant, leaving their souls crushed flat like an empty beer can.

With his life force coursing through my body, my consciousness returned in a rush. And for the first time ever, I was swept away on a tidal wave of hideous memories, memories of atrocities committed not only upon others, but upon my own defenseless self. I saw the things he had done through his eyes. I felt the things he felt while he did them. And I tasted the abhorrent satisfaction he had gleaned from each encounter.

And when it was over, all I could do was collapse on the ground next to his rigid, empty shell, shivering and weeping and howling in unbearable anguish. It would be days before I found the strength to rise up and take flight.

#   #   #

Instead of heading to my apartment, Mike – to my utter disbelief – brought the Tahoe to a stop outside the warehouse on Fourteenth where the dead woman's body had been found. Several cops and CSU techs were still milling around, but nowhere near as many as I would have expected.

I turned to him, wide-eyed. "What the fuck am I doing here, Mikey?"

In all the years we'd worked together, I had never visited an active crime scene with Mike. So, I was more than a little freaked out. I spent most of my time planning, causing, and escaping situations like this. I had zero experience with just strolling right on into one.

He reached into the center console again and pulled out a lanyard with a red laminated card hanging from it. "Put this on."

I looked at the badge skeptically – it had a big white "V" emblazoned across the front and the words "VISITOR – ESCORT REQUIRED". There was a meaningless five-digit number at the bottom. I glanced back at Mike, feeling my eyes widen even more. My voice sounded panicky in my own ears. "I can't go in there, Mike. Look at the way I'm dressed. Look at my eyes. I'm a walking, talking fucking *cold case*, Mike, and this place is crawling with –"

Mike reached over and gently guided the lanyard around my neck, drew the edges of my cloak tighter around my shoulders. "Calm down, Charlotte. You will stay right beside me. You will do exactly what I say, when I say it, and you will not touch a goddamned *thing*." He tried his best for a reassuring smile. "We bring in experts to look at crime scenes all the time. They hauled the body off a little while ago, and by now the CSU guys will be wrapping things up in there."

I nodded slowly, and Mike smiled again and opened his door to step outside. I reached into a pocket with shaking hands and pulled out a pair of small, round, blue-tinted glasses. I sometimes used them at the club to help conceal some of the more outlandish shades my eyes took on at times. With a deep breath, I opened the truck door and stepped out onto the curb, staring up at the drab brown brick edifice with an expression of what I'm sure must have looked like mortal terror on my face. But Mike gave my shoulder a squeeze and led the way toward the main entrance beyond the yellow-tape perimeter.

The second I crossed the threshold, my skin began to tingle like I was snuggling up next to a fuzzy blanket fresh out of the dryer. There was a *lot* of residual power here, the same kind of power that had made me who – or *what* – I am today. I guess *magic* is the appropriate word, but I never liked using it. It made what I am seem – I don't know – less *wicked* somehow. When I think of magic, I think of fairy godmothers and boy wizards and "Bibbidi-Bobbidi-Boo". What was done to me didn't deserve a name as sickly-sweet as *magic*. It had taken something far blacker than that to drag my soul kicking and screaming back into this mortal coil.

I was already attracting more than my fair share of attention as I crossed through the darkened warehouse in Mike's wake. The outfit definitely didn't help. It was hotter than blue blazes in there, and all the cops and techs milling around were already soaked to the skin. I guess they couldn't risk opening the doors and windows yet to admit any sort of breeze for fear of contaminating the evidence. And here I was walking around in stiletto heels with every square inch of skin covered in black cloth and sporting a hooded cloak to boot.

"Hey, Sarge!" A younger man's voice called out from across the room. I glanced that way, and spotted a tall, well-built blond man in his early thirties coming towards us at a trot. He was wearing a dark grey sport coat with a blue paisley tie that had been pulled down a few inches, and the top button of his collar was open. A gold cross glinted from inside his white dress shirt. When he got a good look at me, he slowed considerably but kept coming, stopping just a few feet away.

The thought suddenly occurred to me that maybe Mike and I should have done a little more talking before we got to this point. I had no idea how he was going to introduce me or explain my presence there, let alone my unique appearance. But, as usual, Uncle Mike was two steps ahead of me.

"Detective Tommy O'Connor," Mike said, indicating the newcomer. "O'Conner, this is Miss Chandra. She's helped the Department out from time to time, whenever one of our cases appears to involve elements of the occult."

O'Connor reached out his hand in greeting and I shook it briefly, trying desperately not to let even a flicker of power pass between us. Easier said than done when I was standing in a bubbling cauldron of mystical energy. From the look on his face, I wasn't entirely successful.

"Miss Chandra, huh?" he said after a beat, looking me up and down with an obnoxious grin pulling at the corner of his mouth. "And what are you supposed to be? Some kind of hoodoo priestess, or –"

I started to answer, but Mike cut across me. "Detective, you will afford this young woman the same respect you'd show any professional consultant, or I *will* have you back in blues and writing parking tickets this time next week."

The smug smile melted away, and O'Connor looked properly abashed. "Sorry, Sarge." He nodded to me. "My apologies, ma'am."

Mike turned to me with an exasperated sigh. "Detective O'Connor here has been shadowing me for almost a year now, supposedly training to be my future replacement. Assuming I don't send his ass back to patrol before he makes sergeant, he'll probably be leading homicide in the Fourth District after I hang up my spurs."

O'Connor put on a shit-eating grin, folded his hands reverently. "I could only succeed you, Sarge. I could never *hope* to replace you."

Even I had to roll my eyes at that one.

"Nobody likes a kiss-ass, O'Connor," Mike said. "Why don't you show Miss Chandra what we've found here?"

O'Connor led the way over to where the power circle had been scrawled across the dust-covered concrete floor. I stopped several feet away, and Mike followed my lead.

"Don't cross into the circle, Mike," I warned under my breath. "There's still an awful lot of energy in there."

"What kind of energy?"

I shot a sideways glance at O'Connor, who was beginning to stare at us both like we'd started foaming at the mouth. "My kind," I said with a significant widening of my eyes.

Mike looked between the young man and me for a moment before nodding firmly. "Keep going."

"Okay," I said, after a moment's hesitation. "This is exactly what we thought it was.

These are part of a Romani resurrection ritual."

"Romani?" asked O'Connor.

"A European people. Folks used to call them gypsies years ago – offensively, too, I might add," Mike replied, surprising me and O'Connor both.

I shook it off. "Yeah, well, these symbols are part of the ritual used to bring a dead person back to life," I said, indicating the spot where Karen Wagner had been laid out. "The body is placed within the markings and, after the ritual is performed, the next full moon will charge the circles. At midnight, the spell will bring them back to life."

"Bring them back to –" O'Connor sneered, his voice dripping scorn. "So, we should do…. what? Put out a BOLO for zombies?"

"O'Connor…" Mike growled softly.

"Sarge, what the fuck are we talking about here? *Magic?* Raising the *dead?*"

"It doesn't matter what *we* believe, O'Connor. What matters is what the people who *did* this believed."

O'Conner turned back to me. "Well, I don't know if you've noticed, *Miss Chandra*," he said with obvious derision. "But Karen Wagner didn't get up and wander off. I watched her body – her *dead* body – get loaded into a coroner's wagon over an hour ago. So, whatever 'black mojo' you think was happening here, it clearly didn't – "

A dreadful thought suddenly occurred to me, and I began cursing myself for not having seen it sooner. I grabbed Mike by the sleeve and dragged him out of earshot of O'Connor. The young detective stopped mid-bitch and watched us with intense curiosity but didn't try to move any closer.

"Mike," I hissed. "I think we have a *very* big problem."

He looked down at me, dark brow furrowed in confusion. "What do you mean?"

"Where did they take that woman's body?"

Mike shrugged. "City morgue. Why? What's the problem?"

"Do you know what last night was?"

"Tuesday?"

"No, Mike," I whispered, glancing back over my shoulder at O'Connor, who now seemed to be finding excuses to drift our way. "Last night was the first of August. And at about one-thirty yesterday afternoon, the moon was completely full. *That's* why the power circles are still carrying a charge."

He shook his head. "I don't follow."

"If this woman was murdered and someone used the same… I don't know – the same *sorcery* on her that they did on me, then at midnight–"

"She woke up," Mike said, his voice barely above a whisper. He glanced at his watch. "Jesus Christ, it's after one a.m. now."

I nodded gravely. "And if her experience is anything like mine, anybody within arm's reach of her when that happened is in some very deep shit."

"Mother of God…"

"Mike, we have to–" I never finished the sentence. He grabbed me by the hand and started dragging me towards the door.

"O'Connor, you're in charge here," Mike shouted over his shoulder. "Meet me back at HQ when you're finished. I want a full report waiting when I get there."

"Sure, Sarge, but where are you–"

"Just *do* it!" Mike didn't bother answering any more questions. We just headed for the front door at something slightly less than a sprint. We reached the exit and Mike threw the door open. We jumped in the Tahoe and Mike fired up the engine. Just as he was tearing away from the curb, I caught a fleeting glimpse of Detective O'Connor watching us though the cracked, grimy windows of the abandoned warehouse, his face a mask of frustration.

Mike grabbed the handset for the police radio under the dash. "Dispatch, this is Twenty-Five Ninety-Four."

"Copy, Twenty-Five Ninety-Four. Go ahead, Sergeant."

"Dispatch, I need you to check the status of a body delivery to the City morgue. Victim's name is Wagner, Karen. Her body should have arrived there shortly after midnight."

"Copy, Sergeant. Standby."

The silence on the other end of the transmission seemed endless. Mike and I exchanged nervous glances as he wove his way at high speed through the largely deserted early-morning streets of the City, lights and sirens helping clear the way anyway.

When the voice on the radio returned, both of us were holding our breath. No idea why *I* was, but whatever. *"Sergeant, the morgue reports no body deliveries in the last six hours. They did confirm they were contacted at eleven-fifty p.m. by Detective O'Connor and informed that a homicide victim was en route, but the coroner's van never arrived. Should I tell them it's on the way now?"*

Mike sighed heavily. "Negative, Dispatch. Advise all units to be on the lookout for a missing coroner's van. Advise them to approach with extreme caution if they find it."

"Uh... copy, Sergeant. Will advise all units."

Mike turned to me, his face grim. "So now what?"

I shook my head. "Now we hope somebody finds that van quickly. And while you're at it, you might want to say a prayer for the poor slob who was driving it..."

Four

IT DIDN'T TAKE LONG TO find the coroner's van once they started looking. Hell, the morgue was barely a mile from the warehouse crime scene, right next door to the old Police Department headquarters building on Clark. The van was only a block away from its destination, sitting up against the curb in what – to a passerby – probably just looked like a shitty park job. The driver was dead in the back. Karen Wagner was not.

Mike and I rolled up to the scene, which by now was bookended by two patrol units with lights ablaze. An unmarked white Impala pulled in right behind us, and Detective O'Connor climbed out, headed straight for Mike's truck. He approached from the sidewalk side, leaning into the open window and resting his elbows on my door. His nearness forced me to sit back in the seat as he talked across me.

"What's the story here, Sarge?" he said, eyeing me sideways.

"What the fuck are you doing here, O'Connor?" Mike asked testily. "Did I *not* leave you in charge of the crime scene at the warehouse?"

"CSU's finished – they didn't find shit. We had just sealed off the site when I heard the van had been found and I figured *this* is where I needed to be. My victim is here."

"Actually, she's not."

O'Connor blinked but recovered quickly. He jerked his thumb towards the coroner's van. "She's not in there?"

"The only body in there is the Deputy Coroner. *Your* DB appears to have left the scene."

"Somebody stole the corpse?"

Mike just stared at him for a second. "Maybe."

"Well, what else could –" O'Connor stopped cold, shot a brief, incredulous glance at me before turning back to Mike. "Oh, come on, Sarge. You're not actually buying this resurrection ritual bullshit, are you?"

"*'There are more things in heaven and earth, Horatio, than are dreamt of in your philosophy'*."

Now it was my turn to blink at Mike in surprise. Mike was extremely intelligent – brilliant even – but I never exactly pictured him going in for the long-hair stuff. Mike Benjamin quoting Shakespeare was nothing I ever expected to hear, in life or in death.

Mike looked at me with a grin. "*Hamlet.* Act One, Scene Five."

"Who are you, and what have you done with Mike Benjamin?" I said with mock sincerity.

"Come on, Char – *Miss Chandra*. Let's have a look." Mike climbed out on his side, but I had to let my blue glasses slide down and give O'Connor a dose of the old crimson death-stare over the top of them to get him to take a step back and let me out. We crossed the short distance to where the van was parked, and for the second time in as many hours, Mike held the yellow police tape up to let me step into an active crime scene.

The back of the van was standing open, and the Deputy Coroner was lying face-up on the stretcher where his erstwhile passenger had been, his head towards the rear. The body bag the victim had been in was ripped wide open, the zipper broken, the black plastic shredded. It was partly underneath the coroner's body and partly draped onto the floor of the van.

I took a step forward, reaching towards the dead man's head. Mike grabbed my wrist before I could get to him. I looked at him sharply.

Mike shook his head. "You can't tamper with the scene. And definitely not without gloves."

I wiggled my fingers in their black silk wrappings.

Mike smirked. "*Real* gloves, genius." He whistled to a patrol officer, who retrieved a pair of cobalt blue nitrile gloves from a box in the open trunk of his cruiser. As I pulled them on over my own, I saw O'Connor rolling his eyes and turning away with his hands planted on his hips in an openly belligerent stance.

I moved in close again, eyeing the dead man's face from a few inches away. Over my shoulder, I could hear O'Connor arguing quietly with Mike that I shouldn't be mucking around in a crime scene, gloves or no gloves. I shut them out and concentrated on what I was doing.

Ignoring Mike's warnings, I reached up and gently turned the man's head from side-to-side. I soon found what I was looking for: ten small, yellow patches of skin, five along each side of his face, each about the size of a nickel. The flesh there was thickened and rough, like freezer burn.

Normally, when a grave wight feeds in a controlled manner, the skin is just *lightly* frozen. But the voracious feeding frenzy of a revenant left burns like the ones I was seeing, as if someone had pressed dry ice against the skin of the victim.

The thought crossed my mind that if I could remove my gloves, I might be able to pull hard enough – even now, as the body was beginning to stiffen with rigor mortis – and draw out whatever residual energy was left in his mind to get an image of what had happened in this man's final moments. But I dismissed the idea out of hand. For one, I didn't need to see what happened – I *knew:* Karen Wagner had awakened inside a body bag, torn her way out while the driver struggled to get to the side of the road, and then she attacked and fed upon the closest living being in a mindless, animalistic state. And two, I was pretty sure O'Connor would lose his shit altogether if I tried to take any more liberties with his case than I already had.

I stepped away from the van and turned back to the detectives, both of whom were watching me with varying degrees of unease. I said nothing, just nodded to Mike as I pulled off the rubber gloves.

"You're certain."

"Yup. Burn marks on the sides of his face. It was her."

O'Connor huffed and blustered, but he stepped around me to examine the coroner's body up close for himself. When he returned, a baffled expression had settled onto his handsome features.

Mike patted his shoulder. "O'Connor, call the coroner's office. Tell them to send someone over."

"What for, Sarge? They're already here." I winced, certain O'Connor would never have said something so stupid and insensitive under normal circumstances. The look Mike gave him should have incinerated him on the spot. The younger man swallowed hard, dipped his chin, and headed back towards his car.

As soon as O'Connor was out of earshot, Mike turned back to me. "What do we do now?"

I looked at him funny. "What are you asking *me* for? You're the one with the shield, right?"

"I need you to think, Charlotte. What would you do in her position? Where would *you* go?"

I didn't need to think. I remembered what I had done in her place.

Karen Wagner's resurrection and my own were vastly different experiences. In some ways, you could argue that I got the better end of the deal. I was lucky enough to kill the man who had taken my own life after weeks of grotesque abuse. Karen's consciousness returned to the knowledge that she had just killed a twenty-six-year-old man with a beautiful young wife and a newborn baby girl. She hadn't the slightest idea of what she was or how she got that way. And while Reginald Hargrove had been an idiot, at least he knew what it was he had been *trying* to do – the basics of what a grave wight is and how they survive. When I emptied his soul, all that knowledge came with it. It also came with graphic, first-person-perspective memories of the kidnapping, rape, and murder of seven teenage girls, including myself. But I at least understood that I was no longer a normal, living, breathing human being. I understood that the life I had known was now over.

But that hadn't stopped me from wanting to go home.

# # #

We pulled up to the curb in front of a small, two-story house on Lovella Avenue in Richmond Heights just after seven a.m. It had pale blue vinyl siding, and a single sprinkler was sweeping back and forth across the front lawn. A faded American flag jutted out from a column supporting the roof over the porch, and there was a grey Mazda coupe parked in the driveway.

The very picture of suburban banality.

Before getting out, Mike turned to me. "Charlotte, I want you to stay put."

I frowned over the top of the sunglasses I had donned as soon as the sun came up. "Mike, if she's in there, she's just fed. She's not likely to hurt anybody. Least of all, *me*."

"It's not her I'm worried about. If she showed up at her front door in the last hour or so with blood-red eyes and some insane story about waking up in a body-bag, her family might be more than a little freaked out. And if someone… well, if someone who looks like *you* shows up right after…"

I wanted to argue, but he had a point. Best to let Mike get the lay of the land before I went marching in there, eyes a-blazing. But if she *was* in there, she was going to need my help. There was no sane frame of reference for understanding this. She needed someone to explain the facts of her new life to her and – God help us – to her family, somehow. I remembered those early days all too well – the confusion and the pain and the despair. I wouldn't wish it on the worst of my victims. "All right, Mikey. You go first. But if she *is* in there, you need to come get me right away."

He nodded firmly. "I will. But for now, just sit tight." As he crossed in front of the Tahoe and headed up the walk, I called after him. "Hey, Mike?"

"Yeah?"

"I've been meaning to ask: *Miss Chandra?*"

He grinned. "You like it? I thought it was appropriate."

"Why?"

"I looked up names that might fit while I was waiting for you to show up at the club last night."

Last night? Jesus Christ, that shift seemed like a week ago. "How does that fit?"

"It's Sanskrit," he said. "Means 'moon'."

Once again, Mike Benjamin had proved he could still surprise me after all these years. "Huh," I said, nodding. "I *do* like it."

Mike started off towards the house again. "I thought you might. Besides, it was either that or introduce you as Miss Cherry Bomb."

He didn't turn back to see me flip him off.

# # #

Nearly twenty minutes had passed since Mike had gone inside, and there was still no sign he was coming out. I could hear snippets of their conversation, but my slightly dulled senses from the recent feeding meant my ears weren't as sharp as they sometimes were. I gathered that the husband hadn't seen his wife since she left for the grocery store two days ago, and she hadn't made contact with him at all. Mike – not surprisingly – didn't raise the fact that his wife's body had been found and subsequently lost again over the last several hours.

I was just about to lose my patience and dial Mike's phone when I caught a flash of movement out of the corner of my eye. Something darted from the neighbor's back yard to

the right of the Wagner house and disappeared behind the building. A barefoot something wearing a green dress with pale yellow flowers.

I quickly threw open the passenger door and headed off across the lawn at a trot. I crossed the driveway and turned back along the right side of the house, following a little footpath made of round paving stones set flush with the ground. The backyard wasn't fenced in. There was a beagle tied up on a lead outside, and he was barking madly in that ear-piercing, high-pitched yowl of theirs. Glancing around to make sure no one was watching, I quickly approached him and, slipping off my right glove, gave him a gentle rub behind the ear. His knees buckled and he sank to the ground, snoring softly.

I shook my head to clear it. Animal energy was just a little *different* somehow. It left what, for a living human, might be analogous to a sour aftertaste on the palate. It fed the hunger – bought you a little time, steadied your control a bit – but it couldn't hold the need at bay all the way through a full moon. I had been in desperate spots before, times when pickings were slim and I had been forced to feed off animals in a pinch: rats, feral cats – hell, even *cows* once or twice. But I had never had the heart to take a dog before. I guess I was just weird that way.

But one way or another, the hunger had to be fulfilled – something only the taking of a human life could do. The last time I did the math, my number was somewhere over three hundred. I was probably the most prolific serial killer in American history by now. I just tended to be more selective about my victims, and nobody ever suspected they died of anything but natural causes.

Convenient, huh? In a profoundly depraved sort of way, of course.

I surveyed the rest of the yard. There was only one obvious hiding place: a small, stick-built storage shed at the back of the lot. I rose and approached it slowly, moving as quietly as possible. As I reached the door, I could see a padlock lying broken on the ground, and there were fresh splinters on the door where the hasp had been ripped away. I leaned forward and listened carefully. A soft, muffled sob could be heard coming from inside the shed.

I suddenly found myself in a predicament: if I moved in too slowly, she might hear me and panic, maybe slip past me before I could get a grip on her. Too quick, and she might lash out in terror. I decided the latter course of action was less risky for her, and I didn't think she'd be able to hurt me much before I got her corralled. But I needed to keep things quiet.

Removing my sunglasses, I steeled myself and reached out, yanking both doors open, darting inside, and slamming them shut behind me. My eyes didn't need time to adjust like a mortal's would, and I quickly spotted Karen cowering in the furthest back corner of the shed. She stared up at me warily with wide scarlet eyes but didn't seem inclined to make a run for it. Especially after I opened my eyes extra wide so she could see they were just like hers.

"Karen?" I whispered softly, my eyes locked on hers like lasers. There was almost nothing there in the way of recognition or acknowledgment. And she was trembling so violently, I honestly couldn't tell if she was nodding, shaking her head, or just plain vibrating. "Karen Wagner, right?"

Finally, her eyes seemed to clear and focus at the sound of her full name. "Wh- wh- who are you?" she managed, her voice barely audible, even to me.

I smiled reassuringly. "My name is Charlotte. Charlotte Baum."

"Wh- wh- *what* are you?" Her voice cracked, a sob breaking through. "What am *I*?"

"We're the same, you and me," I said, moving closer. She shifted suddenly, trying to scuttle even deeper into the shadows. I stopped moving again. "I won't hurt you, Karen. I *can't* hurt you. I promise, okay?"

"But I… I hurt *him*."

I sighed, dropping down to one knee just a few feet away. "I know. But that wasn't you, Karen. Not really."

"Yes, it was," she said, the horror in her voice rising. "*I* did that. I… I *took* him. I took *what* he was. *Who* he was. *Everything* he was." She was sobbing again. "And I… I *remember.*"

I glanced down at the floor, trying to control my own surging emotions. I had been there. I had been that broken, humiliated creature huddling in the darkness. And it still hurt. "It wasn't your fault, Karen. Someone did this to you, the same way it was done to me." Not exactly true, but close enough. "Do you remember who?"

She shook her head vigorously.

"That's okay," I said. "That's normal. So, tell me: what's the last thing you *do* remember? From… from *before.*"

She stopped moving, became as still as stone. Her eyes lost focus, seemed to turn deep inside. "I was… grocery shopping?"

I nodded. "That's right. You were shopping. Were you inside or outside?"

"Outside. I was – I was loading the minivan. Trying not to smash the bread or the eggs."

"Then what happened?"

"I put the last bag away and went around to get in. As soon as I closed the door, I… I realized someone was in the seat behind me."

I closed the distance between us now, reached out to take her hand in mine. The shivering began again in earnest. "Did you see them?"

Again, she shook her head so hard I thought it might wobble off her neck.

"You can't remember *anything* about them?"

Her eyes glazed again, but she recovered a bit faster this time. "Short," was all she said.

"Short?" I frowned. "You mean the person who attacked you was *short?*"

She nodded.

"And that's all you remember?"

Another nod.

"What happened then?"

Her eyes widened suddenly, and she started to squirm and shift again, as though she was sitting on a griddle. "No. No, no, no…" I gripped her hand even tighter in mine, placed my other hand gently on her shoulder.

"Karen, this is very important. Do you remember what they did to you?"

She suddenly turned and stared straight into my eyes. "Nothing. They just… *touched* me."

Oh, holy shit….

#   #   #

I sat on the floor of the shed with Karen at my side as the sun began to beat down on the shingled roof overhead. After telling me what she could, she seemed to have slipped into that catatonic state I remembered so well. I grabbed the phone from my pocket and called Mike.

"Charlotte," he snapped, answering on the first ring. *"Where in the hell did you go?"*

"Not far."

"Well, you're not in the truck. I know this because I am sitting in the truck alone, and I told you to wait in the truck."

"I did, Mikey. But something came up."

"Exactly where are you?"

I glanced back at my semi-conscious companion. "Well, at the moment, I'm in a storage shed in the Wagner's back yard. And I'm not alone."

There was a long silence. *"Karen?"*

"Yup. She's here with me. And she's… *changed.*"

"Son of a bitch…"

"You have any bright ideas on how I might be able to get her out of here in broad daylight without being seen?"

I could almost see him thinking as he sat behind the wheel of the Tahoe. *"Okay, how about this? I'll go back inside and tell Mr. Wagner that missing persons just contacted me, and they'd like him to come downtown to look at some photos. The kids are at his mother's house – he didn't want them around with the police coming and going like they've been. I'll get him out of here, and then I'll have O'Connor come back to pick you up."*

I scoffed. "That should go over well."

"Cut him some slack, Charlotte. He's a good cop. A little stiff maybe, but he's steady and not easily rattled. He'll deal."

"If you say so, Mike. I hope you're right about him. You had goddamned well better be."

"What's that supposed to mean?"

I took a cigarette out of the rumpled pack with hands that were shaking and lit it. "Because, Mikey," I said, taking a drag. "Our problem is even bigger than we thought. Remember how you said Karen's death looked a lot like one of mine?"

"Yeah?"

I blew smoke out through my nose, leaned back against the wall of the shed. "Well, that's because I'm about ninety-nine point nine percent certain Karen and I aren't the only grave wights in town anymore…"

Five

MIKE PUT THE CALL IN to O'Connor and went back inside the house to hustle John Wagner downtown. I heard the Tahoe drive off, settled in to wait. I assumed Mike had told O'Connor where to find us, but it would take at least fifteen minutes for him to get here from where we'd left him downtown by the morgue.

I spent the time trying to re-engage Karen in conversation, but she had retreated too far within herself to be much of a talker. I mostly spent the time chain-smoking and trying not to worry over the implications of having the number of walking corpses roaming the streets of St. Louis suddenly triple over the last several hours.

Before long, I heard soft footsteps approaching across the lawn. I didn't hear the beagle barking, so either his owner put him up or I had accidentally killed him. Man, I hoped it was the former. I removed my cloak and wrapped it around Karen's shoulders, pulling the cowl up over her head. Then I settled my side-shielded sunglasses over her eyes. She managed to mutter a 'thank you', but that was the limit of her chattiness.

There was a soft knock on the door of the shed. I sighed. "O'Connor?"

"Yeah, it's me. Miss Chandra?"

I rolled my eyes. "Yeah. Okay, O'Connor. Here's what I need from you: First off, I need you to *not* ask a lot of questions right now, okay?"

"Okay."

"Second, I need you to open the door just a crack and hand me your sunglasses."

"Why do you want my *sunglasses?*"

"That's a question, O'Connor. The things you're supposed to avoid, remember? And yes, I need your sunglasses. You're a cop. Therefore, I can safely assume you *are* currently wearing sunglasses."

There was an audible sigh. "I am."

"Then crack the damn doors and hand them to me, please."

There was a brief rattling of the wooden doors, which immediately triggered a tensing of Karen's body under my arm. I reassured her in soft, soothing tones. Squinting into the searing shaft of sunlight that sliced through the narrow gap that opened, I watched as a hand clutching a pair of mirrored aviators slipped into the shed. I snagged them, staring at them briefly before putting them on. "Nice shades, O'Connor," I said with a slight sneer. "Couldn't you find anything just a tad more clichéd?"

The detective's hand pushed back through the opening, palm up. "You want them or not?"

I grinned in spite of myself. "They'll do. Now, here is the third and most important thing I need from you. I need you to open the door slowly and – no matter *what* you see when you do – I need you to keep your shit wired tight. Are we clear?"

"We're clear," he said, but the note of uncertainty in his voice was unmistakable.

"All right. Let's go." I helped Karen to her feet as the doors swung slowly open. O'Connor stood there, framed in a blinding rectangle of sunlight, staring at Karen and me like a damned idiot. He may not have been able to see her face, but the green floral pattern of her dress under the black cloak was pretty hard to miss.

"What in the name of all that is holy…"

"O'Connor," I said, in a soft warning tone. "This is the part where your shit stays together. Remember?"

His mouth worked open and closed several times like a goldfish, but no added stupidity came flopping out. "So, what do we do now?" he asked, his voice squeaking a little.

"Just step back and lead the way back to your cruiser. I'll handle Karen.

You get the back seat ready, and we'll sit back there. Got it?"

"Got it," he said, and moved quickly to comply. Mike was right about him. Given what he had just witnessed, a lot of cops would have lost it. Credit where it was due, O'Connor was handling the situation about as well as I could hope.

We made our way quickly to the front yard – with a tiny sigh of relief, I saw the dog was gone and not still lying in the grass – and crossed the lawn to the white Impala. O'Connor got the right rear door open, and I gently guided Karen inside. I got her to slide over to the driver's side and dropped into the seat next to her. "All right, O'Connor, let's go."

He nodded, still in a daze, but shut the door behind me and hustled around to the driver's side. He dropped into the seat and fired the engine up. He looked back at me in the rearview mirror through the metal grating between us. "So exactly *where* are we going?"

For a moment, I was stumped. That was actually a damned good question. So, I just blurted out the first thing that came to mind. "Apartment building on the southeast corner of 13th and Monroe. You know it?"

"Yeah, I know it. What's there?"

"Home…"

#   #   #

Forty-five minutes later, I was sitting at the kitchen table in my tiny, one-bedroom apartment, staring at Detective Tommy O'Connor through a cloud of mentholated smoke. I had settled Karen into my own bed, and she had immediately dropped off to sleep. It didn't look like she'd be waking up anytime soon. I hung my cloak and gloves on the hooks behind the door and shed my long-sleeve shirt in favor of a plain white tank top.

For his part, O'Connor was eyeing up my apartment with uncertainty. I couldn't blame him. The building was old, the neighborhood was in steep decline, and the streets weren't safe at night for mortal-kind. But the rent was cheap, and the landlord didn't ask for references. So long as you paid, you stayed. But even I'll admit, on the surface it looked pretty rough.

O'Connor shifted his attention to me. "So…"

I just stared back at him blankly.

"Do you want to explain to me what's going on here, Miss Chandra?"

I stubbed out the butt of my cigarette in the nearby ashtray. "Not really, no. But I guess you're in too deep to keep you in the dark any longer."

O'Connor just leaned forward on his elbows, staring at me from a few feet away, hands folded in front of him.

"First of all," I began, "my name isn't Chandra."

He nodded, grinned. "I figured that out for myself." He pulled his coat aside to show me the badge on his belt. "Detective," he said with a wink and a nod and a click of his tongue.

"Okay, *Detective,*" I said, stalling for time as I worked up my nerve. "My name is Charlotte Baum. Mike Benjamin was my father's partner from 1983 to 1997."

"Your dad was a cop?" he asked.

I nodded.

A light seemed to go on behind his eyes. "Oh, yeah. I remember now. Your dad was Charlie Baum."

Again, I just nodded.

"Oh, *man.* Your dad was a *legend* in the old Sixth. The way the old guys go on about him and Mike – they were the real deal back in the day." He frowned, looking away for a second. "What was it they used to call them?"

I smiled slightly, shaking my head. "The Killer B's." Now *there* was a neuron that hadn't fired in a long, long time.

"Yeah," he said, chuckling. "That was it. 'The Killer B's' – Baum and Benjamin. Well, I'll be goddamned…"

I flashed him a sad smile. "Don't guess that nickname would go over too well nowadays."

O'Connor sat back in his chair, shook his head glumly. "No, it would *not.*" He frowned suddenly. "So, if I remember the story right, your dad was–" He pulled up short, blushed fiercely. "Shit…. sorry."

"No, it's okay. You can say it. He was killed in the line of duty."

"Yeah. That was – what – '97 or '98?"

"September 12th, 1997."

O'Connor's brow drew down even tighter. "And that was just a month or two after…"

I just stared at him, eyebrows raised, scarlet eyes wide.

He swallowed hard. "After both of his daughters were abducted and believed to have been murdered."

I grabbed another cigarette – I was going to need a new pack soon if I kept going at this pace – and snapped my Zippo open. "And murdered they were, Tommy-boy."

It was at this point I could see all the little pieces of the puzzle snap into place behind his eyes. He just stared at me for a solid minute, unable to speak or move. Eventually, he began to shift nervously in his seat. "So, you… you're…"

"Dead as a doornail, Detective. Just like that poor lady in there," I said, tilting my head towards the bedroom door. I puffed my cigarette to life, turning the lighter in my fingers as I watched the flame flicker and flare before closing it again with a flick of my wrist.

"But how is that–" He fell silent, answering his own question before he asked it. "The Roman resurrection ritual."

"*Romani*. And yes – somebody did the same thing to me twenty-six years ago that was done to Karen Wagner last night."

O'Connor began to shake his head, as his brain began to reject the information it was being given. "No, no, no, no – see, that's not possible. That's not – I mean, stuff like that's not *real* – it's all just…."

I pulled down one lower eyelid with the middle finger of my right hand. "These ain't contacts I'm wearing, Detective."

"But you – you're *here*. Now. Talking to me. You're obviously still *alive*."

I laughed aloud. "Am I?" I reached out with my bare hand to take his, but he quickly pulled it back.

"Gimme your hand, you candy-ass. I promise I won't bite it."

Haltingly, O'Connor let his hand move back across the table. I reached out slowly and took his right hand in my left, once again carefully keeping the power locked down tight. I guided his fingertips to my right wrist. I held them there, pressed firmly against my skin for a good twenty seconds or so. "Feel that?"

He gulped air. "No."

"Exactly." I took his wrist and shoved his hand back across the table. "You've had basic EMT training, right, Detective? What did they teach you about room-temperature people without pulses?"

O'Connor didn't respond right away. I think he was trying to decide whether to panic, run screaming from my apartment, or both. He surprised me by doing neither.

"So…" he said softly, almost childlike. "Do you have any… special powers? Like, walking through walls or flying or anything like that?"

I shook my head, stifling a laugh. "I'm a wight, O'Connor, not a ghost."

"You're a *wight*," he said tentatively. "And what exactly does a 'wight' do."

I decided to go thin on details. "Well, I'm pretty goddamned hard to kill, what with being dead already. I heal pretty fast. And my senses are a hell of a lot better than yours are."

"How? I mean, how *much* better?"

"Well," I said, warming to the conversation. "I can see in near pitch dark the way you see at high noon. That's why I needed your sunglasses back at the Wagner place. My eyes don't do so well in bright light – sunshine worst of all."

"And?"

"And I can read the lettering on a postage stamp from about a half a mile away. My ears can hear sounds even dogs can't pick up. And my sense of smell is pretty good."

"How good?"

"Good enough to tell that you had Italian for dinner last night and you've got a Payday candy bar in the pocket of your sport coat."

He reached into his left breast pocket and tossed the sweet treat on the table. I just smirked. "You want it?" he asked, shaking his head. "Can't say I'm all that hungry right now."

"No, thanks. One of the laundry list of *downsides* to being what I am. Can't eat. Liquids only. And nothing with milk or cream in it."

He glanced around the kitchen. After a moment, he rose and crossed over to the fridge, pulling the door open slowly. Inside there were cases of bottled water, soda, and even a six-pack of Guinness bottles. The alcohol did nothing for me, but I still liked the taste.

"Well, there *is* no food in here," O'Connor said.

"Very astute, Detective."

He pointed to the enormous glass jar of Dum-Dum suckers on the counter. "What about this?"

I shrugged. "Even grave wights can have a sweet tooth. I just can't chew them up. And they keep me from smoking." I smirked, toying with the Zippo in my hand, opening and closing it over and over again. "Most of the time."

O'Connor made his way over to sit down at the table again. I noticed he'd grabbed one of my beers. He held it up. "You mind? I could use a drink right now."

"I won't tell if you won't."

He popped the top off with a bottle opener on his keychain. "Thank you, Charlotte."

"*Don't* call me that," I barked, snapping the lighter closed, the distinctive sound adding a sharp emphasis to my words. "Not ever."

O'Connor stared blankly at me.

I took deep breath and released it. "Nothing personal – it's just not a good idea," I said firmly. "Don't want you to get in the habit. Especially if we're going to be seeing more of each other." I took a long drag on my cigarette, released the smoke with a sigh, "Detective, Charlotte Baum has been dead for over two decades now. It's best she stays that way. I keep telling Mike to stop using the name, but I'm afraid forty-year-old habits die hard."

O'Connor took a swig from his bottle, nodded. I could see him visibly processing my admission of my true age. "Okay. So, what *should* I call you? Miss Chandra?"

I scoffed. "No, that was Mike's idea. And I probably wouldn't answer to it half the time anyway. Might look suspicious." I thought about it for half a second before grinning widely. "How about you call me by my *professional* name? That's one I'll answer to."

O'Connor seemed prepared to let the word 'professional' slide without comment. "And what's that?"

"Just call me Cherry…"

\# \# \#

It was mid-afternoon before Mike called to say he'd just dropped John Wagner back at his house after they'd spent the last two hours flipping through useless mugshots. He was on his way back to the City. I told him where we were, and that O'Connor was still here with me.

"How much did you tell him?" Mike asked.

"Enough to explain Karen. Covered the basics. Left the advanced studies for later."

"The feedings?"

"Didn't come up."

"Good. That's probably best for now. But we're going to have to bring him all the way in if he's going to take over for me."

I scowled. "Take over? What the hell is that supposed to mean?"

"Charlotte, I turn sixty-five in December. The department is going to put me out to pasture. Mandatory and non-negotiable."

"So?"

"So, at that point I no longer have access to the information you need to… carry on your work."

I looked across the table at O'Connor, who was slumped in his seat and finishing up the last warm dregs of his beer. "You sure that's the right way to go?"

"You want to run an ad? Recruit? Talk to every cop in the Department, see who'll get with the program?"

"Guess not." O'Connor was watching me now, his curiosity piqued by hearing only one side of the conversation.

"Charlotte, he's handled everything we've thrown at him so far. And he's still there. And, besides, we've talked. It's one of the reasons I picked him as my successor. He's as pissed off and frustrated with the whole system as any of us – almost as bad as I was when we started all this."

"There's an awful big gap between not liking the way things are and choosing to do something about it, Mikey."

"Well, then it's my job to find out if he's willing to bridge that gap or if we have to start looking somewhere else."

I chewed on that for a second before I suddenly remembered the other thing I wanted to ask him. "Oh, hey, Mike, would you mind stopping at the corner and picking me up a pack of cigarettes on your way? American Spirit menthols. I'm down to nothing here."

"I'll make sure you're covered."

"Thanks, Uncle Mikey," I said in a sing-song voice.

"See you soon, Charlotte."

#   #   #

Mike showed up at the apartment twenty minutes later. As soon as he walked in, I held out my hand for the cigarettes – I'd smoked the last one in my pack while we waited – and he handed me a half-dozen Blow-Pops. I glared at him through narrowed eyes.

"Told you I'd take care of you," he said with an evil grin.

I huffed, rolled my eyes, and turned my back on him. "Do you have any idea how hard it is to get one of these goddamned things lit?"

"Smoking is bad for you, Charlotte. That's why I quit years ago. You should, too."

I unwrapped one of the suckers – *grape, the heartless bastard* – and popped it in my mouth without looking back at him. "Still dead here, Mikey. Not getting any deader."

A long moan came from the other side of the wall – Karen was starting to come around.

I ducked into the room. The men let me handle the physical exam while they watched from the doorway. No sense in letting either of them get too close in case she had awakened in a confused state and lashed out again. But she seemed to be in full control of her faculties and, as I knelt beside the bed, she actually managed to sit up, shoulders resting against the headboard.

"Karen," I said quietly. "How are you feeling?"

"Better, I think." Her voice was harsh and raspy. "Could I have something to drink?"

I glanced at O'Connor, who nodded and darted back into the kitchen. He returned a moment later with a bottled water and handed it to me. I popped the seal and gave it to Karen. "Go slow at first, all right? Your body may not–"

But before I could even get the words out, she had turned the bottle straight up and taken two or three big swallows. Her expression suddenly became pained and an instant later she leaned over the side of the bed and up-chucked it all back out onto the floor.

" – be quite ready for it just yet," I finished, patting her on the shoulder. O'Connor didn't miss a beat. He disappeared again for a moment and returned with a towel he'd retrieved from the bathroom next door. I took it with a nod of thanks. "Yeah, that's gonna happen from time to time."

Karen wiped her mouth on the towel, and I took it back. I tossed it over the wet spot on the floor.

"What's wrong with me?" she asked.

I sighed heavily. "That's going to take a little bit more explaining." I turned to my companions standing in the doorway. "Would you guys give us a minute?"

Mike nodded. "Sure thing, Charlotte. We'll be right outside if you need us." He pulled the door shut behind them, leaving me all alone to explain to Karen Wagner why the life she had led up until this point – the life she shared with a loving husband and four young children – was now irrevocably, unequivocally over…

#   #   #

By the time I reemerged from the bedroom and pulled the door shut behind me, nearly an hour and a half had passed. Mike and Tommy were sitting at the kitchen table. From the empty bottles standing there, it seemed that between them they had killed the rest of my Guinness.

Mike rose first. "How is she?"

"Well…. I'm afraid she's dead, Mike."

Mike scowled, but I just shrugged. "Too soon to tell. She isn't taking it too badly, considering. But that doesn't mean she's not a complete trainwreck."

Mike nodded, glanced over at Tommy then back at me. He held up his phone. "I'm sorry, Charlotte, but O'Connor and I have to go. Call just came in – another body in the basement of a burned-out house on the west side of Hyde Park. Looks bad. Worse, it looks like it could be related to the rest of this mess."

"I can't leave her here alone," I said, shaking my head.

"Well, we're going to need you on this, that's for sure," Mike said. "But from the look of things, you've got some time. We don't need to worry about this DB getting up and running off anytime soon."

He held his phone up to me. On it was a photo of a young Black woman sitting on the floor, her arms suspended from shackles mounted into what looked like rings drilled into a cinder block wall. There were no outward signs of trauma, but I saw nothing to suggest the occult.

I shook my head. "Doesn't look like a resurrection ritual at all. What makes you think it's related?"

He drew the phone back and swiped his finger across the screen. When he turned it around again, my stomach dropped. "Because this is on the other side of the same room," he said grimly. "And that *does* look like a resurrection ritual."

I stared at the screen up close, used my fingers to zoom in. He was right. The circles and symbols looked older and dryer, but the same as we had seen at the warehouse. "So, she wasn't the one being brought back. She was just left there."

"Left to wait for whoever *was* brought back to…" Mike gave Tommy a nervous sideways glance. "*Attack*," he finished.

Yeah, I guess "feed on" still wasn't terminology we wanted our young detective friend exposed to just yet.

"Charlotte, I hate to ask this, but we can't take Karen with us, and we can't have an officer come by and sit with her either. Not when every cop in St. Louis has her description and thinks her dead body was stolen out of that van. And I will *need* you at the crime scene." Mike raised an eyebrow. "Is there *anybody* you know who you could trust to stay with her for a bit? Even just an hour or so?"

I shook my head vigorously at first, but then a thought crossed my mind. It was a terrible idea, but it was the least terrible among the almost complete lack of options we had left. Worst case scenario, it would probably just mean the end of my career at The Daily Grind. "Yeah, I think I do," I said. "You go on ahead. Text me the address, and I'll be there as soon as I can."

59

Six

I EXPECTED NO LESS, BUT when Momma Wanda answered my call and told me she would come straight over, I was intensely relieved. I had no idea what the fuck I was going to tell her when she arrived, but she was already on her way by the time I hung up the phone.

Momma Wanda is what is known in the business as a "house mom". She worked for the club, taking care of the girls. Officially, she was the "dressing room manager", tasked with making sure the girls had everything they needed to keep working. She provided food, costume and makeup help, hygiene products – whatever. House moms typically have god-awful reputations, and a lot of dancers outright hate their guts. A lot of them are women who have aged out of the business – embittered, petty, and viciously jealous of the younger girls who had taken their place. And mostly, the girls hated them because they outright *demanded* a share of the dancers' tips.

But Wanda was the exception that proved the rule. She was – without qualification – the sweetest, kindest, and most authentically generous woman I have ever known, at least since my own mother passed away. And she was the closest thing to a real mother many of the girls at The Daily Grind had ever known. She provided sound advice and emotional support, helped mediate the inevitable conflicts that arise in the close confines of a dressing room full of women, and had even helped a few girls get clean and sober when they hit rock-bottom. I knew for a fact she had taken a few special cases under her own roof when they had nowhere else to go. The girls at the

Grind tipped Wanda because they wanted to – I had never *once* heard her ask a dancer for money.

An hour after I made the call, I was standing by the curb outside my building in dark glasses, watching as a black Ford Taurus rolled to a stop in front of me. Wanda practically leapt out of the driver's seat and came hustling around the front of the car to gather me into a back-breaking embrace. Then she held me out at arm's length to look me up and down before shaking her head worriedly.

Wanda was tall and solidly built, with long, sturdy legs and strong shoulders. Her skin was a smooth tawny beige, virtually unlined despite probably being somewhere in her early- to mid-sixties. Her voice had a distinct musical lilt and slipped back and forth between English and Louisiana French with an easy, effortless grace. And, as always, the powerful scent of Oscar de la Renta perfume preceded her wherever she went.

"Are you all right, *cher*?" she said, laying her hand on my cheek. "You've never asked me for help of any kind before, so I *knew* it must be serious."

"It is," I said. "But I'm fine, Momma. I just – I need your help with… someone else. She's upstairs in my apartment."

"Well, then go on and lead the way, *cher*. I have never turned away a child in need, and I ain't about to start now."

I led the way back into the building, pulling off my glasses as we stepped into the shadowed hallway and began to ascend the rickety stairs to the third floor. By the time we got there, Wanda had begun sweating through the thin fabric of her dress, but her enthusiasm didn't seem the least bit diminished.

As we entered the apartment, I rounded on her gently. "Now, Momma, I need you to understand something first. This woman, she… well, she's been through a lot in the last couple of days. She's not herself, and I'm afraid if she's left alone, she might hurt herself or get into some kind of trouble."

"Now, *cher*, how about you just step aside and let me have a look?" She began to work her way past me, heading for the bedroom door. "I've been a club mother for twenty-seven years, *jén dam*. If it can go wrong with a woman, I have most *assuredly* seen it before."

She reached for the door, but I grabbed the knob. "Momma, *this* is gonna be something new. I just don't want you to–"

"*Tifi*, you had better move your skinny ass out of my way and let me see what's ailing the poor baby girl on the other side of that door."

I sighed, but turned and pushed the door slowly open anyway.

"Karen," I said softly as we entered. Karen rolled over towards us and sat bolt upright in the bed, retreating up against the far wall. "This is Wanda. She's a friend. She's going to keep an eye on you for a bit while I run out. But it'll be okay. You just need to–"

Karen scooted back even further against the headboard, wrapping her arms tightly around her knees. She began trembling violently, nearly as bad as she had when we'd first met in the storage shed.

"*O, dous Jezi, cher*," Wanda said, shoving me to one side. "You're scaring this poor thing right out of her wits. You and all your blathering on." She sat down on the side of the bed, and I winced as she took one of Karen's bare hands in her own and reached up to brush the hair back from her face.

As Karen stared at her anxiously, ruby-red eyes shining, I started talking fast. "So, Momma, Karen and I are… well, we're cousins. And see, her eyes, that's um… well, that's normal. Like mine. It's a genetic trait, sort of like…. well, it's kind of like albinism. So, when we–"

Wanda slowly turned and looked at me like I was the biggest idiot on the face of the earth. "*Cher*," she said sharply. "Asking somebody for help and then lyin' to their face is just plain old bad manners. Just *exactly* who do you think you're talking to?"

I blinked, confused for a moment. "I don't–"

"My name is Wanda Dee Quebodeaux, *tifi*. Lafourche Parish, Louisiana – born and raised." she said, her accent seeming to thicken by the minute. "Do you honestly believe it is even the *least* bit possible that I don't recognize a *grave wight* when I see one?"

I was staggered. I must have stood there for half a minute before I realized my mouth was still hanging open. "Wait – you *knew?* You knew the whole time?"

"Of course, I knew," she said, with a dismissive wave of her hand. "My *maman* and her *maman* – going back nine, maybe ten generations – they all plied the trade from time to time. I wasn't born with the knack, *malheureusement*, but I was raised up in and around the occult since I was *nan kouchét.*"

"But at the club, you–"

"*Cher*, you have been workin' in that hellhole for – what? – five, maybe six *years* now? This profession tends to wear on a woman. And here you sit having aged not one single day in all that time. Always skippin' shifts when the moon gets near to full. And a person would have to be stone blind not to see those eyes of yours didn't come from any costume shop. Those red ones, nor the pink ones neither."

"But then why – why were you always giving me such a hard time about keeping my weight up and eating right and all that crap?"

"Well, just because *I* know, doesn't mean the whole world needs to. And I might have made a show of it around those other girls, but I never *did* try to take you home and fatten you up, now, did I? *Bondye konnen,* if I thought I coulda done anything to fix that board-flat *derrière* of yours, don't you think I'd have done it already?"

I laughed reflexively, a stupid grin spreading across my face.

"And, let me tell you, you didn't always make it easy, keeping them other girls off your tail. Sometimes I just about had you figured for a showboatin' fool. Spinnin' round that pole like a bayou hurricane, doing things on that stage no mortal girl has any cause nor right to be doing."

To say I was flabbergasted would have been the understatement of the century. Here I'd tried so hard for so long to keep my secret safe, when there was someone I knew and adored right next to me the whole time who would have understood everything I was going through. In the end, I just smiled and gave Wanda a crushing hug of my own.

"Do you think you'll be okay here for a while?" I asked as she patted my back. "I may be gone until dark."

Wanda shooed me towards the door. "You run along now, *cher*. This child looks well fed, and we've got some catching up to do, now. We're gonna need to get a whole lot better acquainted, if we're to be carryin' on together from here…"

# # #

The house where Mike and O'Connor waited for me was a little more than a mile west of my place in an even seedier part of town. If that's possible. Along both sides of the narrow streets surrounding the scene, about one building in four was boarded up or burned out. Hardly a night went by when I didn't hear shots fired from that direction as I sat by the open window in my kitchen.

I even hunted in this neighborhood some nights, snatching up gang members who perpetrated the drive-by shootings that occurred throughout the City's North Side almost every night. Shootings that sent stray bullets tearing into these houses and – all too often – the helpless residents within. If I got hold of somebody who just played at being a hard ass and had never really hurt anyone, I'd just have a peek inside their head and leave them safely tucked into the bushes nearby to sleep it off. If what I found displeased me – well, they still ended up in the bushes. They just weren't getting up again.

I phoned Mike from outside the crime scene tape this time, and he sent O'Connor to collect me with the same red visitor badge from the warehouse and another pair of nitrile gloves. Poor Tommy had been forced to deal with a lot over the last twenty-four hours, and the stress was showing. His face looked drawn and haggard, and his blue eyes were couched in dark circles that I hadn't noticed back at my place. He'd been on duty since early yesterday evening, although as a cop he ought to be used to long hours. But the parade of incomprehensible bullshit was still marching steadily on by, and whatever he had seen in that basement had clearly rattled him even harder.

My suspicions were confirmed the moment I entered the blackened ruin of the house where the latest body had been found. Most of the second floor had burned away ages ago, but a large portion of the first floor was intact, as was the basement beneath. My skin began to prickle with that same feeling of residual energy I'd felt upon entering the warehouse where Karen was found. It intensified as we stepped through the basement door and made our way down the short flight of stairs by the light of Tommy's flashlight, until by the time my feet touched solid ground, I felt like I had ants crawling all over my body.

The CSU had set up portable lights all around, but the gloom in the basement seemed almost preternaturally deep. Mike spotted me and waved us over. He was standing next to where the dead girl from the photos was still suspended from her shackles and chains.

"What do you know so far?" I asked, grimacing as I stared down at the corpse, which was already beginning to swell in the relentless summer heat.

"Our victim's name is Tasha Davis, seventeen," Mike said, shining the light from his phone on the little spiral notepad he always carried. I couldn't repress a tiny smile in spite of the circumstances – Dad had always carried one just like it. "She was reported missing last week by her family. They suspected she had run off with her boyfriend – one Lester Carter, twenty-two – also currently missing. His family never filed a report, since apparently it wasn't unusual for Lester to be gone for several days at a time. But they haven't seen him at all since Tasha disappeared."

I knelt down next to the girl's body, tried to lean in as close as I could without disturbing even so much as a speck of dust. Again, there were no obvious signs of trauma or assault, and her clothes were all still on, even her white leather tennis shoes. I didn't see any signs of cold-burn lesions on her face, but when I moved the collar of her blouse aside with a pen I borrowed from Mike, I could see her entire neck was one gigantic mass of yellowed flesh. I shook my head. "This revenant didn't take hold of her the same way Karen did the deputy coroner. They must have wrapped both hands around her throat as if to throttle her and taken the life force that way."

"Life force?" Tommy said, his voice unnaturally loud in the small, bare space. Several of the techs working the scene glanced up before returning to their duties. Having seen me at two separate crime scenes already, most of them seemed far less interested than before.

"Not now, O'Connor," Mike said quietly. "We'll explain later."

Yeah, that'll go well. I didn't know how much longer the subject of the feedings could be put off with the young detective, but *this* sure as hell wasn't the time or place. "Anything more on the boyfriend?" I asked, trying to steer the conversation in another direction.

"Well, if he's still out there, you probably would have crossed paths with him sooner or later. Been running with a street gang called the Three-One-Four Set since he was thirteen. In just the past two years, he's been a person of interest in at least five drive-by shootings, one of which killed an eleven-year-old boy walking home from school. Didn't look to be accidental, either – kid was hit three times in the chest, twice while he was on the ground. His older brother was in a rival gang, and we think his murder was payback."

"But no proof."

"Nothing."

"Jesus fucking Christ…." I sighed heavily. My next move wasn't going to be popular. "Mike, I *have* to try something."

He frowned. "Like what."

"I want to try to pull something from her memory. But I need to lay hands on – or at least *a* hand on – to do it. *Bare* hands."

Mike glanced around at the room. "Are you sure this is necessary?"

I shrugged. "Only if you want to know who killed her."

He motioned to Tommy to move in closer, then knelt down to try to insert himself between me and the several other people in the room.

O'Connor stayed standing. "Sarge, you can't let her do this. It'll contaminate– "

"Tommy," Mike said softly, with just a hint of menace. "Kneel down next to me. *Now.*"

O'Connor wanted to argue. He hesitated for a long moment, but eventually dropped down on his haunches next to Mike. "I am *so* going to lose my shield over this bullshit…"

"You will if you don't keep your mouth shut and do what I tell you to," Mike said.

He was bluffing, but Tommy was too off balance to see that. We were gonna be *way* outside of acceptable police procedure here.

Once I could no longer see the others in the room and they couldn't see me, I peeled off my right glove and reached out a bare hand towards Tasha Davis's head.

"No gloves?" Tommy asked, his voice almost plaintive.

I shook my head. "Doesn't work that way, hotshot. It has to be skin-to-skin. And once a body has been dead this long, the chemicals in the brain degrade so badly, I'll be lucky if I can get anything at all."

Mike glared him into silence again.

I placed my hand gently along the side of the girl's face, my palm against her temple and my fingers splayed back along her scalp. I closed my eyes and began to pull. There was nothing at first – I thought for a moment she had been gone too long. But then there was a flicker of light in my mind's eye. It guttered like a dying candle, then flared again suddenly. I pulled even harder on the threads connecting my mind with hers and, just before they snapped, I received a single, horrifying image: a young Black man with eyes as white as bone, mouth open wide in a scream, hands wrapped tightly around my throat.

As the connection was broken, I fell back hard onto my ass in the dust. For a few seconds, all I could see was that final image burned into my retinas. Then my vision swam and cleared, and I was staring up at Mike and Tommy who were on either side of me, faces tight with concern. O'Connor kept glancing around to see if anyone had noticed the sudden movement.

"Are you all right?" Mike asked.

I shook my head, but just to clear some lingering fog. Then I nodded. "I saw him. The revenant."

"No idea who it was?"

"Just a face. But… I got the distinct impression that she knew him. She was terrified, but beneath that was a feeling of confusion. As if she didn't understand why *this* person in particular was trying to hurt her."

Mike fiddled with his phone. When he turned it around, there was a mugshot of a young, handsome Black man. The same man I'd just seen in Tasha Davis's memory. "That's him. The boyfriend?"

Mike nodded, grimly.

"He was the one in the circle of power. Somebody killed him, placed his body in the circle, and left his girlfriend here for when he woke up."

Now O'Connor was really starting to lose it. "Sarge, what the *fuck* are we doing here? You're letting civilians like…. Vulcan *mind meld* dead victims now?" He rose to his full height, planting his hands on his hips, his eyes glinting in the dim lighting. "Look, I don't care if it costs me my shield anymore," he hissed. "If you two don't level with me – *right now* – I swear to Christ, I'm going to the Ex-O with this."

Mike glared at him hard for a second, then turned to me. I just nodded. "Not here though," I said, getting to my feet.

Mike glanced at his watch. "All right, it's after two already, and we haven't eaten since last night." Mike looked up at O'Connor. "How about we go grab lunch someplace quiet and talk?"

Tommy looked down at the victim for a beat, then nodded.

"Detective Carson," Mike called out over his shoulder. A short, stocky young man in a grimy white dress shirt excused himself from his conversation with a CSU technician and walked over.

"Carson, you're in charge here. O'Connor and I have to run down a lead. This is your scene now, so do it right. Got it?"

"Got it, Sarge," the young man said, grinning just a bit. Probably the first time he'd been the lead detective on a crime scene before.

"All right," Mike said, patting the man on the shoulder. He headed for the stairs with me and Tommy trailing in his wake. "Keep me posted."

"Will do, Sarge."

Seven

WE ALL PILED INTO MIKE'S truck outside and headed down St. Louis Avenue to Crown Candy Kitchen. It was one of the oldest continuously operating restaurants in the City of St. Louis – over a hundred years old – and always attracted a huge lunch crowd. People sometimes stood in line around the corner for an hour or more in the shade of the green and white awnings just to get inside. We got lucky – it was well after peak lunch time – and we managed to get a table right away. We sat down in the last booth along the back wall of the small space, a beautifully crafted wooden piece in antique white, flanked by tall coat-hook posts on the outside corners.

This wouldn't have been my first choice for a 'quiet' lunch spot, but I guess Mike was thinking more along the lines of a public place away from the crime scene where O'Connor would be less likely to make a scene. I also noticed that he let O'Connor slide into the little booth first before sitting down next to him, firmly pinning him in.

Mike and O'Connor ordered sandwiches and fries while I stuck to a cherry soda – a *real* cherry phosphate from the oldest soda fountain in St. Louis. When it arrived, I snagged the maraschino from the top and handed it to Mike by the stem. I can't eat them, but I knew Mike loved them. He popped it straight into his mouth, snapping off the stem and twisting it idly around one finger.

We sat there in silence for a while, until it seemed O'Connor could take no more. "Okay," he said finally. "We're here. I'm calm. I'm controlled. So how about you two tell me what the *fuck* is going on?"

Mike seemed stumped as to how to start, so I just waded in. "Tommy, look. There are a few facts about my… *condition* that we may have left out of the Cliff Notes version I gave you back at the apartment."

"Such as?"

"Well, I've already told you what I am. You've seen – more or less – how someone like me comes to be. And I've told you that I cannot eat solid food."

"Yeah," he said, brow furrowing. Then his eyes widened suddenly. "Oh, don't tell me you have to drink blood to survive…."

I sighed and rolled my eyes. "No, Tommy. Not a vampire, remember?" I said quietly. "But… it is true that a grave wight does not live on suckers and cherry sodas alone."

"So, what then?"

I glanced at Mike. He hesitated, then nodded. I turned and stared straight into Tommy's dark blue eyes with my crimson ones. "Life force." I said, spreading my hands out in a helpless sort of gesture.

"*What?*"

I shrugged. "I don't know any other way to describe it. It's the living essence, the spark… the *soul* of a human being, for lack of a better term."

"Wait," Tommy cried, rising off his seat just as Mike shoved him back down hard. "Are you telling me you eat *souls?*"

The waiter standing at the end of the table holding two plates of food stared at the three of us blankly.

I raised a hand to my forehead and just stared at the wall while Mike got the food settled in front of them. The waiter stared for a moment longer before wandering off.

"You want to keep your voice down, O'Connor?" Mike snarled as soon as the server was out of earshot. I glanced over his shoulder, relieved to find the booth behind us was empty at the moment.

"But how…" Tommy stuttered. "What kind of… Okay, so whose *souls* do you eat?"

"The last one was Chester Hamlish."

Tommy blinked, began to look back and forth between Mike and me. "Hamlish? The dead guy in the hotel room last week? The one with the busted window?"

"Yup," I said, taking a sip from my bendy-straw.

"But that wasn't even a homicide. The ME said it was natural causes. Not a single mark on–" Tommy's voice stopped short.

Wicked girl that I am, I gave him one raised eyebrow and a sly smile.

Tommy looked like he wanted to throw up or climb bodily over the table to escape, but Mike had him pinned in tight. "So, you just go around draining the life out of people at random?"

I shook my head. "There was nothing *random* about Chester Hamlish."

I could see the lights go on behind Tommy's eyes. He looked to Mike, then sat back hard in the booth. "Chester Hamlish was a suspected serial killer."

For the first time, Mike decided to chime in. "Not suspected, O'Connor. We had that motherfucker dead to rights. Caught him with the fingers of two dead boys in his freezer. Apparently saving them for later if he got hungry."

Tommy blanched, swallowed hard, said nothing.

"But then his attorney got the search warrant thrown out, along with any evidence that was collected while it was being served," Mike growled. "And that son-of-a-bitch *walked*."

"It took a few years to get to him," I said. "And it cost two more kids their lives. But he won't be hurting anybody else from now on."

Tommy was frowning deeply. He stared at me hard. "But how did *you* know what he was? All the information about him? None of that detail was in the papers."

I smiled, leaned forward. "Did you ever watch *Dexter*, Tommy?"

"Yeah. A few seasons. I liked the novels better. They just didn't–"

I cut the book club review short. "Well, what I can do makes Dexter look like Dilbert. And while I may not work in a crime lab, I do have somebody in Homicide who is… shall we say, *sympathetic* to the cause."

Bright boy that he was, Tommy turned straight to Mike. "So, you feed her the info on these people, and she goes in and takes them out?"

Mike swallowed a bite of his BLT, nodded. "That just about sums it up."

Tommy shifted in his seat, squirming like a kid who needs to hit the restroom. "How long has this been going on?"

"I showed up on Mike's doorstep two moons after I was brought back,"

I said. "Once I got him past where you are now, we started talking about how to keep my new 'addiction' under control. That was twenty-six years ago."

"Two *moons*?"

I sighed heavily. This was probably going to be the last big hurdle. "A grave wight must feed at least once during every lunar cycle. The full moon lights the fuse. It burns for the next twenty-eight days. And with each day that passes without feeding, a little bit of my humanity is stripped away, and I become more like one of them."

"One of who?"

"The revenants. The mindless monsters who killed that deputy coroner and Tasha Davis. By keeping my feeding schedule regular, I get to live like a real girl most of the time."

By now O'Conner was leaning forward in his seat, face buried in his hands over the untouched plate in front of him. I exchanged anxious glances with Mike as he finished off his own lunch and started snatching cold fries from Tommy's plate. It was a full minute before the young detective dragged his hands down his face and just stared at me with a lost look. "Am I to understand that with Sergeant Benjamin's complicity and assistance, you've picked off at least one human being a month for twenty-six years."

"Yes."

"That's… three hundred and twelve people."

"Give or take," I said with a shrug, mildly impressed with Tommy's math skills.

"And *every* one of them was guilty. *Every* one of them deserved to die. All three hundred of them?"

"You can't lie to the hunger, O'Conner," I said firmly, shaking my head. "When I touch someone, I see all the evil they've ever done. And I see *exactly* what they are now. If they felt any remorse for what they did. If they enjoyed it. And – *most* importantly – if they intend to do it again, given the chance."

He glared at me hard. "And what if you're wrong?"

"I'm not. *Ever.* If I hook into someone and I see innocence or remorse or even just a *sliver* of regret…. I can just throw them back in the pond. No harm done."

Now he rounded on Mike. "How can you be okay with this, Sarge?

You're a cop. A

good cop. The justice system–"

Mike looked at him like he'd lost his mind. "The *justice* system?" he asked, incredulous. "O'Connor, you've been on this job a good long while now. Long enough to know better. You know the justice system in this country is broken beyond repair. We've got innocent people sitting on death row and *known* murderers walking free in the streets. Rapists, child traffickers, gang-bangers – and most of the time, there's not a goddamn thing we can do about it."

"But I can," I said with a grim half-smile.

For a long time, Tommy said nothing. When he finally spoke up, I could tell he was teetering. "Sarge, how could you let yourself get involved in this?

Mike didn't hesitate. "It was Char – *Cherry's* father. My partner, Charlie Baum."

"I know – he was killed in the line of duty. But that doesn't excuse–"

Mike turned to Tommy, his dark features as hard as cut stone. "The asshole that killed him – big-time drug dealer named Christopher Macklin, went by C-Mac – had all but publicly boasted he was going to take us both out. We'd been harassing his low-level dealers and pulling his product off the streets for months. He had to get us off his back. So, he and three of his crew put a dozen rounds through the back window of our cruiser while we were sitting outside a convenience store off Tucker. I was hit twice in the shoulder. Charlie took one to the base of the skull."

O'Conner looked down for a moment, and Mike kept going. "Charlie and I never saw a fucking thing. So, we had nothing. No witnesses – at least none willing to talk. No surveillance footage back then. No vehicle description. Every cop and criminal in the City knew who did it – but this guy was going to *walk*. DA wouldn't even let us hold him without something tangible to hang a charge on."

I let out a long breath, tried to keep the tears from my voice before speaking. "I was resurrected four days after my dad died. Like Karen and this guy back at the newest crime scene, I killed the first person I encountered. In my case, it was the psychopath who had kept me doped up and locked in his basement for six weeks, while he…." I took another deep, shuddering breath, tried to steady myself. "So, you can imagine I wasn't too broken up about it. But he was just the first."

Mike swallowed hard. "Charlotte, you don't –"

"No, Mike," I snapped. "I do. If he's in, he's *all* the way in." I glared at Tommy across the table. "I knew what I had become because the guy who *killed* me knew. And I knew what I would have to do to survive. But I couldn't. I couldn't take a life like that. So, I did nothing – just wandered the streets for a month, eventually reading about my dad's murder in the papers. And the whole time, the hunger got stronger and stronger."

Tommy's face went paler still.

"One night, I was asleep in the doorway of a vacant building in North City, barely in my right mind with the madness. And the precise moment of the full moon came, just as an eighty-year-old man walking his dog passed me by. And…. I *took* him."

"You killed him? You drained his… drained his *soul?*"

I choked down a sob and carried on – thank God, the restaurant had all but emptied out by now. "It wasn't me that did it. At least that's what I told myself – that it was the monster. But I couldn't take it. I couldn't live like that. So, I decided to end it. For good this time."

Tommy jaw tightened as he processed that for a moment. "You tried to kill yourself."

I fought to stop the tears from welling up, failed miserably. I angrily wiped them away, pissed at myself for breaking down in front of O'Connor. I nodded sharply. "A few weeks after my dad's funeral." It was a struggle to get back my control, but I somehow managed to keep talking. "Knowing what I'd become, how I'd have to live out what might be an immortal existence taking other people's lives to survive? Dealing with all the sick, demented *filth* that I pull out of their heads? You bet your *ass,* I tried."

"But… but how–"

"I broke into a sporting goods store one night. Stole a big-ass handgun and a box of ammunition to match," I said quietly, as the tears began again in earnest. "Then I walked as far out into the woods as I could, sat down at the base of a tree, stuck the barrel under my chin, and pulled the trigger."

"Holy *shit,*" Tommy gasped, eyes as big as dinner plates. "Why –"

My temper flared violently for an instant. "Tommy, do you honestly think I *want* to live like this? Look, once a month I have two choices – find a victim who deserves it or lash out uncontrollably at one who doesn't. I don't get a vote. And don't think for one fucking *second* that the thought of putting myself in the ground where I belong hasn't crossed my mind every single day since I woke up in that psycho's basement."

"But it didn't work?" He scoffed humorlessly. "Well, fuck, obviously, it didn't work."

"Nope. Blew a hole through the top of my head the size of a softball. And all I managed to do was knock myself out cold. When I woke up a few hours later, I could barely move. I couldn't even form a coherent thought. And the pain – oh my God, the pain was *incredible.* I ended up lying there for almost a day in agony. But eventually, the hole closed up, my brains got unscrambled, and I found I could walk again. So, I got up, chucked the gun in a pond nearby, and just headed back into town."

"And that's when you went to Mike."

I nodded, wiped my running nose on a napkin. "He was on leave, still recovering from the shooting. He took me in, actually *believed* the insane story I was telling him. He listened to me without judgment. And together we worked out.... *this*."

Tommy looked at me hard. "You never tried again?"

"Never. But I think about it. Every… single… fucking… *day*."

For the second time, a long silence fell over the table. Tommy's jaw worked furiously, his thoughts turned deep inside. I didn't have to lay hands on him to know he was wrestling with some pretty hefty demons in there somewhere: his duty as a cop, his oath to uphold the law, and – overriding everything else – his sincere desire to help people. To protect and serve, as the old saying goes.

In the end, he seemed to come to some kind of accommodation with himself. Some moral high ground on which he could stand and still look at himself in the mirror. "Okay," he said quietly, carefully. "I'm in. But only for the duration of this case. When it's over… well, then I guess we'll see."

I nodded as Mike dropped a hand on Tommy's shoulder. "That sounds like a good plan, Detective," he said.

Tommy turned to me again. "Dexter, huh – not Dracula?"
I laughed despite the tears. "Not even Count Chocula, Tommy...."

Eight

THE GUYS FINISHED THEIR LUNCH and Mike dropped me back at my apartment. We agreed there was probably nothing more I could contribute at the Hyde Park scene, and my continued presence there would just raise more questions. They promised to let me know if anything new turned up, and I promised to keep them in the loop on Karen's progress. I hopped out of the back seat of the Tahoe and, waving goodbye, turned and headed for the front door of my building as they sped away.

As I approached, I could see smoke rising from a vacant lot about halfway down the block and there was a strange odor on the breeze, like somebody's grill was putting a little too much char on their burgers and dogs. Shaking my head, I opened the front door and went inside. I removed my glasses and took the stairs two at a time, eager to let Wanda get back to her own life and maybe even catch a few winks in the recliner in front of the TV. I had been awake for nearly twenty–four hours now. I could go much longer under pressure. But I found it helped bolster my control over the hunger and made going into work a little easier if I stuck to a regular schedule. Well, as near to regular as a dead woman who works nights at a strip club can get.

As I topped the last flight of stairs, I stopped dead in my tracks: my apartment door had been blasted through the frame and lay diagonally across the third-floor landing. "Momma!" I screamed, clearing the obstacle in a single bound. I scanned the outer room, but nothing appeared to be amiss. I headed for the bedroom, silent heart in my throat.

Wanda was face down on the floor next to the bed. I darted to her side and carefully rolled her over. There were no visible signs of injury, but that didn't mean shit when there were creatures like me in the mix. I reached up and touched the side of her neck. An enormous wave of relief washed over me as I felt the steady thump of her pulse under the skin.

I did a quick sweep of the apartment, but to no avail: Karen Wagner was gone.

Returning to Wanda's side, I brushed the hair back from her face and began patting her gently on the cheek, speaking softly to her as I did. After a seemingly endless moment, she began to stir.

"Momma? Momma, are you okay?" I asked, my voice uncharacteristically shaky. I don't rattle easy, but it had been a miserable fucking day so far.

With my help, Wanda managed to struggle to a sitting position. "*Bondye mwen – sa ki sot pase*," she muttered, her eyes finally focusing on mine. "Jus' give me a minute to catch my breath, *cher*," she said, her voice dry and thin. "I'll be fine – takes more than a little bump on the head to put Wanda down for the count."

"Momma, what happened? Where's Karen?"

"I just stepped out to use the ladies' room, and when I came back, she was sitting up there waiting on me," she said, waving a hand towards the bed.

"She *attacked* you?"

"She surely did. Eyes all milky white and snarling at me like a damned tiger."

I shook my head. "Momma, that's impossible. She just fed last night. She can't possibly have progressed to revenant mode that fast."

"She can if the wight-master called."

That one just about floored me. "What do you mean, *wight-master?* I've never – "

"*Cher*, a grave wight is irrevocably bound to the will of the person who raised them. If the master calls, the wight *must* answer."

I shook my head. "But how can that be true? Nobody has ever–" And then it hit me: of course, I'd never heard my master's call. I'd sucked the life out of the sick sonofabitch the second he was within arm's reach. Reginald Hargrove had been too stupid to ask any questions beyond the resurrection ritual itself and his ignorance had killed him.

The thought gave me a shiver. If he'd have known the power he held over me, been just a little more careful about my awakening, then he'd have had the most obedient, submissive slave a diseased prick like him could ever have hoped for. And all these years, I'd never known how close I had come to a life of endless abuse and torment.

"I killed the man who brought me back me, Momma. Drained him dry as soon as I woke up."

She nodded solemnly. "I figured as much. And that's why you've got your own free will, *cher*. That's what *moun fou* like him get, messin' about with powers they don't understand. But poor Miss Karen…"

"Karen was under the control of whoever performed the resurrection ritual."

"Well, whoever it was, I guess they had no cause to want me dead. That girl coulda sucked out my soul like a crawfish head and tossed this old shell to the side in a heartbeat."

I sighed heavily. "And now we've got another indestructible living weapon walking the streets of the City, with absolutely no idea who's pulling her strings."

Wanda looked at me funny. "*Indestructible? Cher*, how in the name of the *bon Senye Jezi* can you *be* a grave wight, and *still* know nothin' about 'em?"

"What's that supposed to mean?"

"Look, you may have been *lucky* so far, but you are in no way 'indestructible'."

I stared at her. "Wait – so you're saying…. you mean a grave wight *can* be killed?"

"*O wi*, I surely do," she said with a nod. "It ain't easy, but it most definitely can be done. Elsewise, there'd be red-eyed folk wandering all over this world."

"But *how?*"

"Oh, there's three or four different ways to do the deed. Decapitation works, assuming you can get in close enough to swing a blade. Thing is, you only get one chance. You miss or don't cut all the way through, and that's gonna be *lanmo ou.*"

"Anything else?"

She shrugged. "Some kinds of poisons, from what my *maman* taught me. Mostly ones with a big dose of mandrake root in 'em. Of course, the quickest way to do it is fire."

"*Fire?*"

"*O, wi.* You can get close to it, but if you ever get yourself good and lit up, there'll be no puttin' you out."

With a terrible realization, I leapt up from the floor, turned, and ran down the steps as fast as my legs would carry me.

#　#　#

By the time I got Mike on the phone and got him and Tommy headed towards the vacant lot, Karen Wagner's body was charred almost beyond recognition. The fire had burned with an unnatural intensity – like white phosphorus – consuming not only flesh and bone, but the very earth beneath it. If not for the tattered remnants of her green and yellow dress that had somehow escaped the blaze, there would be virtually no way to know for certain that it was her. Hell, that it had ever been a human being at all. Except that *I* knew it was.

Beside the body was the warped and twisted shape of a yellow bottle of Ronsonol lighter fluid, the same one that had been sitting on the dresser in my bedroom this morning, the same one I had used to refill my Zippo just yesterday. The pack of matches lying in the grass was from The Daily Grind. I picked them up and stuffed them into my pocket. No sense throwing any shade in that direction.

Two patrol units arrived first, with Mike's Tahoe just a few seconds behind. It came to a screeching halt, and both he and Tommy hopped out and came racing across the lot at a dead run. They halted alongside me, each of them retreating a step as the terrible heat radiating from the spot where Karen's body lay washed over them.

"Jesus Christ, Charlotte," Mike said, holding his hand up to shield his face. "What in God's name is that?"

I gestured helplessly at the smoldering remains. "Karen."

Tommy looked pale, bending forward with his hands on his knees to steady himself. I thought for a moment he was going either going to puke or go down. "What the *hell* happened?"

"She overpowered the woman I left to care for her, took a bottle of lighter fluid from my apartment, and did… *this.*"

"Is your friend all right?"

"Seems to be. Turns out she's known exactly what I am since she first met me years ago. And she let me in on a few secrets about my kind, too – things even *I* was unaware of."

"Such as?" Mike asked.

I glanced around at the uniforms who were beginning to cordon off the area, keeping the ghouls and rubberneckers at bay. "No, Mikey. Not here. Too many ears. We need to regroup and think this thing through from the beginning. How long before you get to a point where you can talk?"

Mike glanced at his watch. "Technically, Tommy and I should have been off-duty hours ago. As soon as the day-shift detectives arrive on scene, we'll turn it over to them."

Tommy looked agitated. "But, Sarge, shouldn't we stay with this one? This is – or *was* – our vic. Maybe we should –"

I shook my head. "They're not going to find anything here, Tommy. Karen walked into the middle of this lot, doused herself in lighter fluid, and set herself ablaze. She didn't need any help to do it." My voice was shaking again, my emotional control slipping. "She just needed me to leave her alone…"

#   #   #

After seeing Wanda safely to her car, Mike, Tommy, and I sat down at the little table in my kitchen. Both of them were staring at me expectantly, so I took a deep breath and just dove right in.

"Wanda said that when Karen attacked her, she was in full-on revenant mode. The way I understood things, that shouldn't have been possible. But Wanda said that all grave wights are bound to the will of the person who raised them – she called them 'wight-masters'. If they call to them, the wight has no choice but to come – to do exactly as they're told."

"So how is it *you* never had to answer to anybody?" Tommy asked.

"Because I killed the man who resurrected me. Apparently, if the wight-master dies, the wight regains their free will."

"But if Karen was a revenant, why didn't she kill your friend?" Mike asked.

I shrugged. "She wasn't told to, I guess. She was just supposed to knock her out and escape."

Tommy was shaking his head again. "Just to commit suicide a hundred yards away?"

I looked down at the floor. "I can't say for certain, but I'm guessing she was no longer of any use to them."

"What's that supposed to mean?"

I turned to my uncle. "Mike, you said somebody called you directly to tell you where to find Karen's body, right?"

Mike nodded grimly.

"And they mentioned me by name during the call."

"They did."

I sighed heavily, dropping my face into my hands. "Mike, Karen Wagner was a misdirect – a wild goose for us to chase. They resurrected her in *your* district – practically within rock-throwing distance of *my* home. They called you and told you exactly where to find the body with plenty of time to spare before she rose. And they knew you, of all people, would recognize the markings of the resurrection ritual."

"But why?"

Tommy surprised me by answering first. "To draw Cherry out into the open."

I nodded firmly. "That's my guess, too."

The light of understanding flared in Mike's dark eyes. "They knew you'd be the first person I'd call when I realized what had happened in that warehouse."

"And I'd wager they were watching from somewhere not too far away. Maybe even milling around amongst the gawkers behind the crime scene tape."

"Son of a bitch...." Mike rubbed his hands across his face. "But

Charlotte, you and I – and I guess Wanda, now – we're the only people who knew the truth about you. What's changed?"

I shook my head. "I don't know. But there's more."

He sighed wearily. "Now what?"

"My thinking is this: Karen was like a time bomb, set to go off at midnight. They didn't leave anybody in the warehouse for her to go after. They wanted her to rise either in a room full of cops or on a slab in the morgue. Her primary purpose was to spread chaos and confusion in the ranks while they finished their real work."

Mike slumped in his chair. "Raising Lester Carter."

"Yup. And you'll notice that they were very careful to provide *him* with a meal for when he came around. They wanted him satisfied and controllable. And remember: Lester Carter was a violent, remorseless killer *before* they gave him the power to take a life with the touch of a hand."

"We were *supposed* to find Karen," Tommy said. "They let us focus our attention on her, while – hell, Cherry, you even brought her into your *home*. If they really were controlling her–"

"Then they know where I live, who's been helping me, how I've survived, who my friends are – the works."

Mike was quiet for a long minute, deep in thought. "Charlotte, why did the fire kill Karen? I thought you were immortal."

I sighed. "That's the other bit of bad news Wanda dropped on me today – or *good* news, I suppose, depending on how you look at it. Turns out, I *can* be killed after all. Fire appears to be the quickest way. You saw how she went up. No *human* body burns with that kind of heat. It's because of what she was."

"But there are other ways, too?" Tommy asked.

"Separating my head cleanly from my body is supposed to do the trick. You know, I kinda always wondered about that one. I figured even if it didn't kill me, how in the hell was I supposed to get it back on? Would it just grow back? And what would I do with the extra head? And how –"

I glanced up at my companions, suddenly aware of their mortified stares. My tone had been facetious, but the look of horror on both Mike and Tommy's face was genuine enough.

I just kept going, "But obviously, somebody would have to get in close to do that, and they'd be taking an awful big risk that I'd lay hands on them before they could get it done. Wanda also mentioned some kinds of poisons containing mandrake, too." I shook my head, a rueful smile pulling at my lips. "I guess even Supergirl has her kryptonite."

"I'm not finding any of this funny, Charlotte." Mike said with a scowl.

"Just gallows humor, Mikey," I said, patting his hand where it rested on the table, careful not to let the power stir. I rose and went to the fridge, took out three bottled waters and grabbed a Blow-Pop from the jar on the counter.

"Okay, so do you have any suggestions on how we should proceed?" Mike said, twisting the top off the bottle I handed him.

"First off, I think you guys should call in the canine units and start doing sweeps of every derelict building in the City."

Mike scoffed. "That's somewhere north of six *thousand* buildings, Charlotte. And what exactly would we be looking for?"

"More scenes like that one in Hyde Park. Doesn't make sense to go to this much trouble for one resurrection, Mikey. I'm guessing you're gonna find other victims. In this heat, some of them will start to report themselves." I took a sip from my bottle. "And I'd go through the missing persons reports for the last twenty-eight days. Maybe focus on people with a history of violence, cruelty – anything that makes them stand out. If they happen to be bigger and stronger than most, that should move them to the top of our list, too."

"Okay, you've lost me now," Mike said, shaking his head in confusion. "What list?"

"Cherry's right," Tommy said, nodding thoughtfully, peeling the label from his own bottle. "That's exactly the type of people I'd target if *I* was going to try to do it."

"Do what?" Mike asked, becoming exasperated.

I unwrapped the sucker – *Yeeech...seriously? Watermelon?* – and popped it in my mouth, waiting for Tommy to impress me again. He didn't disappoint.

"Raise an army," he said, gazing straight into my eyes.

I nodded.

Maybe Mike was right about Tommy after all....

\# \# \#

In the week that followed, the dogs turned up two more resurrection sites, and neighbors called in a third. All of them in the Fourth District and all of them with similar characteristics: each of them had an empty power circle on the floor and a revenant victim either tied up or caged somehow nearby. I was able to get a residual image of the attacker from the mind of the first victim they found – a petite little thing named Sofia Rossi, but the others were too far gone. We matched the face of the one I *did* get to a bodybuilder who never came home after a night at the gym in late July – Vincent Lagorio. Guy was a fucking behemoth – six foot six and two hundred and eighty-five pounds. Could have played defensive line in the NFL. I sincerely hoped the rest of them weren't *that* goddamned big. Turns out he was also engaged to Sofia.

But otherwise, the heart of the City was unnaturally quiet. It was almost as if the bad boys and girls sensed that something new was cruising these streets like a shark in the shallows, and nobody wanted to be the next one to get pulled under. And now the clock on my own personal time bomb was ticking down fast. Pickings would have been slim on the streets even if Mike hadn't all but forbidden me from running around on my own.

Over Mike and Tommy's vehement protests, I decided to return to work. They figured out a schedule between them – without consulting me, of course – that allowed one or the other to pick me up and drop me off at the club each night. I didn't like it one damned bit – they were far more vulnerable out in the open than I was. But Mike actually swore he'd have me locked up if I tried to ditch them even once. Not sure how he figured he was going to *do* that if I decided I didn't want to go, but the level of concern evident in the otherwise empty threat convinced me to play along, if only for *his* peace of mind.

After twenty-six years of playing lone wolf, suddenly I had a whole damned pack surrounding me. I can't say the feeling was entirely unwelcome, but I damned sure didn't want anybody getting killed on my account either....

Nine

FROM MY FIRST SHIFT BACK at The Daily Grind, it became crystal clear that even Momma Wanda had gotten in on the bodyguard racket. From the minute I walked in the door until she passed me off to whoever's turn it was to drive me home, she was never more than arm's reach away unless I was on stage or interacting with customers. And even then, I could see her peering out between the swinging doors of the dressing room – not really watching my performance but scanning the crowd for anybody who looked even the slightest bit off. I got the distinct feeling she had tucked something nasty up her sleeve. She claimed to have no talent for the occult, but I was betting she could bring a lot more to the table in a pinch than just hugs and sage advice.

I, for one, was just glad to get back into the swing of things, the comfort of the routine. It might sound bizarre to a layperson and maybe even more so to some people in the business, but I really *loved* the thrill of being onstage. I'd spent more than half of my life hiding in the shadows. Up there I was the star of the show. Instead of fading into the background, I was free to attract people's attention – *demand* it, even – and let them feel just the tiniest hint of the immense power I carried inside. I could hold the crowd in the palm of my hand, mesmerize them, make them my own. And whenever I touched someone and *didn't* take their life – well, there was an odd kind of power in that, too. Morbid, maybe, but undeniable, nonetheless.

And unlike the other girls, I didn't really have an alter ego, a 'real person' I needed to be outside the club. No identity I needed to protect. No family to be ashamed of what I do.

Outside, I was nobody. No life. No name. Not even a headstone. Just a faded footnote – an obituary more than a quarter of a century old.

But up there on that stage – I *was* the Cherry Bomb.

Most dancers stay out for just a few songs at a time, but I don't get winded like a regular human. Plus, I usually need to collect as much cash as I can on stage, since I won't do the private dances that take place in the little curtained cubby-holes in the far corner of the club opposite the dressing room. That's where the real money gets made, but it was simply too dangerous when it got later in the cycle. And it would have been a bad precedent to set now. For the sake of my self-appointed guardians, I kept my performances to a more reasonable length before collecting the scattered cash lying along the tip rail and heading for the relative safety of the dressing room.

My fifth shift back, a week or so after I returned to the club, I finished a three-song set and climbed down from the stage, hands full of rumpled, sweat-soaked paper bills. I had just about reached the back hallway when a ripple went over my skin like ice-water trickling down my spine. That made the third time that night I'd felt it. I turned and scanned the room with a predator's eyes. Eyes that had slowly bled down over the past several days to a bright bubble-gum pink. Eyes that had started to become sharper and more focused than normal – a sure sign that the hunger was growing. In about a week, without a proper feeding, the irises would fade to a shade I'd only seen once or twice in my afterlife – the pale, delicate hue of spring cherry blossoms. Beautiful, yes, but, oh, so *very* dangerous. And if the full moon arrived before the hunger had been fed, my eyes – as featureless and white as new-fallen snow – might just be the last thing some poor innocent bystander ever saw.

I spent a full minute standing there, clutching my clothes in front of me, head swimming with an acute awareness of enormous power somewhere very close by. But as was the case each time, I couldn't identify the source of the strange sensation. After a while, I gave up, shook my head to clear it a bit, and pushed through the swinging doors marked CLUB STAFF ONLY in big block letters.

Wanda was waiting for me, bustling me inside and getting me settled at an open station as far from the other girls as possible. I snagged a fresh pack of cigarettes from my purse. But by that time, I was shaking so badly that Wanda eventually had to take the Zippo from my trembling hands and light the cigarette for me.

"What on earth is going on with you tonight, *cher?*" she asked, her voice little more than a stage whisper. "You look like you're barely able to stand up straight on your own out there."

I could only shake my head. "I don't know, Momma," I said softly, glancing around to make sure no one was close enough to overhear. "Maybe it's just the cycle getting too far on. Mike still hasn't identified a target for me yet. And I haven't been able to find *anything* on my own."

"You're still keeping it under control though, *non?*"

"Yeah," I said, nodding. "For now. But this is probably going to be my last night to work until this situation sorts itself out. In a week – ten days tops – things are gonna start to get pretty damned interesting. Mike's been so busy trying to identify exactly who was raised at the last two resurrection sites, he hasn't been able to do any legwork for me. I just hope he remembers that ignoring my issue is going to escalate our problems to whole new levels."

Wanda reached out and took my hands in hers. I flinched, clamping down on the hunger that rose up like a serpent in my breast. She hid it well, but I could tell even she was shocked by just how cold my hands were becoming, even through the fabric of the gloves. "*Cher*, your uncle has taken good care of you all these years. I don't think he's likely to start neglecting you now."

Kennedy came sauntering over from the other side of the dressing room, garbed in a ridiculous red-leather bondage set that must have taken her and Momma an hour to get her into. "Hey, Cherry! You doing all right? You look like curdled shit, woman. What the fuck is going on with you lately?"

I smiled hollowly, trying to put on a good face. "Had some family trouble. Personal stuff to take care of."

Her soft brown eyes narrowed and darkened. "Everything all right?"

"Yeah. Everything's fine now."

Most people would have called bullshit on me, but Kennedy knew me well enough to let it go. She just gave me a tight hug and held my shoulders for a beat. I was careful to hug with my arms and not my hands, keeping my fists closed tight behind her back. I know she had to feel some of the chill regardless. "Well, if you need anything, you call me. Cause I got your back, all right?" She held out her fist. I grimaced but bumped it and blew it up anyway. ""Time to go separate some fools from their hard-earned money" And with a flourish, she was gone.

I suddenly felt that same deep-rooted weariness that had overtaken me so often in recent weeks settling into my bones. I rested my elbows on my knees and buried my face in my hands. "Momma," I asked, my voice sounding painfully childlike in my own ears. "I think I need to go home now. Do you mind?"

Wanda had been my ride that night, since Mike and Tommy had been called in to what looked like a murder-suicide downtown. With three bodies on the ground, neither of them had been able to get away to drive me to work. Mike had refused to allow me to go on the train, so I had reluctantly agreed to impose on Wanda's kindness once again. "Not one bit. Let me get Jasmine over there into that ridiculous getup she's puttin' on, and we'll go, okay?"

She patted me on the shoulder and hurried off to a nearby station where the young lady in question appeared to be in a wrestling match with a white sailor-style skirt and top. She had her blue-black hair tied up in long, sweeping pigtails on either side of her head and was having difficulty getting the little cap that completed the outfit to stay settled in between. She was working the midnight-to-six shift, and in – or *out* of – that getup, she stood to make some damn good money tonight.

While Wanda got that situation under control, I quickly changed into my usual street clothes, swapping out my stage gloves for the sturdier pair I wore in the second half of the lunar cycle. I pulled on my boots and headed for the backstage door. I said goodnight to the other girls as I passed, earning a condescending sneer from a relatively new dancer named Misty as she headed for the main floor. Apparently, she thought wearing the cloak, gloves, and boots outside of the club constituted taking my on-stage persona a little too seriously.

Piss off, you miserable bitch, I thought, not really in the mood to deal with anybody's backstage bullshit tonight. *At least I can walk the streets in the daytime and* not *look like a stripper. Good luck tucking those ridiculous bolt-on tits of yours into* any *outfit that* doesn't *make you look like a streetwalker.* I was way out of line, and I knew it. But in my defense, she was a *very* difficult person to like.

Wanda joined me after a few minutes, and we headed out back to the employee parking lot. Vic was a stickler for security – especially for staff – and the lot where the dancers and other club employees parked was surrounded by an eight-foot security fence topped with coils of razor wire. A key card opened and closed the automatic gate. Within a few minutes, we were passing through the fence line and headed off across the main lot towards the highway.

As we neared the turnout, that familiar feeling of power – *my* kind of power – swept over me again. I spun around in my seat, searching for the source. But the only remarkable thing I saw was a gorgeous bright blue 1970 Cutlass with hood scoops, mag wheels, and white rocker panel stripes. If it were mine, I'd have parked it a lot closer to the building, not all the way the hell out here by the road, away from the security lights and cameras and bouncers. But there was nobody behind the wheel and no sign of anybody loitering nearby, and soon Wanda's lead foot had the club and everything around it fading quickly in the rearview mirror. So, I just shrugged it off once again and leaned back in the passenger seat, closing my eyes.

"You sure you're okay, *cher*?" Wanda asked, eyeing me sideways again.

I sighed. "To tell the truth, Momma, I don't really know anymore. I've been getting these dizzy spells and cold chills running over my body on and off all night. It got really bad right after my last set."

"Well, with most of the girls, I'd jus' say they were coming down with some kind of bug. But I don't guess that's got much to do with it in your case."

"I've never been sick a day in my life… or *death*, I guess I should say. I'm not sure it's even possible, is it?"

She shook her head. "I suspect you've just been neglecting yourself – not sleeping like you should. All this fuss and bother goin' on and I know you've been wearing yourself out tryin' to fix it. Probably been running on fumes for a while now. What you need is some rest and to get your strength up again."

I nodded weakly. "What I *need* is somebody deserving of a sudden, tragic demise. But we seem to be running low on murderers and child molesters right now. The cupboard has been strangely bare these last few weeks."

Wanda grinned. "Well, maybe you just need to lower your standards a bit, *cher*. Hell, I see plenty of folks runnin' around out there every day doing nothing but takin' up space and messing things up for the rest of us wherever they go."

That actually coaxed a chuckle out of me. "I don't work that way, Momma."

"Oh, come on, *cher!* Jus' *think* of the possibilities: Able-bodies folks parkin' in handicap spots. Those *moun fou* you see weaving all over the road and gettin' folks killed 'cause they're too busy textin' or talkin' on the phone. People talkin' all *through* a damned movie you paid good money to see. Old folks drivin' down the highway with one blinker on the whole time. Then there's the ones that don't bother using their damned blinker at *all*. Tailgaters. Folks ridin' down the street on motorcycles so loud they're 'bout to rattle the fillings out of your teeth. And telemarketers – *Bondye mwen*, sometimes I wish *I* could just drain some of them dry right *through* that damn phone. And I'd throw my good-for-nothin' ex-husband your way, but *nobody* deserves to have to go pokin' around inside the head of that *vye moun fou*...."

By the time we'd turned onto the interstate, Wanda's rant had me laughing so hard I was rolling in my seat.

#   #   #

Wanda dropped me off outside my apartment a little after one in the morning. I waved goodbye as I watched her drive off into the darkness. I turned and headed up the short length of broken sidewalk that led up to the front door of my building, so exhausted that each step felt like I was dragging a ball and chain. I opened the front door with my key, taking care to lock it securely behind me. There were twelve apartments in the building, four on each floor, and the last time I looked, eight of them were occupied, including mine. The lock wouldn't slow me – or anybody *like* me – down for more than a few seconds, but in this neighborhood, it was best to take as few chances as possible under any circumstances.

I made my way up the stairs, a herculean feat in and of itself, and fiddled with the lock on the new door the landlord had installed – at my expense, of course – a few days after Karen had blasted the last one from its frame. I'd spent a few nights with the broken door propped up in the opening and held in place by pushing the recliner up against it. It wasn't secure by any stretch of the imagination, but I didn't have much to fear from garden variety burglars or rapists. Hell, at this point I'd *welcome* a violent home invasion. Get this damn monkey off my back for another month.

As soon as I was inside and had locked the door behind me, I went straight to my room and collapsed onto the bed. I think it probably took three whole minutes for me to fall fast asleep.

#   #   #

I was startled awake sometime later by the constant vibration of the cell phone on my nightstand. It took me a few seconds to find the damned thing, not because of the dark – my eyes were well beyond the point of being able to see in almost total darkness – but because I had been sleeping so soundly, I had awakened in a bit of a confused state. I managed to lay hands on the phone at last and glanced at the caller ID: *Mike. Fuck me...*

"Mikey, what in the name of God are you calling me for at–" I pulled the phone away from my head for a second to check the time, "Four-fourteen in the morning?"

"Charlotte, where are you right now?"

"In bed trying to get some very badly needed sleep. Why, where are you?"

"A bit out of my jurisdiction, I'm afraid," The phone went quiet for a moment, and I could hear him barking orders to somebody nearby. *"Look, O'Connor is heading your way now. Can you be ready in fifteen minutes?"*

"I guess so. Where the hell am I going?"

"The Daily Grind."

If he wanted my attention, he had it. I sat bolt upright in bed, instantly wide awake, every nerve ending tingling. "What – *why?* Mike, what's happened? Is Momma okay? Is she–"

"She's fine, Charlotte. But we've got two bodies on the ground here and another girl who's gone missing."

I shook my head, trying to process what I was hearing. My stomach tightened into a ball as I contemplated the obvious next question. I had to ask it anyway. "Mikey, who died?"

There was another brief silence on the line, probably as he checked his little notebook. *"Male, Caucasian, thirty-two – name of Oliver Goldblatt. Looks like he was a customer. Other body is female, Caucasian, real name Barbara Bennett. Goes by the stage name 'Misty Mountains'."*

I felt like I was going to throw up on the floor of my bedroom, just exactly where Karen had not too long ago. "Jesus fucking Christ...." I muttered, wiping a hand over my eyes. "And the missing girl? She's one of ours, too?"

"Afraid so."

"Who?"

The silence on the other end of the line was palpable. *"Charlotte – it's Kennedy."* Another agonizing pause. *"I'm sorry, Charlotte. Wanda said you're friends."*

I could barely bring myself to speak at this point. But I shoved down the anger and the terror and just tried to lower my head and keep bulling forward. "And the bodies?"

"Not a mark on them. But no burns, either."

I shook my head, though he couldn't see me. "No, there wouldn't be. This wasn't a revenant attack, Mike. Way too early. This was murder, plain and simple. And I think it was something else, too."

"What's that?"

"A message."

#   #   #

I was waiting at the curb when Tommy pulled up in Mike's black Tahoe, red and blue strobes flashing in the grille. I went to slide into the passenger seat, and Tommy had to snatch a small pile of manila folders out of the way before I could sit down. As I buckled up, he stacked them on top of the armrest of the truck, pinning them under his elbow.

"You all right, Cherry?" Tommy asked as he gunned it and pulled away from the curb, turning left onto Thirteenth and heading south towards the approach to the Musial Bridge.

I sighed heavily, sliding down into the seat. "No, Tommy, I'm really not."

He was quiet for a moment. "I'm sorry about your friends."

"Misty wasn't a friend," I said, shaking my head. "Truth be told, I couldn't stand the bitch. But she didn't deserve *this*."

"But the other girl, Kennedy? She –"

I glared at him fiercely, and he wilted just a bit under the power of my unnaturally colored gaze. "Yes, Kennedy is a friend. But she's only *missing*, Tommy. And at this point, that's *all* this is." I threw my hands up in frustration. "Fuck, maybe she just finished a set and cut out without anybody seeing her leave. It happens. A customer creeps a girl out and she flat refuses to go back out onto the floor." I knew I was talking out of my ass, trying to convince myself more than Tommy. But I refused to let the cops just write her off before we'd even started looking.

"I'm sorry. I didn't mean to imply–"

"No, it's okay," I said, turning my eyes back to the road. "Look, I'm exhausted, I'm confused, and more than a little pissed off. It has nothing to do with you."

He fell silent, concentrating on his driving as he carefully made a hard left through the

red light at the empty intersection of Thirteenth and Cass.

"Tommy," I asked. "What the hell is Mike doing over on the East Side, anyway?"

He pursed his lips, kept his eyes on the road. "They activated the Major Case Squad after the last of the revenant victims turned up. It's being treated as a regional serial killer investigation now, Cherry. As of yesterday, Mike and I have been detached to the MCS for the duration."

"Jesus H. Christ," I said, rubbing my tired eyes. "This thing is spiraling out of control so fucking fast. It was hard enough keeping the paranormal aspects of this mess under wraps when it was just the three of us. Now we're going to have twenty-odd investigators from all over Hell's half-acre poking around and pulling at threads. And here you guys come with Morticia Addams in tow, all black cloak, black gloves, and bunny-rabbit eyes."

"It'll be all right, Cherry. These guys are professionals. I'm sure they won't–" He turned suddenly to glance at me. "Wait – *bunny-rabbit* eyes?"

I turned to face him and opened my eyes as wide as I could. In the light of each passing streetlamp, he leaned in closer to look. I guessed he hadn't been paying much attention earlier or even the last couple of times he'd shuttled me back and forth to the club. And whenever he'd seen me before that, my eyes had been ruby red, as had Karen Wagner's. The only significant amount of time he'd spent around me had been in the first few weeks after a feeding. He'd never seen this softer pink shade before.

"Whoa…" he said with a crooked grin, marveling at the change. "That is *so* cool."

"It really isn't, Tommy. Not when you consider that pink is somewhere between the bright red of a freshly fed grave wight and the pure white of a starving revenant." I shook my head firmly. "A week from now, if this clusterfuck hasn't worked itself out, you will not think this is very cool at *all*. Especially if you and Mike are forced to put me down."

He swallowed hard. "Mike would never let that happen, Cherry."

"Well, he might not have much of a choice." I stared at him hard for a long minute. "Don't make him be the one to do it, Tommy. You understand me?"

He opened his mouth, but nothing came out at first. "Cherry, I can't –"

"*Promise* me, O'Connor. Swear it on your life."

He said nothing for the longest time. "Yeah. Yeah, I promise. If it comes to that…."

I nodded, releasing a breath I wasn't aware I had been holding. "Good. Remember, you'll be doing me a favor. I can't live with taking an innocent life. Not again."

He slowed as he made the last left onto the bridge approach, but just as he reached the straightaway, a homeless man pushing an old shopping cart stepped off the median and directly into the path of the truck. Tommy grabbed the wheel with both hands, dodging into the right lane and slamming on the brakes. He shot past the man, only missing the front edge of the guy's cart by a fraction of an inch. As he swung back into his own lane, all the folders he'd had tucked under his elbow went flying into the passenger side floorboard.

Tommy glared in the rearview mirror as I turned in my seat, both of us shaken by the terrifying near miss. The old man actually flipped us the bird as we sped away.

"Stupid motherfucker," Tommy snarled, returning his attention to the road ahead.

"Cut him some slack, Detective," I said, starting to gather up the scattered papers that now littered the floor of the truck. I had no idea which ones went with which folder, so I just tried to stack them all face up in a neat pile. "He probably just–"

My voice caught in my throat and for a moment I was stunned into silence. In my hand I held a photograph of a beautiful classic muscle car – bright blue, hood scoops, mag wheels – a 1970 Oldsmobile Cutlass Supreme. I held the picture up to Tommy.

"You know this car?"

He glanced over briefly, nodded. "Yeah. That one goes in Lester Carter's folder."

"Wait – *this* is Lester Carter's vehicle?"

He frowned and nodded. "Yeah. Why?"

I sighed heavily. "Because *this* car was parked outside the club when Momma and I left tonight."

Tommy snagged the picture, his eyes flicking back and forth between the photo and the road ahead. "Are you sure?"

"Absolutely."

Swearing violently, Tommy floored the accelerator, reaching over to add sirens to the strobes as he did. The Tahoe leaped forward, and he grabbed the handset of the police radio. "We better give Mike the heads up, let him get a fresh BOLO out on that car." He shook his head grimly, taking a deep breath. "Holy Mary, Mother of God – Sarge is going to flip his shit when he hears this…"

Ten

WHEN WE FINALLY PULLED INTO the lot of The Daily Grind, I knew Mike's was not the only shit getting flipped tonight. The last thing a strip club owner wants to see is his building surrounded by cop cars, crime scene vans, and yellow tape – all of it clearly visible from the nearby interstate. My boss, Vic, should be about halfway to stroking out at this point. With two dead bodies in a private suite and one of his own dancers abducted from *inside* the club, it was going to take *months* for his business to recover from this. Assuming it ever did. The pandemic had wounded the club badly a few years ago – this shitshow might just finish it off.

Tommy pulled up at the edge of the chaos surrounding the place, giving us a chance to approach the building with at least a little discretion. By now, some of the other girls *had* to have noticed that my rides to and from work of late had been in unmarked police vehicles. Half of them probably had me pegged for a narc already. *If they only knew...*

We found Mike standing near the open rear doors of an ambulance, talking to my buddy Jerry, the head bouncer. Jerry had a sort of shell-shocked look on his face, as if his mind was still struggling to catch up to whatever had just happened. A paramedic was bandaging a bleeding wound on the back of his scalp. I broke away from Tommy and headed towards him at a jog, greeting Mike with a nod.

"Jerry," I said, sitting down beside him on the bumper of the ambulance. "Are you okay?" He looked at me funny for a moment, seemed to lean away from me a bit. "I'm fine, Miss Cherry," he replied, his voice noticeably changed from its usually friendly, jovial tone. "Just took a knock on the head, is all. Some fella come bustin' through those doors with Miss Kennedy by the arm, her pitching a fit the whole way. So naturally, I stepped in to put a stop to it."

"Did he hit you?"

"Nope. Just stopped and stared at me for a moment. Then he reached out his arm and I went to block it – that's the last thing I remember. Musta cracked my head on the sidewalk when I went down."

"You get a good look at him?"

"Yes, ma'am. Black fella, about my height – maybe a bit shorter. Stocky build, strong. But he…"

I leaned in. "He what, Jerry?"

"Well, Miss Cherry, meanin' no offense, but he had bright red eyes, just like yours." He suddenly seemed to notice the recent change in my eyes for the first time. "Well, at least the way yours usually look. Red, though – not pinkish the way yours are now."

I suddenly realized the reason for the subtle changes in Jerry's demeanor: he was afraid of me.

Mike was already pulling up pictures on his phone. He showed one to Jerry – the same mugshot of Lester Carter I had seen back in the basement where Tasha Davis's body had been found. "This him?"

Jerry leaned in, squinted. "Yeah, that's the guy all right. Except like I said, his eyes was all red, not dark like they show there." He turned and gave me another uncertain look, as if really questioning my appearance as something more than an on-stage persona for the very first time.

The touch of fear I saw reflected in his eyes hurt a lot more than I expected.

Mike tilted his head towards the club, and I said goodbye to Jerry, patting him reassuringly on the shoulder as I stood. He jumped a bit but managed a weak smile.

Mike kept going straight through the front doors of the club, and I followed with Tommy close behind. As soon as we were inside the club proper, he turned to face us, all business. "O'Connor said you saw Carter's

Cutlass parked outside tonight?"

"I did. And there's something else."

"What's that?"

"More than once during my shift, I felt something… *odd*. A kind of cold chill and dizziness that shook me up pretty bad. It wasn't the *same* feeling I had walking into the warehouse or that house in Hyde Park the other day, but it was… *related* somehow."

"You think it was Carter?"

I nodded. "I do. I think I can sense when other… *people* like me are close by. I've just never been around any before."

"But you never saw him?"

"No, and I *looked*. But by this time in the cycle, I can usually hide from living eyes if I want to. Maybe we can hide from each other, too."

Tommy stared at me, frowning. "What do you mean, *hide?*"

I sighed, looking around. The CSU guys were swarming the private suite area, but nobody appeared to be paying us any attention at all. "This isn't the time or place for show-and-fucking-tell, but you need to understand this, Tommy. Mike knows, but I don't think he's ever seen it in action before. And this will work a whole lot better than me trying to explain it." I turned to Mike. "I'm going to try to use the glamour to get a close-up look at the crime scene."

Mike turned and looked over his shoulder. "CSU is crawling all over the place, Charlotte."

I nodded. "And not one of them is expecting to see *me*."

Mike sighed, nodded. "Fine. But the same rules apply. Don't disturb anything – don't *touch* anything."

I flipped him a mock salute. "You two just try to act natural – don't make it obvious you're watching anything in particular."

Mike grunted testily but didn't try to stop me. As he and Tommy stood in the middle of the club floor, pretending to compare notes and eyeing me sideways, I let the glamour wash over me and slipped to the other side of the nearest stage. I took a roundabout path toward the private dance suites at the far end of the room, moving with a stealth and lightness that only apex predators can manage. I slid past each tech in turn, stutter-stepping and dodging and even crouching down at times to avoid physical contact. But not one of them so much as glanced my way. I got within ten feet or so of where the bodies were lying, but CSU was shoulder-to-shoulder in the narrow, curtained entrance. I had to settle for observing from a distance.

A few moments later, I returned to Mike and Tommy, let the glamour slip away.

Tommy's eyes were as wide as dinner plates. "That was – without question – the most insane thing I have ever seen," he whispered, turning back to look towards the suite area. "Nobody saw a fucking thing, and you passed a foot in front of their faces! But we saw you every step of the way." He turned to look at me again. "You want to explain that?"

I shrugged, shook my head. "I can't give you specifics. I just know how I've learned to use it over the years. The bottom line is, I can't *truly* be invisible. I think the glamour takes advantage of people's tendency to only see what they *expect* to see and filter everything else out. *You* could see me because you knew I was there. But the folks around the private suites –"

"Weren't looking for you." Mike finished.

Tommy was starting to regain his composure. "Like a blind spot, but one *you* can consciously control."

I considered that for a beat. "Close enough. But there's a catch: it only works until I've fed. Once the hunger is sated, the glamour is gone. For at least a week or so after the next full moon, when the hunger starts to build again."

Mike got back to business. "Did you recognize the male victim? Is he a regular?"

I shrugged. "I've seen him around – I wouldn't say he's a *regular*, but he's definitely been here before."

Mike glanced at his notebook. "Apparently, he really *is* just a regular guy – husband, dad, day job."

"Just like Karen."

Mike nodded. "We used his face to unlock his phone, located his next of kin. Seems his wife and kids went to visit her sister in Rolla this morning and he stayed behind to work. Or so he said."

"We get a lot of guys in here looking for a few hours of playtime while the wife's away."

"He was in there with both of the girls? The missing one, too?"

Tommy grinned at Mike. "Come on, Sarge. You never fantasized about a little *ménage à trois?*"

"Fuck you, O'Connor."

I nodded. "Again, nothing unusual. It's expensive, but the girls make sure the customer gets his or her money's worth."

"Two women," Tommy said thoughtfully. "And sometimes *three*. Can you even imagine...."

I glared at him.

He started, blushed furiously. "No. I just meant... I wasn't suggesting–"

Mike planted his hands on his hips. "You said you could *feel* Carter in the club earlier. But you couldn't see him. But *he* could see *you*?"

"I was working, Mike – performing. I *want* people to see me, remember? The whole thing would be a gigantic pain in the ass if I couldn't turn it on and off at will. People don't throw cash at invisible strippers."

"But Carter had to be close if you could sense him."

I just shrugged. "We're in uncharted territory here, guys. Yesterday I didn't even know it was *possible* for me to sense another wight nearby. I haven't the slightest idea what kind of range that sensitivity has. But I *do* think it must have something to do with the hunger level of the wight in question."

"Why do you say that?" Tommy asked, frowning.

"Because I never felt it around Karen. She was freshly fed. I gotta figure that's why I never noticed anything unusual when I was near her. It's like... I'm not sensing the wight – I'm sensing their *hunger*."

Mike was deep in thought. I could see the wheels turning place behind his eyes. "So, Carter came into the club and just watched you from somewhere nearby, waiting."

"He must have followed us out, too. I could sense him somewhere near his car when we pulled away."

"Then he came back into the club and picked out his targets. And once he fed on those two bodies over there, he couldn't hide anymore. That's why the bouncer was able to see him."

"What about security cameras?" Tommy asked. "Would *they* have seen Carter's movements through the club?"

"The club has cameras on the main floor, of course, but you won't see anything up until the moment he killed Misty and her customer. Don't ask me why, but I've never had a problem with video cameras until *after* I've fed." I shook my head. "Carter must have seen enough to figure Kennedy was somebody I really cared about – one of the few. Somebody that would rattle me hard if she was taken." The thought caused my stomach to drop. "Mike, has anybody checked in with Wanda? She said she was going straight home from my place, but that was hours ago, and–"

"I called her again myself, Charlotte, not ten minutes before you pulled up. She wanted to come straight down here, but I convinced her the best thing she could do to help was to stay safe. So, she's at home behind locked doors with what she assures me is a *very* large caliber firearm."

I smiled gratefully. "I don't doubt she can take care of herself, but can you please set a watch on her? Just as a precaution? She lives just a few miles down the road. Her address–"

"I'll go, Sarge," Tommy said suddenly. "I'm doing fuck-all here – might as well make myself useful."

I turned to him, sincerely touched by the offer. "Thank you, Tommy. *Really.* Thank you."

Mike nodded. "Go on, kid – I'll send relief as soon as I can cut somebody loose."

I gave him the address. He headed out the front door at a trot.

As hard as I had fought it, I was really starting to like young Tommy O'Connor. A lot of guys would have folded up shop or run screaming from everything that had been dumped in his lap lately. I'm pretty sure they don't cover grave wights and resurrection rituals in the police academy curriculum. But Mike was right – Tommy was a good cop with a decent head on his shoulders, and he'd spent enough time on the street by now to understand there *are* things out there that aren't in the manual. I still wasn't convinced he'd ever sign on with the program Mike and I had been running, but I felt like the odds might be improving.

When he was gone, I dropped wearily into a chair at one of the tables around Stage One. "This is getting awfully personal, Mikey. If Wanda hadn't left here with me tonight–"

"I know," he said, taking a seat next to me. "You do seem to be the common thread running through this whole fucked up mess."

"The warehouse was bait – we know that. They involved *you*, knowing you'd involve *me*. And they had a shot of taking you off the board in the process. I don't think it went *exactly* to plan, but they rolled with it. And it ended up giving them a chance to hit me at home – put eyes and ears inside my apartment through Karen. Now they've hit me at work, involving just about everybody I care about."

He nodded. "And I've been too busy chasing corpses to find a new target for you. Now they've shut down the club, which takes away your backup source of bad guys, too."

"It feels like I'm losing everything I care about – like I'm being…." I gestured helplessly at the stage. "*stripped* of everything that matters in my life."

Mike sighed as if preparing himself to deliver bad news. "And that's why I'm going to do what I can to move you out of harm's way."

I frowned. "What's that supposed to–"

"Charlotte, I don't want you going home. The next logical step is for them to come after you directly. And I'm not going to have you sitting alone in that apartment, waiting for them to come."

"I'm not going into hiding, Mike. You can't make me."

Mike sighed, reached for my hand. I yanked them back, holding the power tightly at bay. A sad smile crossed his face, and his hands dropped to his lap. "I'm not taking you out of the fight. But you can't be a sitting duck, either."

"What am I supposed to do?"

Mike looked at the floor. "Do you think your friend Wanda would–"

"Uh-uh, Mikey," I snapped, sitting up straight. "Absolutely not – no *fucking* way. If somebody's coming for me, I'm not going to be hiding behind Momma's skirts when they do. If anything happened to her because of me, I'd–"

"Okay, you're right," he said, holding up his hands. "Bad idea. It *would* put another civilian in danger – *further* in danger in her case. But I've only got one other idea. And I *really* don't think you're going to like that one, either." His mouth thinned to what might almost have been a rueful smile. His eyes met mine. "And neither will he."

I stared at him blankly for a minute before my exhausted brain finally caught up. "Oh no, no, no, Mike," I said, shaking my head vigorously. "You *cannot* be serious…"

#   #   #

"Sarge, you *cannot* be serious!"

The two detectives were standing in the front lot of The Daily Grind in the pale orange glow of the coming dawn. I was a respectful distance away, smoking and sulking like a spoiled teenager.

"Tommy, I don't have a lot of options here," Mike said, glancing back at me over his shoulder. If he thought he was standing far enough away for me not to overhear their hushed conversation, he was about a week late and a hundred yards too close for that now. But I played deaf.

Tommy had just returned from Wanda's place – he had confirmed she was safe, at least for now. Mike had the MCS detail a unit to stake out her place 24/7 for the foreseeable future so he could pull Tommy back into the field. The more I thought about it, the less good I believed even full-time police protection would do. Whoever was out there calling the shots, they wouldn't send Carter again since he couldn't stay out of sight. A cop wouldn't stand much of a chance against a wight even if they *could* see one coming, but it was better than doing nothing.

"Tommy," Mike said softly. "We can't let her go home, and she'd be no safer with me – the anonymous call I got the night Karen Wagner was resurrected means they already know about the connection between Char–" He sighed. "Between *Cherry* and me. You're all I've got."

Tommy glanced at me over Mike's shoulder. I averted my eyes, feigned a sudden, intense interest in the club's sparse, dried-up landscaping.

"She's family, Tommy," Mike said earnestly. "All the family I've got left. And somebody is trying to take her away from me. So *please* – can you help me out here?"

I felt a sudden tightness in my throat, swallowed hard. That was the most naked emotion I'd seen from Mike in a long, long time. He and I had all but come to blows over this idea a few short hours ago, but I had finally relented for his sake.

Tommy looked down for only half a second, then nodded firmly. "Yeah, Sarge. I got this. Nothing's going to happen to her on my watch."

"Thanks, Tommy," Mike said, gripping the younger man briefly by the shoulder. "I owe you one." He turned and they started walking my way. "As soon as I clear a couple of things with the site CO, I want you and Tommy to take my Tahoe and head back to headquarters. I'll catch a ride back with CSU."

"What about Kennedy, Mike?" I asked.

He sighed. "We're doing everything we can. Every cop in two states is looking for that Cutlass. Flashy ride like that, somebody is bound to spot it before long. Besides, why would Carter have *taken* her instead of just killing her outright unless he had a reason to keep her alive?"

I just stared at him hopelessly. "There are a lot of horrific things a creep like Lester Carter can do to a girl like Kennedy that don't involve murder, grave wights, or resurrection rituals, Mikey."

He nodded, looked down for a moment. "I know. But we'll find her. I promise."

"You damned well better…"

Eleven

THE SUN WAS WELL OVER the eastern horizon when Tommy and I pulled into the parking lot of Police Headquarters on Olive. I waited outside on a bench in the bright morning sun with my hood up and sunglasses on while Tommy ran inside to leave the keys to Mike's vehicle with the desk officer. He returned a few minutes later and together we crossed over onto the employee lot. As we walked, I amused myself by trying to imagine what *kind* of car a 'Detective Tommy O'Connor' would drive. There were *so* many different kinds to choose from. A Camry maybe? Or a VW Beetle? Perhaps some kind of Hyundai or Kia. Hell, if I were lucky, I might even get a *Prius*.

I didn't get a Prius. Instead, Tommy strolled right up to a mint '68 Mustang GT. Fastback, Dark Highland Green, blacked out grill, grey five-spoke wheels, quarter-window louvers – the works.

Tommy O'Connor drove a Bullitt.

"Nice wheels, Detective."

He grinned like a proud papa as he unlocked the passenger side door and held it open for me. "You like it? It's a–"

"I *know* what it is, Tommy. My dad was a huge Steve McQueen fan – made me sit through that movie a thousand times." I slid into the passenger seat. Even the interior was spotless and authentic, right down to the stock four-speed shifter and black leather-wrapped Shelby steering wheel. That had to have cost a pretty penny. "Dad always wanted one of these. Never shut up about it."

Tommy closed the door behind me and jogged around to the driver's side. For a moment there, I half-expected him to go sliding across the hood. But he just climbed inside and fired up the engine, the throaty growl of the exhaust echoing wildly between the nearby buildings. Then he disappointed me again by not peeling out. Instead, he kept it under control and deftly guided the old Pony out onto Olive, then cut a block over onto Pine and headed for the ramp onto the interstate.

"Awfully expensive ride for a guy on a cop's salary, isn't it?" I asked, peering over the top of my sunglasses.

"It originally belonged to my dad. Must be a Seventies cop thing, I guess. He restored it himself – practically built it from the ground up. Took him twenty years' worth of weekends. Then he turned around and gave it to me on the day I got my shield."

"Your dad was a cop, too?"

Tommy nodded. "And my grandfather before him."

"Your dad still around?"

"Yeah. He retired from the force in 2017. Went to work with my granddad and my brothers."

"Oh God – there's more of you at home," I groaned playfully, smacking my forehead with my palm.

He grinned. "One older, one younger."

"What is it they all do together?"

"They run a pub over on Clayton Avenue in Dogtown."

I shot him a glance, grinned. "Wait – your family *owns* O'Connor's Pub?"

He smiled proudly, nodded. "You know it?"

"Are you kidding? Every cop in the City knows it. You can walk in that place any time – day or night – and half the people in there are off-duty cops or their families."

"At least."

"After Mom passed away, my dad used to take us there to meet Mike for dinner two or three nights a week." I chuckled at the memory. "Dad was a widower. Mike was divorced. Neither one of them could cook for shit. We'd probably all have starved to death if it wasn't for O'Connor's Pub."

Tommy grinned. "Best corned beef and cabbage in the City."

"Ugh…" I said. "Well, there's *one* thing I don't miss about solid food."

"*What?*" he cried, staring at me in disbelief. "You don't like it? Or… '*didn't*' like it, I guess?"

"Hell, I can barely stand the *smell* of it. And with my nose, the entire month of March in this town is a fucking nightmare!"

Tommy laughed aloud. "Me? I *love* that stuff. My granddad bitches about serving it – says it's not 'real Irish'. But *that's* what people want when they go to an Irish pub." He paused for a moment, frowning as he rested his hand against his belly. "Jesus, I just realized I'm *starving.*"

You and me both, buddy…. While I didn't struggle with physical hunger anymore, the one I *did* have to deal with was becoming more troublesome by the hour. Like an itch between my shoulder blades, the kind you can never quite reach. I decided to change the subject. "Did your dad work with Mike much before he retired?"

Tommy shook his head. "Just in passing. Dad did his time as a PO, then moved over to Mounted Patrol."

"The *horse* cops?"

He grinned. "Yup – he worked out of the stables just up here on the right. Dad retired as a Sergeant of the Mounted Patrol Unit. He loved the assignment, but then his back gave out and he couldn't ride anymore. So, he decided he'd rather retire early than sit behind a desk for ten years."

"Yeah, my old man probably would have done the same if they ever tried to take him off the street." I shook my head. "I don't know how Mike has kept going all these years. Something in him just won't let him quit, I guess."

"You know, I used to wonder what kept him going, too," Tommy said with a sideways glance and a knowing grin. "I think I'm finally figuring that out."

I turned away and stared out the window, fell silent for a moment as I watched the familiar geometric curves of the old Planetarium pass by outside.

The more time I spent with Tommy O'Connor, the more I found myself pleasantly surprised by how much it seemed the two of us had in common. Despite the radically different paths his life and mine – such as it is – had taken, I reluctantly had to admit that I was beginning to enjoy his company more than I'd thought possible. But then again, Uncle Mike always was a hell of a judge of character. I still hadn't begun to process the idea of moving on without Mike's help. But Tommy was quickly proving to be somebody I could imagine myself working with when Mike was inevitably forced to step down.

Now if only Tommy could imagine himself working with someone like *me*...

#   #   #

Tommy's house was on Kraft Street, near the western end of the Dogtown neighborhood. If the Hill is the heart of the Italian community in St. Louis, then Dogtown is its Irish next-door neighbor. His was one of the hundreds of older bungalow-style homes that huddled close together along the neighborhood's narrow, tree-lined streets – a neatly-kept, unassuming little place with white siding and awnings and two small flights of concrete stairs leading up to a front door that sat several feet above street level. Like most of the other homes in the area, his had a small, detached garage that accessed off a rear alley, where Tommy carefully guided the Mustang under the overhead door and brought it to a stop.

We entered the house through the back, directly into a small, well-lit kitchen. There was a breakfast bar separating the entryway from the main cooking area and a bathroom off to the left. Tommy led the way into a formal dining room, one that didn't look like it was used very often for its intended purpose. Instead, the table was piled a foot deep in places with what appeared to be copies of case files, a laptop, and there were two bankers' boxes stacked in one of the high-backed chairs.

"*Wow* – doing a little homework lately?" I asked, casually glancing at the labels on a few of the files.

"More than a little. Mike's got me looking into missing persons reports going back a month or two, trying to figure out who our other resurrection subjects may have been."

I think my jaw must have dropped a bit. "Surely there aren't *this* many missing persons reports in St. Louis over just the last few months, are there?"

"Well, these aren't just from the City. MCS covers six counties in

Missouri and four in Illinois. So these come from all over the place – St. Charles, Wentzville, O'Fallon, Belleville, Edwardsville – everywhere. Hell, statewide we probably average at least one report a day."

"But this is still an awful lot of files."

"I'm working an angle here. See, you were able to tell us that at least two of the known wight victims were killed by their significant others. So, if we can match up couples among these reports...."

"We might find the other wights," I nodded, impressed. "Good thinking, O'Connor."

He shrugged. "And the boxes over there are records of deaths going back two years for which the ME was unable to establish *any* identifiable cause of death. I was planning on sorting through them later looking for... well..."

"You're looking for other possible wight *victims*," I said, nodding my head. "No, that's smart. I mean, who knows how long our new friends were in town before they decided to make their presence known?"

"Actually, Cherry," Tommy said, rubbing a hand across the back of his neck and blushing a bit. "I was sort of hoping you might be able to thin those boxes out a bit for me while you're here."

"Sure. It'll give me something to do until Mike locates a new target for me. How do you want me to start?"

Again, Tommy seemed oddly embarrassed. He couldn't seem to figure out how to put what he wanted to ask into words, and I wasn't helping.

I must have been off my game because it took a few more seconds for me to realize what he was asking. "Oh," I said softly, embarrassed I hadn't seen it sooner. "You want me to cull out which ones were mine."

He winced. "That would *really* help."

I nodded, although not without a bit of reluctance. I didn't think sorting out a pile of two dozen people whose deaths I was personally responsible for would improve Tommy's opinion of me much. Or his opinion of Mike either, for that matter. But I guess if he was going to get involved, he'd have to see the truth of it sooner or later. At least I'd be able to show him the type of people who got onto my radar – maybe give him a peek into the things they had done to earn the punishment I had dished out.

Tommy glanced at his watch. "Hey, I don't know about you, but I'm not ready to dive right back into this shit at the moment. I could use a shower and a few hours' sleep."

He had a point. I was still running on just what little shuteye I had gotten last night, and these last few days had been physically and emotionally exhausting, even for me. I nodded. "Now that sounds like a plan."

Tommy headed for the front of the house, beckoning for me to follow. There was a long single flight of stairs by the front door that led up to the second floor. We passed what looked like Tommy's bedroom on the left as he led me down the hall to a small but comfortable-looking guest room on the opposite side. Although the sun was bright outside, the room seemed unusually dark until I noticed the carefully covered window on the far wall. "Blackout shades. Just the thing for a cop working the night shift. Dad had them in his bedroom, too."

Tommy smiled. "Don't know how I'd survive without them. Since I started working Homicide with Mike, it seems like what sleep I *do* get usually happens during the day."

"Mike never would take day shifts. With his seniority, all he had to do is ask. But he always wanted to work nights."

Tommy shrugged. "I imagine that's so he's out there on the streets with you."

If I could have blushed, I probably would have. "Maybe so," I muttered, embarrassed I had never properly appreciated everything Mike had sacrificed on my behalf. Hell, he probably would have been Captain by now if not for me.

"You want to hit the shower first?" Tommy asked, jerking a thumb towards the far end of the hall.

I shook my head. "No, I think I'm just going to lie down before I fall down." I glanced down at my wardrobe glumly. "Although I'm afraid I packed a little light. Mike wouldn't let me go back to the apartment, so I haven't even got a change of clothes."

Tommy held up a finger and darted into the hall, returning a moment later to toss a bundle of bright yellow fabric to me. I unfolded it, found myself staring at a t-shirt boldly emblazoned with a full-color picture of Bruce Lee on the front. "It's a little big on me," Tommy said. "It ought to work just fine as a nightshirt for you. We can toss your clothes in the laundry later."

I chuckled a bit. "Well, yellow isn't really my color – washes me out. I think corpse-pale qualifies me as a 'winter'. But thanks for the loaner."

He just grinned. "Keep it. Honestly, I'll get a kick out of seeing you walking around in anything that isn't from the 'Elvira, Mistress of the Dark' collection."

I sneered. "Bite me, O'Connor."

He grinned and retreated into the hall, pulling the bedroom door shut behind him.

I stripped down to just my underpants and pulled the garishly colored t-shirt over my head. I took a quick glance in the mirror on the back of the door. Yeah, yellow definitely isn't my color. With my bright red hair and ivory skin, I looked like a fucking Popsicle.

But that wasn't the most disturbing part of my reflection. Leaning in close, I stared at the irises of my eyes. They had faded quite a bit just since my shift last night at the club. I'd gone from bubble gum to cotton candy in a matter of just a few hours. A quick check of the calendar on my phone – for which I had no charger and about twenty percent battery life left – showed I still had an entire week until the next full moon. But I rarely let the cycle get this far along in any given month, and an ominous sense of gathering momentum was reminding me why that was.

I turned away from the mirror, switching off the lights and sliding under the covers. I could hear the sound of running water in the bathroom down the hall, smell the warm, masculine scent of whatever soap or body wash Tommy was using.

Not that I was feeling romantically inclined towards Tommy or anything – most *definitely* not. I officially declared that part of my life over and done with twenty-six years ago. From what little I remember from my time as a wanton teenage harlot, that intense connection – that overwhelming desire to meld with your partner and make every part of them a part of yourself – might accidentally prove fatal to said partner in my present condition. Besides that, I've always believed that having any kind of actual sex life at all would – for me – technically meet the legal definition of necrophilia.

No, it was just nice to be sharing a space with somebody, even if it was only for a little while. Almost reminded me of being back at home. Almost.

And besides, I couldn't help but be grateful for everything Tommy had put up with on my account recently. Which now included taking me into his home and promising Mike to protect me from whoever or whatever was out there wreaking havoc on my existence.

But as sleep began to quickly overtake me, one final thought drifted through my mind, a realization that had become increasingly clear of late: the clock was ticking. Tommy taking me in – generous and much appreciated as it was – was a decidedly temporary fix. All too soon, the focus would turn to figuring out how to protect *him* from *me*.

# # #

For the first time in a long time, I dreamt of my mother. She was in the kitchen making breakfast while I was getting ready for school, and we were waiting for Dad to get home from his overnight shift. He was running late again, and Mom kept yelling upstairs for Leesy to come down and eat before she missed the bus. She wasn't answering – as if she was already gone. I don't remember much else, other than the powerful aroma of coffee brewing and the anxious feeling in my stomach every cop's family feels as they wait for their loved ones to come home safe and sound again.

As my eyes fluttered open, I realized the coffee smell was real, wafting up the stairs from the kitchen below. I reached onto the nightstand and checked my phone – almost three-thirty in the afternoon. There was a warning message on the screen as the battery level was now critically low.

I climbed out of bed, heard the heavy tread of Tommy's footsteps downstairs. I checked my appearance in the mirror once again – the t-shirt fell to the middle of my thighs, so I figured it wouldn't be indecent of me to walk around in it for a bit while my clothes got clean. I went ahead and put my bra back on, though. I may not be overly busty, but I didn't really feel comfortable jiggling around Tommy O'Connor's house in the middle of the day.

Gathering the rest of my clothes, I followed the coffee smell downstairs. I found Tommy sitting at the dining room table staring at his laptop. He was already dressed for duty and sipping from a big midnight blue mug emblazoned with the silver badge of the SLMPD. I could smell the sickly sweetness of the French vanilla creamer he was using – my enhanced senses were still ramping up quickly. He glanced up as I came in.

"Oh, hey – sorry, Cherry," he said. "Hope I didn't wake you."

I shook my head. "No, you didn't. Six hours is way more sleep than I usually get anyway. Besides, if I'm going to help you get anywhere with these files, I need to get started." I held up the bundle of black clothes in my arms. "You mentioned we might have time to wash these before tonight?"

"Oh, yeah, no problem."

He started to get up, but I waved him down. "I know how to do my own laundry, Tommy. Just aim me in the right direction."

He pointed back towards the kitchen. "The washer and dryer are behind the louvered doors in the back of the bathroom to the right. Detergent and softener are on the shelf above."

"Thanks," I said, heading back that way. I threw everything in the washer together – one nice thing about wearing all black is not having to sort shit out. I headed back to the kitchen where the coffee pot sat steaming on the counter. "Hey, Tommy," I called. "Mind if I grab a cup?"

"Knock yourself out," he replied from the dining room. "Mugs are in the corner cabinet."

I rounded the breakfast bar and opened the cabinet, snagged the first mug on the bottom shelf. This one was Kelly green with the gold harp logo of O'Connor's Pub on the front. I shook my head and smiled a little as I filled it – my dad must have had a dozen just like it at home when I was little.

I returned to the dining room, blowing across the top of the hot black liquid in my cup. "You heard from Mike yet?"

He shrugged. "Nothing worth reporting, but it's still early. And there's over a thousand cops on the street right now, all of them looking for Kennedy."

I slumped into the chair opposite Tommy and began flipping through the files in the bankers' boxes. Browsing through the names on the labels, I quickly turned up eighteen of the twenty-four people I had taken over the last two years. A few of mine had never been found or had been tagged with the wrong COD, so I didn't expect to find them all. I set them aside and began flipping through the rest, finding jack shit before I realized I wasn't hearing

Tommy's fingers tapping on the keyboard anymore. I looked up and found him staring at the stack of files I had separated, his face twisted into a poorly disguised look of horror. I sighed. "You gonna be okay with this, O'Connor?"

"Yeah, it's just – it's a little different when you see them all piled up like that. To see the names and faces – suddenly, it's not just a number anymore."

I glared, felt his judgement hit me like a punch in the throat. "You ever kill anybody, Tommy?" It was a shitass question to ask a cop, but I was pissy. And I was done with the kid gloves.

His eyes flicked up to meet mine, narrowed a bit. He reached out a hand that shook just a bit and took a sip from his mug. "Yeah," he said after a moment, setting his cup down gingerly as if he was afraid of spilling it on the files. "I uh…. I have."

Ooof. Wasn't expecting that answer. "Want to talk about it?" I asked after a beat, suddenly ashamed of my pettiness from a moment ago.

He pushed back his laptop, folded his hands in front of him. As I watched, he began nervously sliding them back and forth, fingers interlaced. He finally sighed heavily. "I spent enough time talking to the department shrinks about it. I guess I can tell you, too."

"Tommy, I'm really sorry. If you'd rather not–"

"No," he said quickly. "It's okay. I've got a handle on it. Most days, anyway."

I waited, watching him carefully.

When he finally began, his voice was soft but seemed to gather strength as the words began to flow. "It was during my second year as a patrol officer, back in the old Sixth. We got an armed robbery call about two a.m. – silent alarm at a convenience store near 70 and Goodfellow. My partner and I were just a few blocks away. We were the first ones on scene."

He paused for a beat, took a deep breath before continuing. "We had just pulled up and stepped out of the cruiser when two teenage kids came busting out the front door. Just – *bam* – no time to think about it, there they were. The clerk had stalled them – convinced them he couldn't open the register. When they saw the lights on the cruiser, they took off. One of them bolted immediately to Joey's side and he took off after while I drew my weapon and held it on the other. I couldn't see a face – just a baggy hoodie and jeans. The backlighting from the store had them in shadow. I still don't–"

He fell silent again. I didn't push, just waited.

"I still don't understand what went through her mind…"

Oh shit…

"I figured she was just gonna take off, you know? But she reached into the front pocket of the hoodie and…. came out with a gun." He sighed, fell silent for a long moment. His gaze seemed turned within. "I waited. I really did. Hell, I just about froze up. But she pointed it right at me, even got off one shot that hit the cruiser window in front of me. I pulled off two rounds and down she went."

I looked down at my hands, feeling absolutely miserable for having broached the subject at all. I suddenly felt utterly ridiculous – sitting in the formal dining room of Tommy's home in a Bruce Lee t-shirt and panties, listening to him describe in excruciating detail the single worst day of his life because I popped off at him.

"I radioed in shots fired and ran to where she fell, kicked the gun away," he said. "I knelt and unzipped the front of her sweatshirt… she'd taken one high in the chest and the other through the throat. She was bleeding out fast. I was still on the radio with dispatch when she gave this gurgling sort of cough and just… her eyes just went glassy, and she was gone."

"Jesus, Tommy," I said, my voice little more than a whisper. "I'm so sorry."

He sighed heavily, looked up with a thin, forced, ghost of a smile. "So that was my big accomplishment – I gunned down a fifteen-year-old girl who had just stolen two eight-dollar bottles of gin and a carton of cigarettes."

I shook my head. "Tommy, it doesn't matter how old she was or what she took. She *shot* at you."

"I know," he said. "But that didn't make it any easier to see her eighth-grade graduation picture in the paper. Or to hear her mother calling me a baby-killer on TV. Or listen to her brother screaming at me as I sat on the stand at his trial."

"No, I don't suppose it would," I said. "Her brother was the one who ran?"

He nodded. "Yup. Seventeen and trying to earn his way into a gang.

Too scared to go it alone, so he brought his little *sister* with him. Gave *her* the fucking gun."

"Was he convicted?"

"If you can call it that. Robbery, second degree. Class B felony. Neither of them ever did pull the gun in the store, so it ended up just being a strong-arm charge. *And* he was a minor. Got five years, served eighteen months."

"And his sister died for nothing. Nobody ever paid for what happened to her."

Tommy just shook his head, his focus still turned deep within. "Well, I guess somebody did." It was killing me to watch him rip himself up over this, knowing it was my fault he was being forced to dredge it up again.

I decided to try changing tack a bit. "Well, you've heard about my first two kills already – including the innocent great-grandfather I took because I waited too long. Before I knew I wasn't *allowed* to deny the hunger forever. But we haven't talked about the first person I killed on *purpose.* "

He glanced up. "Who was that?"

"The man who murdered my father."

Tommy's gaze dropped to his hands again. "Ah. And the first one Mike was a part of."

I nodded. "Yeah. When I landed on Mike's doorstep that night and explained my…. *predicament,* he aimed me straight at the guy. By then I *did* know there could never be a question of guilt or innocence – I'd either see it in the target's head or not. But Mike wasn't wrong – he never has been."

I stood up quickly, reaching down to gather up the pile of folders that detailed my most recent kills. I rounded the table and pulled a chair in close to Tommy's. As I sat down next to him, I absentmindedly rested my hand on his in what was supposed to be a reassuring manner. Instead, he flinched, jerked his hand back and blinked. His eyes swam dazedly for a moment.

"Oh fuck, Tommy – I'm sorry. *Jesus,* that was fucking stupid. It's…. it's getting a lot harder to hold it back."

"No," he said, shaking his head to clear it. "No, it's all right. No harm done." He just stared down at my hands for a second before glancing up to meet my pale pink gaze. "Do you – do you think it would be safe to –"

I could see him tilting his head towards my hands. I swallowed hard and nodded, grabbed the power by the throat and shoved it down hard. "Just go slow."

He slowly raised his hands and gingerly took hold of both of mine. Instantly, I was like a bird dog on point, wrestling with the voracious energy that swirled inside of me, ignoring the ragged scream of the hunger in my mind – begging me to feed. His hands felt almost hot to the touch, and he laughed softly as he rubbed my fingers gently. "Jesus Christ, Cherry. They're *literally* like ice."

I jerked my hands away quickly. "They'll get even colder. In a couple of days, I could burn your skin yellow with a brush of my hand. That's why I usually wear the gloves full-time this late in the cycle – helps keep a leash on it. They're not for my protection–"

"They're for everybody else's." Tommy stared at me for a beat before glancing down at the stack of folders I'd brought over. "So those are all yours?"

I nodded solemnly. "I'd say we should wait, but we've got no time. You ready for this?"

For whatever reason, Tommy suddenly seemed energized with a confidence I'd only glimpsed in him before. As if recounting his own story of when the system had failed so badly – getting a glimpse into the type of people I preyed upon – had given him the courage to at least wade into the shallow end of the murky waters of my existence. I felt like he was finally willing to give me a chance.

I seized that chance with both hands and ran with it.

Twelve

AN HOUR LATER, WE WERE halfway through my stack, working through it in no particular order. I'd glance at the name on the tab, and a surge of foreign memories would rush forward. As the images of these people's crimes welled up from the black depths of my mind, I found myself becoming increasingly sick to my stomach. I fought down the worst of it and kept going.

"All right," I said wearily, laying the next folder open in front of us. "Samantha Cameron, twenty-seven. In 2019, she called 911 with a bullshit story about a home invasion – told the police two Black men forced their way into her home and abducted her children at gunpoint."

I sorted through the folder and came out with a group photo of three smiling kids. "That's David, age six. This is Donald, age four. And the little one is Alissa. She was a year-and-a-half old," I said, indicating each of the faces in turn. "Samantha gave the cops a detailed description of the intruders – Homicide had a sketch artist do work-ups, rewards were offered to the public for information, the whole nine yards. But nothing – no useful leads. A year went by – the kids never turned up and nobody ever demanded ransom."

Tommy nodded. "I remember this one. It wasn't my case per se – MCS came right in – but everybody in Homicide was involved in one way or another. We knew she was lying, but we had absolutely *nothing* to go on."

"Well, she sure didn't waste any time moving on. There was security camera footage of her slobbering all over her boyfriend at some dance club downtown within a week of the kids having supposedly been taken. But in

the year that followed, there was nothing. A bit of circumstantial evidence –
nothing the DA could make stick in court.”

“So, you paid her a visit.”

I nodded. “Spring of last year. I followed her one night as she was
leaving a club, drunk as hell, with a *new* boy-toy she had just picked up.
They went back to her place, went at it for a while. I waited – perched on
the overhang outside her bedroom window. When I was sure they were both
asleep, I slipped inside. I gave him a quick touch just to make sure he stayed
out, then turned to our poor, grieving young mother. She was face down on
the bed with her bare back above the sheets, and I just gently rested my hand
between her shoulder blades and had a little look around inside her head.”

“And?”

“And she did it. Just like everybody *knew* she did. She drugged the
kids’ dinner one night, lined the trunk of her car with clean blankets, and
carried them all out to the garage one by one. Drove forty-five minutes west
and met up with the first boyfriend she’d been spotted with at the club. He
had stolen a car and they rendezvoused in the woods down by the Missouri
River. They transferred the kids’ bodies to the stolen car and floated it out
into the water.”

“Jesus Christ,” Tommy muttered, rubbing his face with both hands.

“Yup. Just like that. She dropped him off at home, drove back to
her place, and waited about an hour before calling the cops. Even had the
boyfriend give her a good whack across the cheek with a gloved fist before
she left his place, just to make it look good.”

“How could somebody do that to their own kids?”

“It’s not all that complicated sometimes. That bitch was just a straight-
up sociopath. She was young, pretty, divorced – had herself a hot new man.
The last thing she wanted was three kids weighing her down. So, she and the
boyfriend worked out a plan and got away scot-free.”

Tommy looked at me, one eyebrow slightly raised. “Well, not *exactly*.”

“No,” I said with a grim, satisfied smile. “I drained that bitch like a
fucking bathtub.”

“And the boyfriend?”

“Well, that’s the *real* kicker. She killed her kids to be with this guy, then dumped him two months later. Once I dealt with her, I called in an anonymous tip on where to find the car and the kids finally got a decent burial."

"I remember that, too. I was standing on the river bank the morning they hauled that car up out of the mud. You let the boyfriend go?"

I shook my head. "Mike and I tracked him down the next lunar cycle. He was living in an RV in the woods down near Cape Girardeau. By the time the cops there found his body, I think his dogs had eaten most of what I left behind." I glanced around. "I guess that's why his folder isn't here."

Tommy blanched but didn't seem to be taking this as bad as I feared. He picked up a folder of his own and dropped it on the table. "Tell me about this one."

I leaned forward, frowning a bit. "You found one of mine on your own?"

"Wasn't that tough, given the details."

I glanced at the name on the tab. "Ahh…. Matthew Oliver Lewis."

"The Roadside Reaper," Tommy said with a nod. "His truck was towed out of the parking lot of The Daily Grind six months ago. Officially termed a 'heart attack'."

I smirked. "Uh-huh," I tapped my finger on the folder. "See, *this* is why exotic dancing is my ideal profession."

"How's that?"

"It's like this: the first memories that flash through someone's mind when I lay hands on them are almost always their darkest, most vile secrets – the ones they fight like hell to hide. But inside they're dying to let them out. Usually, it's just filthy thoughts about the neighbors' teenage daughter or playing doctor with a cousin years ago. Maybe the occasional embezzler skimming cash from the boss's ledgers."

"But sometimes –"

"Sometimes I hook a big fish. Truck driver comes in – early in the lunar cycle, mind you – and pays for a lap dance. The *second* I touched him, I see him butchering prostitutes all up and down his route. Sixteen women in all."

Tommy nodded. "The murders were the subject of a Netflix documentary, old episodes of America's Most Wanted – the works. But they had no suspects."

"After I finished the dance, he offered me two hundred dollars to meet up with him in the sleeper cab of his rig when I finished my shift. I agreed. *He* figured he had just picked up Victim Seventeen. Instead, the piece of shit got me." I sighed. "The ME fed his DNA into CODIS and I gave Mike what he needed to match it to the right victims. Gave the families of sixteen dead girls at least some measure of closure. Not bad for a single night's work."

Tommy spent a full minute or so in thoughtful silence. "Look, Cherry – I see how someone with your…. *appetites* would see your arrangement with Mike as making the best of bad situation. I do."

My stomach tightened into a cold lump. "But?"

"*But*," he said, looking down at the pile of folders. "You guys have been playing a very dangerous game for a very long time. Operating outside the system. Taking the law into your own hands. And working entirely without a net. And I'll admit, you've been lucky so far. It's worked. But sooner or later, this is *going* to blow up in your faces."

"Well, if you've come up with something Mike and I haven't thought of in the last twenty-six years, you have my undivided attention."

"You know I haven't. But that's not the only thing worrying me, either." He paused for a beat, sighed quietly. "Cherry, please don't take this the wrong way. I know this is going to sound horrendous, but I can't stop thinking about it."

"About what?"

"Because what I want to ask is going to sound like I'm *suggesting* something. And I'm not – I swear to fucking *God*, I'm not. I don't want anything to –"

"Jesus Christ, Tommy – spit it the fuck out!"

He rubbed his eyes, clearly fighting the urge to drop it and say nothing. His conscience finally got the better of him. He spoke slowly, cautiously – clearly not wanting to set me off. "Look, you already told me you tried to kill yourself once. But you couldn't figure out how," He stared at me hard. "Now that you *know* how to do it… what's going to stop you?"

I was stunned. Not that he was saying this out loud to me, but that he had managed to precisely articulate the nagging worm of an idea that had been crawling around in my subconscious since the day Momma Wanda told me I *could* be killed. I finally had a way out of this disgusting excuse for a life. I didn't *have* to do this anymore.

I thought about it for a split second longer, then gave him the one and only answer I had been able to come up with so far.

"Mike." I said simply, finally. "I'll live for Mike."

He nodded. A long silence held sway before he finally broke it. "Cherry, please believe me when I say I understand why you've done the things you've done. Hell, at this point I'm not even sure I think it's *wrong* – that it isn't even the *morally* correct thing to do. Christ, if I knew who had killed someone I cared for – my dad, one of my brothers, a friend – and I *knew* they were going to get away with it? I don't know how I could live with that either."

I sighed. "Well, when you say your prayers tonight, Tommy O'Conner, you make sure to ask the Good Lord nicely that you *never* have to find out."

#   #   #

Tommy and I puttered around with the rest of the files on his dining room table for a little while longer, finding nothing new in the same pages we'd been staring at forever. The grandfather clock in the living room chimed softly, and Tommy shot a startled glance at his watch. He rose quickly. "Dammit – it's getting late, Cherry. I have to start getting my shit together. Mike and I are starting early – he should be here any minute to pick me up."

I picked up my phone to check the time, but it was completely dead now. I showed it to Tommy. "You don't have a charger that'll fit this, do you?"

He took the phone, glanced at the bottom of it, and shook his head. "Nope. All I've got is iPhone stuff. Nothing that's gonna fit that."

"Shit," I cursed. "Mike won't let me go home, so I guess I'm going to have to run out somewhere and get one."

Tommy grinned, looked me up and down. "Look, not that your ensemble isn't quite fetching, but your regular clothes are still in the washing machine. And I don't think you want to be walking the streets in that getup. Besides – and don't kill the messenger, here – Mike gave me strict orders to keep you indoors and out of sight."

My temper flared violently again. "So now I'm under *house arrest*?"

"Like I said, Sarge's orders," he said, raising both hands in surrender.

"And I meant what I said about the 'don't kill the messenger' part. Please don't." He couldn't suppress a small, wicked smile.

I shook my head and stormed off for the laundry room. "Don't even joke about that, O'Connor. I'm gonna have a hard enough time not kicking Mike's ass when he gets here. Don't make me have to kick yours, too."

Mike arrived a few minutes later, and he and I had it out. *Big* time. Tommy stood at a respectful distance, but not too far away – probably figuring he was going to have to pull me off his partner at some point.

"Charlotte, I cannot have you out wandering the streets alone," Mike said, folding his arms stubbornly across his broad chest. "Forget the fact that you're like a daughter to me. You're also the only resource we have who knows anything at all about this resurrection shit."

I glared at him hard. "Not true. You've got Wanda, now. And besides, I'm not gonna be a hell of a lot of help sitting here in O'Connor's living room while you're out there working this case."

"Look, I've thought about this a lot," he said with a sigh. "And if my suspicions are correct and the point of all this is to take you out and then take over your – I don't know, your *hunting grounds* – then there's a very good chance there are at least four more wights out there right now, all of them hunting for *you*."

He was right, of course, but he clearly wasn't seeing the whole picture. I moved to stand just inches in front of him. I'm not very tall – five foot six, minus the heels I wore at work – and Mike towered over me. But I could see him lean back a bit as I moved in. "Ignoring the fact that Kennedy is still out there somewhere, suffering God knows what at the hands of these motherfuckers – have you taken a *good* look at my eyes lately, Mikey?"

He did, his mouth thinning to a grim line. "I understand, Charlotte. And we're doing everything we can. We still have a week until the next full moon. You'll be fine until–"

"Until you come by to pick up your partner one of these nights and find out I've already sucked him dry."

Tommy looked away and covered his mouth suddenly, but he couldn't hold back and tried stifling a burst of laughter behind his hand.

Jesus, I walked straight into that one.

I reached over and frog-punched him on the upper arm hard enough to leave one hell of bruise. "Not what I meant, and you know it, shithead."

He rubbed his arm, wincing, but the smile never left his face. Mike glared daggers at him though, and he settled down quickly.

I rounded on my old friend again. "Mike, I *have* to hunt. This isn't negotiable."

"And you *will*," he said, taking me by the shoulders. "Look, just give me another day. Two tops. I got a call on the way over. A patrol unit may have spotted the Dodge dually pickup that disappeared along with its owner, Vincent Lagorio – that hulk you ID'd from the third resurrection site victim. Those missing vehicles are the best chance we have of finding these people."

I sighed. "And what the fuck am I supposed to do in the meantime?"

"Just sit tight. As long as we don't get a call-out, I promise it won't be long. And I'll call as soon as we know something."

I held up my phone. "Not on this, you won't. It croaked, and my charger is back at my apartment."

Mike glanced at Tommy. "House phone?"

Tommy shook his head. "Who the hell has a house phone anymore, Sarge?"

"*I* do, asshole," Mike snapped, without real anger. "Charlotte, I have a charger that'll fit your burner in my desk down at Headquarters. We'll swing by and pick it up on our way back. Okay?"

"Fine," I said, after staring at him hard for a long moment. "But I'm telling you this right now, Mike: in two days, whether you've found these people or not, I'm hitting the streets to hunt."

Relief swept over his dark features. "Thank you, Charlotte." He turned to Tommy. "Come on, O'Connor. Let's go."

They were almost out the door when Mike stopped suddenly, turned, and pulled me into a crushing hug. I was so startled I kind of froze – I just sort of stood there and took it. But after a few awkward seconds, I got over it and hugged him back just as hard. Tommy looked away, his face flushing. It was becoming all too clear that Mike was scared – *really* scared – for my safety. "Trust me, Charlotte," he said softly. "I won't let you down."

"I know you won't, Mikey," I said as I let go and looked up at him with a small smile. "You never have."

They swept out the back door and were gone into the night.

#   #   #

As soon as the guys left, I headed straight upstairs to take a shower. Tommy had kindly laid out a neatly folded towel and washcloth for me, along with a new bar of good old-fashioned Ivory soap, still in the wrapper. I guess he figured I wouldn't want to go around smelling like whatever manly-man product he had been using earlier. He was right.

I stripped off the yellow shirt and my underwear and showered in water hot enough to scald a normal human. I stood in there under the spray until the water started to go cold, then shut it off and grabbed the towel from the vanity. I quickly dried my hair and body, wrapped the towel around my torso, tucked the edge under my arm, and softly padded back along the hall, down the stairs, and all the way to the laundry area off the kitchen.

I pulled my clothes from the dryer and quickly dressed in my usual attire – my *only* attire at the moment. I decided to skip the panties. I'd rather go commando than put dirty ones back on. It was just too damned hot outside to be recycling underwear.

After dropping my towel in the laundry room hamper, I made my way back to the living room. I watched television for a bit, then I thought about starting in again on the case files. But curiosity got the best of me, and I decided to amuse myself by nosing around Tommy's house.

There was only one room on the first floor I hadn't been in yet – it turned out to be a small office space next to the dining room. There was an old desktop computer in there, and built-in shelves loaded with paperback books, board games, Blu-Rays, and – to my surprise – an old school police scanner like the one my dad had kept at our house. Many a night, my mother and I had sat in the living room with that thing chattering in the corner, praying we wouldn't hear my dad's call number being bandied about.

I fiddled with the knobs for a second, but nothing seemed to work. Then I spotted the end of the power cord in the dust underneath the unit. I snatched the scanner off the shelf and searched for an open outlet. Jamming the plug into the wall, I was pleasantly surprised to hear the scanner crackle to life behind me.

I started twisting the dials and flipping switches until I finally got it tuned in correctly.

The words I heard sent a lightning bolt of fear straight through my chest.

"– 3285 Choteau Avenue. Repeat – All units, all units, be advised: suspect vehicle at abandoned building at 3285 Choteau Avenue. Homicide unit is on scene – officers are holding position awaiting backup. Responding units coordinate with site commander Sergeant Benjamin on arrival. Responding units will hold position and await supervisor's orders."

As nearby patrol units began responding to the call, I stood there in stunned silence for a moment, my rage spiraling out of control. Mike knew what he was up against, but he was still trying to keep me out of the fight. The stubborn ass was going to get himself and everyone else in there killed trying to keep a dead girl safe from harm.

Like hell, he is…

There was no way I was going to let them go into that building without me. But it had to be at least three or four miles away as the crow flies, and getting there on foot would take too long. By then, it could all be over, and Mike and Tommy might well be dead.

Then, out of the corner of my eye, I spotted Tommy's car keys sitting in a shallow bronze bowl on the counter.

I pulled on my boots, fastened the cloak across my shoulders, and drew my gloves up over my forearms. I snagged Tommy's keys as I passed and blasted out the back door at a dead run…

Thirteen

I EVENTUALLY MANAGED TO GET Tommy's Mustang backed out of the garage without scraping the paint on either side of the door opening or ripping off the side-view mirror. I hadn't driven a stick since high school driver's ed – hell, I hadn't driven a car at *all* in twenty-six years. I killed the engine twice before I got it out, and damn near lurched into the neighbor's fence on the other side of the alley when I finally did. But I eventually got it moving forward, bucking and jerking all the way, while the interior began to fill with the unmistakable stench of burnt clutch.

By the time I made it down Hampton and swung onto the ramp towards I-64, I felt like I was almost getting the hang of things again. Almost. But traffic was light, and I pressed the pedal to the floor as I merged onto the highway. I had a little trouble shifting through the gears at the right points, accidentally redlining the engine a few times as my speed began to climb. I was doing just over a hundred when I reached the exit at Grand and, in my haste, I completely forgot how tight that one-eighty turnoff was. I slammed on the brakes and wrenched the wheel to the right, but the ass end of the car broke loose, fishtailed around, and slammed into the guardrail on the shoulder. The engine died again as soon as the car came to a stop. I quickly got it restarted and gunned it again, wincing at the sound of metal scraping metal as the car surged forward and the crumpled left rear quarter panel dragged along the guardrail.

I blew through the red light turning left onto Grand and finally cut over onto Choteau, where I cut the engine and let the Mustang coast to a stop along the side of the road. I was still a block from the old Louie's Cola bottling plant – the 'abandoned building' mentioned by the dispatcher – but I needed to approach unseen. I had to force the driver-side door open with my shoulder – apparently the guardrail had taken a bite of that, too – and set off at a full sprint toward the black bulk of the abandoned factory silhouetted against the night sky ahead.

There were several squad cars surrounding the place now, red and blue strobes casting flickering shadows across the alleyway. I spotted Mike's Tahoe among them, but there was no sign of him or Tommy. Apparently, they were already inside. *Son of a bitch...*

I walked straight past the police perimeter unnoticed and made my way around to the north side of the plant. There were no doors on that side, but I had spotted a small lean-to shed beneath a long row of windows that were all propped a few inches open. I leapt onto the roof, and immediately began to struggle through the narrow gap under the sloped glass of the nearest one. I barely managed to squeeze through and dropped about ten feet or so to the factory floor. Instantly, my skin began to prickle with the now familiar sensation of another grave wight – perhaps several of them – lurking somewhere close by.

I took a moment to take stock of my surroundings. The building itself was enormous – the roof probably covered at least two or three acres – and there were several levels of catwalks and stairways crisscrossing overhead. The factory floor was broken up into dozens of smaller areas by the old bottling lines, which had been left in place when the plant was idled. Add to that the dozens of pieces of large equipment scattered about, and trying to move through the building quickly was going to be damned near impossible.

The more analytical part of my mind noted that, from a tactical point of view, the situation couldn't have been much worse. We had an unknown number of bad guys moving freely about through a gigantic space with literally hundreds of places from which to ambush the handful of police officers who had entered the building. They knew the interior layout better than the cops did. They could see in near total darkness – Mike and his people could not, and their flashlights would betray their exact locations.

And, lest I omit the biggest obstacle the police were now facing, at least a few of our adversaries might be completely fucking *invisible*.

In short, the place was a goddamned *kill box*.

I had to get Mike and his people out of there fast.

I could hear footsteps ringing against the metal grating of the catwalks overhead, and decided the best way to get my bearings would be from above. I skipped the steps and just launched myself straight up into the air, grabbing onto a handrail twenty feet above the factory floor. I vaulted over the rail, landing on the walkway with almost no sound at all. From my new vantage point, I could see lights moving about in at least three locations – one set far away on the uppermost catwalk, another along the east wall near where I could see Carter's Cutlass parked just inside an overhead door, and still another weaving between the bottling lines near the center of the factory floor. It seemed that the police were working in pairs, trying to cover each other's backs as they moved through the darkness.

I held my breath, focusing my hearing on each pair of officers in turn. When I got to the two on the upper catwalk, I heard a familiar voice speaking softly to his companion – *Tommy*. I raced towards the far end of the building, moving up a level and turning right to cross over the top of Carter's car and head their way. I was directly above the Cutlass when, without so much as a flicker of energy, something huge landed on the walkway in front of me with a resounding *clang*. As the hulking figure rose to its full height, I realized it could only be one person: Lagorio.

I jumped straight up into the air, aiming the toe of my boot at the monster's square, heavy jaw, but he casually swatted the kick aside with an arm the size of a normal man's thigh. I landed badly and before I could get up again, Lagorio raised one foot and brought it down hard onto the right side of my chest. I heard the crunching sounds as several of my ribs were staved in, the sharp ends ripping into my lung and setting my whole side aflame. The pain was blinding.

I tried again to make it to my feet, but Lagorio reached down and latched onto me like taking a dog by the scruff of the neck, lifting me high over his head before whipping me out over the handrail. I plummeted thirty feet straight down to land hard on the roof of Carter's Oldsmobile, blowing out the windows in all four directions.

I managed to stay conscious, rolling off the crushed roof and dropping face-first onto the concrete floor below. I started to crawl away over shards of shattered glass from the car windows, but Lagorio landed with a thud about ten feet in front of me. He started towards me at a leisurely pace, obviously enjoying what he was doing. I could see his face clearly now – his eyes were almost entirely white, but nevertheless he seemed completely in control of his actions. A phrase suddenly leapt into my mind: *the wight-master calls.*

As I watched, Lagorio reached into the small of his back and came out with a Bowie knife that had to be nearly the length of my arm. I turned over onto my back and began scuttling back towards the car, glass grinding into my elbows, the jagged edges slicing the skin of my hands and forearms to ribbons. As Lagorio continued his ponderous advance, my shoulders bumped against the rocker panel at the bottom of the car door, just in front of the rear wheel.

For the first time since I tried to take my own life that night in the woods, the thought crossed my mind that I was about to die. And this time it would be for good. Not that I would have minded so much, but if I died, Mike and Tommy would no doubt be right behind.

I quickly looked around, searching for a weapon of some kind, but saw nothing I could use. Lagorio stopped just a few feet away, stabbed out with the Bowie knife straight towards my face. I dodged to the right, and the knife drove straight through my left shoulder and deep into the rocker panel of the Cutlass. I clamped down on a scream as Lagorio bent over me and grabbed the handle of the knife, trying in vain to yank the blade free for another try. But it was stuck, the serrated top edge snagged in the torn metal.

Still pinned in place, I pulled my knees to my chest and kicked out hard with both feet, driving the heels of my boots into the big man's groin. He staggered back, slipped on the glass shards scattered across the concrete floor, and fell flat on his back.

I knew I had one chance to get free. I yanked down hard on the handle of the knife, freeing the serrated edge, and with every ounce of supernatural strength left in my body drove my shoulder hard against the wide hilt. It tore free of the car and my shoulder in a single pull, ripping another ragged scream from my throat.

I leapt to my feet and launched myself at Lagorio, just as he was sitting up and gathering himself to get up off the floor. I hit him square in the chest with both knees and, with my good arm, drove his own blade straight through his temple. It blasted out through the opposite site of his head in a splatter of fluid and brain matter. Lagorio fell back to the floor, his body twitching and flailing.

He wasn't finished, of course, but it gave me the few seconds I needed to struggle to my feet. I jerked the knife free of his skull, laid it against his throat and, pushing hard against the handle and the smooth section of the back of the blade, shoved it straight down through his neck until it clanged against the concrete floor. Lagorio's head rolled to one side as it parted ways with his neck. As it did, I watched in fascination as his sightless eyes suddenly darkened, returning in a matter of seconds to the soft hazel color they had been before his resurrection.

I struggled to my feet again and stood looking down at the mutilated body of my assailant, momentarily horrified by what I had done. Killing like this wasn't my style, and that Sasquatch should have squashed me like a grape. But he was new to his powers, and I had twenty-plus years of experience in getting the most out of what they had given me. With a surge of almost revenant-like fury, I lashed out with my foot and booted the severed head halfway across the factory floor where it finally bounced and clattered to a stop.

As my wits slowly returned, I realized that the altercation had almost certainly not gone unnoticed by the other people in the building. Oddly enough though, nobody had come rushing up to arrest me yet. I secured the big knife under my belt, made sure the camouflage glamour was still in place, and started stumbling towards the nearest stairwell.

The first thing I saw as I rounded the car was a dark figure in a police uniform and a bulletproof vest lying in a heap a few yards away. My stomach dropped, and I hobbled over to check on them. But it was too late. Steam was still rising from the spot on the back of the man's neck where the skin was just now beginning to thaw. Lagorio must have fed on him just before attacking me – that's why I never felt him coming. I had the awful suspicion that his search partner was probably lying somewhere nearby as well.

I moved away from the body and began to ascend the stairs, every move I made pure torment. I couldn't raise my left arm more than a foot or so away from my torso, and I could feel the shattered ribs in my right side grinding together with every step. Since I didn't need to talk at the moment, I shut down my breathing, trying to ease the pain. It helped a little, but not much.

It took what seemed like an eternity to climb to the uppermost floor where I thought I had heard Mike and Tommy earlier. The second I reached the top landing, I heard Tommy's voice screaming frantically from across the way.

"Officer down!" he screamed, his voice teetering on the edge of hysteria. "Somebody get the EMTs up here. *Now*!"

Ignoring the terrible pain in my side, I raced towards the sound of his voice as fast as my legs would carry me.

Fourteen

DETECTIVE SERGEANT MICHAEL BENJAMIN WAS lying on his back, his head resting in Tommy's lap. His bulletproof vest had been sliced cleanly in half. Someone had shoved a blade into his belly just inside his left hip, beneath the protection of the vest. The blade had been ripped upwards diagonally, cutting through the vest like tissue paper, splitting his ribcage, and opening him up from groin to armpit, partially spilling his insides.

Somehow – God only knows how – the stubborn old son-of-a-bitch was still alive.

The wound was gaping open, and blood was pulsing out of his torso with every failing beat of his heart and raining down through the metal grating to the factory floor far below. But he just wouldn't let go. His eyes focused on me and softened as I screamed his name and dropped to my knees beside him, my face directly over his.

"Oh my God, oh my God," I wailed. "Mike? Mikey, just hold on. Help is coming, okay? Just… just hang on."

The faintest of smiles crossed Mike's lips. I looked up at Tommy, who just stared at me helplessly for a second before shaking his head once.

I resisted the sudden urge to reach out and backhand him across the face as hard as I could. How could he even *think* such a thing? Of *course*, Mike was going to be all right. He was… *Mike.* The rock in my life. The man who had brought me back from the dead in a far more meaningful way than Reginald Hargrove ever had. The only family I had left in the world.

Mike raised his left hand and seized me by the wrist with a strength that surprised me. He pulled me close, placing my hand directly over his heart. I was weeping hysterically now. "No. No, Mike. No, I won't. You're going to make it. You *have* to. You're going to be fine. They'll fix you up and–"

"Charlotte…" Tommy whispered in my ear from just inches away, his voice barely audible, even to me. I could tell he was crying, too.

I stared down at Mike's face, tried to keep his eyes focused on me. His dark skin was quickly turning a horrible ashen gray and his breathing was becoming rapid and very shallow. His grip on my wrist tightened, though, pressing my hand even harder against his breast. His throat was choked with blood, but his eyes pleaded with me: *End it. Now. Please!*

"I can't, Mike. I can't do it. How can I–"

"Charlotte," Tommy said again, reaching up to grip my shoulder. "How can you *not*?"

Mike managed to nod once more. Sobbing, I stared straight into his warm, kind brown eyes. He nodded again, weaker this time. He was fading fast. He wouldn't last more than a few more seconds now, every one of them in unspeakable anguish.

So, with my tears falling steady on his face, I closed my eyes, pulled off my glove and – resting my hand gently against his butchered chest – carefully let the power begin to flow down through my arm. I eased gently into his mind rather than smashing through it as I usually did with my victims. With the most delicate of touches, I took hold of the life force within him that was already flickering and fading by the moment. And, ever so gently, I began to pull.

I can barely put into words the sensations I felt as Mike's living essence began to flow into my body, slowly at first and then in a powerful rush. My mind was flooded with vivid images. As always, it was the most painful, shameful things first. His guilt over the death of my father. The night my sister and I had disappeared. Standing by my father's side through my mother's illness and death. The bitter failure of his own marriage. The face of the one man he, too, had been forced to kill in the line of duty years ago.

And then, utterly without warning, my mind was suddenly filled with a warm, benevolent glow, and I experienced something I had never felt from

135

any of my victims before: the *good* memories. His friendship with Tommy. The love and brotherhood he'd felt with my dad. The courtship of his wife and the early days of their marriage. My birth and that of my sister. And overriding everything else – his unconditional love for me. I always knew he cared about me but, somewhere along the way, in his mind he *had* adopted me. He'd never had children of his own. To him, I wasn't *like* a daughter – I *was* his daughter.

The flow of energy began to wane, slowing to a trickle, then a steady drip. But just before it stopped altogether, a single image raced forward from his mind. The last thing he thought of. One last thing he wanted me to see.

With a gasp, I fell back onto my ass, the connection seeming to dissolve rather than snapping as it usually did. Mike was gone, and if his death was going to devastate me, what he had just shown me would probably take what precious little was left of my sanity and smash it into dust.

Because Mike had just shown me the face of his murderer. And he knew who it was.

#   #   #

Friday, July 25, 1997

I snatched my keys from the little table next to the front door and stepped out onto the front stoop of the shabby townhouse we rented on the west end of Forest Park, slamming the heavy door behind me. The brutally hot evening air was almost unimaginably oppressive.

'Summer in St. Louis,' I thought 'Christ, it's like a goddamned Turkish bath out here.'

The buildings and streets and sidewalks still radiated the scorching heat of the afternoon – the temperature had flirted with the century mark for several days in a row – and the violent thunderstorm that rolled through around four-thirty had left tepid puddles in the gutters and a faintly visible haze in the still night air that was laden with the not-so-subtle fragrances of mildew and backed-up sewers.

I hurriedly walked the half-block to where my car was parked under the hazy yellow glow of a streetlamp, warily eyeing the deep shadows between each house as I passed. Our neighborhood was a bit dodgy in the daytime – a girl alone at night was a prime target for violent crime. Or so my father reminded me daily.

As I approached my car, I glared at it in disgust. It was a boxy '78 Celica with a rusty bumper, hazy headlights, and a huge dent in the right front fender where I'd drunkenly clipped a light pole in a gas station parking lot last June. I hated the goddamned thing, although in my defense it was a hard car to love. The air conditioning had conked out months ago, and for some reason the driver's side window didn't want to roll all the way down. Driving it during the day over the past few weeks had been a living hell, especially stuck in afternoon traffic on Highway Forty. Nothing like sitting in the blazing sun on blisteringly hot asphalt with the vents hitting you in the face like a hair dryer and a miasma of car exhaust coming in through a half-open window.

And the color – ugh. Toyota called it 'Cashmere Beige Metallic'. My friends and I just called it 'Baby-Shit Yellow'.

Dad bought it for me at a police auction the spring I turned sixteen using the last of the insurance money left over after my mom died. Deep down I knew I should have been more grateful for it – a lot of my friends didn't even have cars of their own and were forced to rely on me for transportation. And there hadn't been much money in the first place. My mom was the picture of health right up until she was diagnosed with stage four pancreatic cancer. She was dead three months later. Since Dad was the one who worked, they hadn't taken out much of a policy on her, and I think the car was his attempt to make up for having to deal with the aftermath of Mom's death instead of celebrating my Sweet Sixteen without a care in the world. We both knew that had been a qualified success at best.

I stuck the key in the door and unlocked it, jerking it open with a rusty screech. I dropped into the driver's seat, shocked at how hot the ripped vinyl still was against the backs of my thighs, though the sun had set over an hour ago. I tugged at the hem of my denim miniskirt to try to put something between me and the seat, but there just wasn't enough material there to work with. I gave up and jammed the key into the ignition and twisted. After a few turns, the engine coughed to life in a cloud of blue-white smoke.

I sat in the front seat for a few minutes, simmering in the damp heat and my own cherished, self-righteous rage. I should have been with my friends tonight, scamming our way into fraternity parties and chasing SLU college boys who usually wouldn't give high school chicks the time of day. Instead, I was stuck picking my pain-in-the-ass little sister up from a slumber party that was supposed to have lasted until noon tomorrow. Dad was on the overnight patrol shift downtown, so that left me to chauffer the little shit home when she decided she wasn't actually going to spend the night.

I pounded the dash in frustration a few times before finally wrenching the steering wheel over and pulling away from the curb to the power steering unit's high-pitched, warbling refrain. I had a general idea where the slumber party house was located but, unfortunately, I wasn't as familiar with the swanky Central West End neighborhood around it. I must have made wrong turns down half a dozen dead-end streets trying to find the old brownstone where Annaliese's friend Carla lived. St. Louis had this bizarre habit of taking through-streets and turning them into half-assed cul-de-sacs by throwing up a line of giant concrete planters across random intersections. It was supposed to cut down on traffic and reduce crime – at least that's what my dad told me. As far as I could tell, its primary purpose was fucking over anybody trying to get from Point A to Point B in a hurry.

I finally spotted the house as I whipped past it in the dark, slamming on the brakes and twisting the Celica into a noisy U-turn to head back the way I came. There were no parking spots on the street for as far as I could see, so I pulled up outside and double parked next to a silver BMW. I turned on the hazard lights and jumped out of the car, hustling up to the front door.

I climbed the steps of the small porch and hit the doorbell, stepping back a pace or two to wait. I could hear the muffled squeals of a gaggle of pre-teen girls inside and was about to ring again when I heard footsteps approaching the door. The porch light popped on, and a woman's face appeared in the little window alongside the heavy wooden door. It disappeared again, and I heard the rattle and thump of chains and deadbolts being undone.

The door swung open, and a frazzled, forty-something woman in a t-shirt and sweatpants looked at me with a faint flicker of hope in her eyes.

"Are you Annaliese's sister?"

I pushed my anger down and tried to put on my best responsible face. "Yes, ma'am. I'm Charlotte Baum. My dad called. He said my sister had decided not to stay?"

The woman's body visibly relaxed. "Yes. But it's a bit more complicated than that, I'm afraid. Please, come in."

She stepped aside and let me pass. My mouth involuntarily fell open. The house was stunningly beautiful inside, although I suspected the generous amount of random clutter scattered around was not the norm. But one thing was patently clear: this family had money and lots of it. I suddenly felt a bit self-conscious, dressed as I was for a college frat party. With my bright red hair cut in a messy, short-cropped bob, red flannel shirt over a black tube top, scandalously short skirt, and Doc Martens, I probably looked like some kind of bottom-shelf streetwalker to these people. But the mother barely gave me a second look. She pointed down a side hallway towards what looked to be a rec room, from which piercing, high-pitched shrieks were emanating at irregular intervals. "There are a dozen fourth-grade girls in there wired up on enough sugar to kill a horse," she said wearily. "I told my husband renting a cotton-candy machine was going overboard, but he insisted. So here we are."

"Is my sister okay?"

The woman smiled gently. "I think she's more embarrassed than anything else. We tried to get her to just take a shower and put on a pair of Carla's pajamas, but she wasn't having it."

We rounded a corner and the hallway suddenly opened into an enormous, beautifully appointed kitchen. A heavy-set man with salt-and-pepper hair sat at a table tucked into a breakfast nook, his face resting despairingly in the palm of one hand. Across from him sat my little sister, dressed in a long white nightgown and sobbing quietly. As I approached her, my nose was assaulted by the stench of vomit, and I saw the whole front of her was covered in a brightly colored stain that looked to be a sort of tie-dye mix of toxic orange, bubble-gum pink, and chewed up pepperoni.

As soon as Leesy spotted me, she slid off her chair and came running. I tried to block her with my hands, but her momentum carried her forward and she wrapped her arms tightly around my waist. I could feel something wet and warm pressing against my legs just above my knees. With an effort, I managed not to retch.

"Char, I want to go home. I want to go home now," Leesy shrieked, pulling me even tighter against her soiled clothes.

The more mature part of my adolescent brain knew that what had happened wasn't exactly her fault, but I was still nursing a grudge against my father for making me cancel my plans to deal with her shit. Still, I managed to force a smile. "We're going. Get your things together."

Carla's mom was on the job. She immediately handed me the little wheeled suitcase with Alice in Wonderland on the front. "Here you go. I gathered up everything she brought, but I'm afraid her sleeping bag is a mess. I was just about to throw it in the washer when you arrived. If it's okay, I'll get it cleaned up and my husband can drop it off at your house tomorrow afternoon."

I sighed, grateful I didn't have to haul the puke-covered thing home in my car. The Celica smelled bad enough as it was in the summer heat without adding that to the mix. I don't know what the previous owner did with the car, but I'm pretty sure it involved delivering Chinese takeout because it smelled like egg-drop soup every time the temperature got above eighty degrees.

"That would be great," I said, trying to peel Leesy off me. "Come on, kid. Time to go home."

Carla's mom escorted us out, with Leesy gripping my hand tightly and sniffling the whole way. We were damned near out the door when my sister suddenly came to a complete halt, her hand jerking from my grip. "What about Sam?" she cried indignantly.

'Son of a bitch...' I thought, balling my hands into fists. Even at nine years old, she still refused to leave the house without that ridiculous stuffed animal. It was a black and white toucan with a huge rainbow-colored beak — a gift from my mom just after her diagnosis was confirmed. Leesy named him Sam after the cartoon mascot of her beloved Froot Loops cereal. I thought it was stupid for a kid her age to still be that attached to a toy, but it was one of the last things our mother had ever given her.

I glanced at Carla's mom. Her eyes were a little wide and she gave me a quick shake of the head.

I knelt down. "Leesy, Sam is covered in throw-up. Carla's mom is going to toss him in the washer with your sleeping bag and you'll get him back clean in the morning. Okay?"

I watched in dismay as my sister's face screwed up in anguish and she began wailing horribly. "No, no, no," she cried. "Sam has to come home with us. I can't leave him here alone! I can't sleep without him, and he'll drown in the washing machine!"

Now my frustration was really starting to boil over. "Leesy, we are not–"

"No!" she screamed, stomping her foot on the oak parquet floor of the foyer.

Carla's mom, clearly as desperate as I was to get Annaliese out of her house, darted off towards the kitchen. When she returned, she had a large brown paper grocery bag in hand, the top of it carefully rolled down and secured with a clothespin. To my utter disgust, I noted the wet spot on the bottom of the bag where it had already started to soak through. I rose and took it from her, wrinkling my nose and holding it away from my body like a dead rat. "Okay, we've got him. Let's go home."

"I want to see him."

"Oh, honey," Carla's mom said soothingly. "Sam is very dirty. You don't–"

Leesy glared daggers at her. "I want to see him. Now."

The woman looked at me pityingly. I sighed. As I went to remove the clothespin, I noticed Carla's mom taking a step back. I gingerly unrolled the top and peeled back the edges of the bag. The stench that came wafting out of there defied description, but I choked down the bile and tilted it towards my sister so she could see the soggy mass of black, white, and foamy pink goop stuffed inside. "Satisfied?" I said, turning my face away into clearer air.

Leesy leaned forward, peered into the bag, and nodded glumly. I quickly rolled the top back down and snapped the clothespin back into pace. I thanked Carla's mom and apologized for their trouble, bustling my sister out the door as quickly as I could. Taking her by the hand, I all but dragged her to the car. I flipped the front passenger seat forward and buckled her in the back, being none too gentle in the process. I went to stick the bag in the trunk, but Leesy screamed and insisted on holding it herself. Shrugging, I tossed the bag into her lap where it landed with a wet slap and slammed the car door closed.

I crossed around behind the car, dropped behind the wheel, and was just about to start the car and pull away when I noticed the bright yellow rectangle of paper tucked under my wiper blade. Seething, I threw open the door again and snagged the parking ticket off the windshield. 'Twenty-five bucks? Fuck, I was only in there like five minutes, tops!'

I jumped back in the car, slamming the door even harder than before, hard enough that the side view mirror shattered, and small pieces of glass clattered to the pavement below. Shrieking in frustration, I stuffed the ticket in the glove box with all the others, started the car, and shot off down the block, tires screeching.

Leesy was quiet for the first few minutes, finally speaking up as I was struggling to figure my way out of the neighborhood again. "Why didn't Dad come?"

I glared at her in the rearview mirror. "Because Dad's a cop and can't leave work. And because you wouldn't stay, I had to cancel the plans I made with my friends weeks ago to come get you."

"What plans?"

I started to tell her it was none of her goddamned business, but instead just stuck to the cover story. "The movies."

She was blessedly silent for a few seconds. In the warmth of the car, the smell of her clothes and the paper bag was starting to make me light-headed. "You weren't going to the movies," she said smugly.

I glanced sharply at her. "Yes. I was."

"No, you weren't," she smiled wickedly. "And I'm going to tell Dad when we get home."

My head felt like it was about to burst. "Like hell you will. You're going to keep your big mouth shut, or I swear to God old Sam there is going right out that fucking window. Stink and all."

She just kept grinning, knowing I was bluffing – nothing would be worth the fallout from a stunt like that. I held my tongue, instead trying to concentrate on reading street signs. I saw one that looked familiar and made a hard right, nearly running down a tall man in dark clothes who was about to cross into the intersection. The move also sent the barf bag sliding across the backseat to smack into the far side of the car.

Seconds later, to my extreme irritation, the Celica's headlights illuminated a row of those ridiculous concrete planters blocking the end of the street, each of them sporting a dead and withered bush that had been burnt to a crisp in the summer sun. I slammed on the brakes, grinding to a stop with just inches to spare.

I turned in my seat and glared at my sister, madder than I could ever remember being at her before. "Look here, you little asshole. I was supposed to be out having a good time with my friends tonight. Instead, I had come pick you up and cart you back home – covered in puke, no less – because you can't act like a normal kid for once in your fucking life and make it all the way through a goddamned slumber party. So how about you shut the hell up before I dump your whiny ass out on the street?"

I don't know if it was the tone of my voice or the murderous look in my eyes, but she actually looked cowed. I felt a sudden flush of embarrassment, but I covered it by slamming the car into reverse and turning around in the narrow space between the curbs. A sudden pang of guilt overtook me and before I started forward again, I threw the cark in park.

As I was about to turn around to apologize, a flicker of movement outside the half-open window caught my eye. In the cracked side mirror, I saw a dark shape approaching rapidly, already even with the back bumper of the car. I turned my head to look back.

Wham!

A blinding white light exploded in my head as something incredibly hard and unyielding collided with my left cheekbone. I found myself awake, but unable to move or speak, just sort of floating in a half-conscious state. I heard the car door creak open. I heard my sister screaming. I felt myself being violently shoved over the armrest and face first into the passenger seat. The door slammed shut again, and just before the darkness closed in, I caught a brief glimpse through my rapidly swelling left eye of a cadaverously thin man clad in black, crowded behind the wheel of my car. Then I felt the Celica start to move.

I felt nothing else for most of the rest of my life.

Fifteen

I AWOKE SLOWLY, EASILY, GENTLY, with the sweet sound of *"La Vie en Rose"* drifting though the room like the smoke from burning incense. Momma Wanda was sitting in a rocking chair in the corner of Tommy's guest room, eyes closed, the ghost of a frown furrowing the smooth skin of her brow. A closed Bible rested in her lap, her place marked with a scarlet silk ribbon, and a string of rosary beads dangled from her free hand. A small speaker sitting next to her on the nightstand seemed to be the source of the soft, exquisite mezzo-soprano of Édith Piaf,

"Momma?" I asked quietly, my voice a dry croak.

Her eyes snapped open, and a smile spread across her features until its brilliance set her whole face aglow. She set the Bible aside and rose from her chair, crossing over the short distance between us to sit on the edge of my bed, still clutching the rosary in her hand.

"O, ou pitit dous," she whispered, reaching up to gently brush wayward strands of hair away from my face. "We were startin' to worry you weren't *ever* gonna come back to us again."

"What are you doing here?"

"Well, when your young man got home the other night after…" Her face clouded for a moment. "Well, *after* – you were still just sittin' in the front seat of his car out there in the garage. You must have been there for hours, eyes wide open and starin' straight ahead and not seeing a thing. So, he looked up my number on your uncle's phone and gave me a call. I've been

144

here ever since."

"He's not 'my young man', Momma. He's just a friend. Mike–" Even saying his name aloud caused my voice to catch in my throat, hit me like a fist to the sternum. "Mike was his partner." It was fairly dark in the room, but the glow emanating from around the blackout shades told me it was late afternoon outside. "Wait – the other *night?* How long have I been out?"

"More than two whole days now. We could get you to sit up and move around when we had to, but there's not been much of anything goin' on behind your eyes in a good long while. And seeing as you don't breathe when you sleep, all we could do was wait and see if you were gonna wake up at all."

I suddenly realized I had almost no recollections at all from that timeframe. The last thing I could recall was a vague memory of Tommy trying desperately to get me to leave Mike's side as the pounding footsteps of the other police officers in the building were closing in and I could hear the sirens of the ambulance approaching in the distance. I couldn't pass unnoticed anymore with a full charge in my system, and there was no way for Tommy to explain my presence there or keep me out of jail if I stayed. I think I must have just gone back out the way I came in, through the same set of windows on the north side of the building.

But the walk to the car, the drive back to Tommy's house, and whatever may have happened after that were a complete mystery to me. Mike's passing – having been the one to end his suffering and free his soul from his torn and mangled body – had apparently driven me into a fugue state again, not unlike the one I'd experienced immediately after my resurrection.

"Where's Tommy?" I asked.

"He's downstairs staring at a baseball game on television, but I don't think he's really seeing much of what he's looking at, either. He's in a bad way himself, I'm afraid."

"But he's okay? I mean, he's not hurt?"

She shook her head, her smile faltering just a bit. "Not on the outside, if that's what you mean. You want to see him?"

I swallowed hard, nodded. Wanda rose from the bedside, pausing for a moment to hand me a bottle of water from a bag by her feet. "I'll go get him.

You two talk for a while, and I'm gonna make us all some tea, *pou kalme nanm nan*." She smiled as she touched me gently on the cheek and headed out into the hall.

As soon as she was gone, I struggled to a sitting position, leaning back heavily against the headboard and settling the sheets across my hips. I glanced down at my clothes, found I was somehow wearing Tommy's yellow t-shirt again. I had no idea how that might have happened, but I certainly hoped Wanda had been the only one directly involved. I took a tiny sip of water, set the bottle on the nightstand.

As a few sketchy details of the catastrophe at the old bottling plant began to coalesce in my mind, I gingerly probed my ribs and left shoulder with my fingers, looking for signs of serious injury – *nothing*. I pulled the collar of the shirt down almost to my left armpit to expose where the brutal knife wound had been, but there was nothing there now but a faint pink scar about four inches long.

"You were pretty busted up in general, but sooner or later you're gonna have to explain that one for me."

I glanced up. Tommy was leaning against the doorframe, hands jammed into the pockets of his jeans, wearing a black Rush concert tee. I quickly let the collar of my shirt slip back into place, covering the expanse of exposed skin. It might seem strange for a woman who takes her clothes off for a living to be shy about someone seeing too much of her bare body, but there is always a distinct difference between a stranger – a paying customer – seeing you naked and your family and friends, the people who make up your life outside the club. Or so I've been told.

"I'm going to assume it has something to do with the Crocodile Dundee knife I found in the floorboard of my car." Tommy said, a wan smile crossing his face.

"You okay?" I asked, noting the wide, dark circles under his eyes, the sunken appearance of his cheeks.

He shrugged. "Not really. You?"

"Not really."

He pushed himself off the door frame and crossed over to the chair where Wanda had been sitting, pulled it closer to be within arm's reach of the bed and dropped wearily into it. He stayed silent though, as if he had no idea what to say or do next.

"How many did you lose in there?" I asked quietly, dreading the answer.

He took a deep breath, and I could see him almost wince as he replied, "Three, counting Mike."

"Fuck – I knew there were two, but I hoped maybe…."

"Judging by where we found Lagorio's body – or *most* of it, I should say," he said, that small, thin smile tugging at the corner of his mouth again. "It looks like he ambushed the two officers we posted next to Carter's vehicle to cut off that route of escape."

I nodded. "After I finished him off, I found one body lying next to the car with the skin of their neck still frozen. Lagorio must have taken him down right before he came after me."

"That would have been Pete Kasun. He fell right by the car. The officer who was partnered with him, Jenny Heller, had her neck snapped and her body thrown thirty feet or so into the far corner under the stairwell."

I processed that for a moment, committed their names to memory. "They have families?"

"Heller was married – no kids yet. She was still a rookie PO. Kasun was single. Transferred to the force two years ago from Denver PD."

I tried to keep it together, but the hollow ache in my chest suddenly became too much to bear, and I broke down. Tommy rose from his chair and sat down as Wanda had, taking me into his arms and holding me tightly against his chest. I completely fell apart, sobbing into his shoulder like a child for what seemed like forever. He didn't seem inclined to complain. I think he wanted desperately to be held and comforted, too.

I eventually got it under control and slowly extricated myself from his embrace. I stared into his dark blue eyes. "I'm so sorry, Tommy."

He frowned, reaching up to take my shoulders and hold me gently at arm's length. "Sorry for what?"

"Sorry for Mike. Sorry for the others. Sorry for dragging you and everybody else into this fucked-up world I live in."

He shook his head. "Cherry, if you hadn't taken that big bastard down like you did, there's no telling how many people we might have lost in there that night." He managed a weak smile again. "That was a nasty piece of work you did there, by the way."

"Fucker had it coming."

"Looked like he got his licks in, too. I don't think I've ever seen someone with a concave ribcage before."

"I hope you never see it again, either."

He released his grip on my shoulders, letting his hands fall into his lap. He was silent for a long time. "Cherry," he said finally, his voice a bit unsteady. "Mike tried to tell me something. Right before you arrived, near the end. It didn't make a lot of sense. But it was something I think he wanted you to know if he couldn't hold on long enough."

I stared at him for a moment, said nothing.

"He said –" He stopped, looked down for a beat before meeting my eyes again. "He just asked me to tell you it was Leesy. That somebody named *Leesy* had done that to him."

I nodded, the tears beginning to spill down my cheeks again. "I know. I saw it in his mind." I fixed Tommy's gaze with my own. "Our wight-master is my sister, Annaliese."

His eyes widened, and he began shaking his head in confusion. "But I thought… I thought your sister died around the same time you did."

"No. The man who killed me traded her off to someone in exchange for the knowledge he needed to resurrect me. We always assumed she was dead, but her body was never found."

"And you're certain? You saw her face?"

I nodded. "She looked a little older than she was when we were taken, but not more than a year or two, I'd guess. And I saw her eyes, Tommy. Pale pink, right about where they should be given the time left until the full moon." I sighed raggedly. "She's a grave wight, Tommy. Just like me."

"And you think *she's* the one who's been orchestrating all of this?"

"I'm sure of it."

"But she's just a *kid*."

I shook my head firmly. "Tommy, she's no more a little girl than I am a teenager. She may look like a child, but she's survived in this world for over thirty-five years now. Hell, Tommy, she's probably older than *you* are."

He pursed his lips. "Yeah, I guess she would be."

I glanced at his casual attire. "So, what's going on? Why aren't you getting ready for work?"

He sighed. "Department put me on administrative leave. I won't be allowed to return to duty until I'm cleared by the Departmental shrink."

"Because of Mike?"

He nodded. "I guess it's policy. Or the fact that my psych profile already had a red flag or two in it, from before. Once you have a breakdown like that, they get pretty dodgy about putting you back out on the streets again."

He had mentioned the shrink before, but not the breakdown. And now was not the time to press. "Any sign of Kennedy at the bottling plant?"

He nodded once. "We didn't find *her*, but we did find evidence that they had been operating out of there for a while. There was some fast-food trash, fairly new. Figure *they* weren't eating it, so the only reason that shit would be there is if they were feeding somebody who *does* need to eat."

"She's still alive, then – or was a few days ago." I rubbed my eyes wearily. "She clearly has value to them. Even if I don't take the bait and try to save her first, they'll either turn her at the next full moon or use her at a resurrection to feed somebody else. Either way, they know I'll do everything I can to stop that from happening."

"Which means we have until midnight Wednesday to finish this."

I scoffed humorlessly. "Jesus, I don't even know what *day* it is anymore."

"It's Friday," He glanced down at his watch. "Friday, August twenty-fifth. Four-thirty-four p.m., to be exact."

"Only five days until the full moon, then," I processed that for a second. "Tommy, about Mike…"

His face looked pained, but he met my gaze. "Yeah?"

"Have they made funeral arrangements already?"

He sighed, nodded. "Looks like they're going to hold a combined memorial service Monday morning at the Cathedral Basilica, with the procession moving to graveside services at three different cemeteries afterwards. The Department wants to do this up right. It's gonna be the biggest funeral the City's seen in decades. We haven't lost three officers in the line of duty in a single year since the Sixties, let alone three in one night."

I collapsed back against the headboard, stared at the ceiling. "Christ, Tommy, I don't know how I'm gonna make it through all this again. I just… I just don't think I can do it."

He reached out and rested a hand on my shoulder. "You'll make it. And you'll be right there beside me the whole time."

I started to panic a bit. "Tommy, I can't. The glamour is gone. I can't hide from –"

He shook his head firmly. "Goddammit, Cherry, you're not *going* to hide. You're gonna put on a dress and you're gonna sit beside me in the front row at the service and I don't give a flying *fuck* who sees you."

"But they *will* see me. They'll know."

"They won't know jack shit. Hell, we'll tell people you're my cousin. Or my girlfriend. Or whatever else you're comfortable with. But, by God, you are going to attend Mike's funeral and not be hiding in a corner like you don't belong there. I swear, I will *not* fucking stand for it."

As the tears started to flow again, I reached out and pulled Tommy close again. We must have stayed that way for five minutes, my head resting on his shoulder, his chin resting on my head. There wasn't anything the least bit romantic about it – just two damaged souls trying to find comfort in one another. And I could have stayed there forever, just he and I keeping the outside world at bay while we grieved for our lost friend.

But the whistle of the tea kettle downstairs broke the spell and we awkwardly pulled apart. "You feel like going downstairs?" he asked.

I nodded firmly. "I've got to get up and back on my feet again. Kennedy and the people who killed Mike are still out there somewhere. And this ain't over yet."

"I know. Come on." He took me by the hand – safe, and at least room temperature now – and helped me to my feet. He held on tight as he led me down the stairs and back towards the kitchen.

\#　\#　\#

Wanda had three mugs set out, each one with a teabag inside. She was carefully pouring water from a black teapot into them, filling them to within an inch or so of the top. "I know our Miss Cherry there don't want milk, but how about you, *jenn gason?* Lemon or sugar maybe?"

"Just a bit of sugar for me, thanks."

She glanced at me. "*Cher?*"

"Just the tea, thank you," I said. She sat a mug down in front of me and I reached out to take the teabag by the string, lifting it in and out of the steaming hot water over and over again absentmindedly.

Wanda turned to Tommy. "Next time I come by here, Thomas, I'm gonna bring you some proper tea. That ol' Lipton stuff you had in there'll serve in a pinch, but a kitchen just isn't complete without a decent box of chamomile and some Mariage Frères."

"Momma," I asked, "how are things with Vic and the club?"

She shrugged. "Shut down, of course. The girls have been picking up shifts at some of the other clubs. They're doing all right. And don't you spend one minute worrying about Vic. That old *dejenere* has more money than he knows what to do with – he'll weather this storm jus' like he did the pandemic. I think he's planning on using the down time to add that silly drive-thru thing he's been goin' on about forever and then throwin' some kind of grand re-opening gala in a month or so."

Tommy glanced up, eyebrows raised. "*Drive thru?*"

I patted his shoulder. "Later, O'Connor." I lifted my mug and grabbed a battered pack of cigarettes and my Zippo from where some kind soul had left them out on the counter near the back door. "You mind if we step outside for a bit, Momma?"

She waved a hand. "*Pa ditou.* You children jus' go on and take whatever time you need. I'll square things away here and then I'll be in the other room catchin' up on my programs."

"Thanks, Momma." I tilted my head toward the door, and Tommy followed in my wake.

Once we were outside, I had to blink a bit in the glare, but the sun had fallen below the level of the trees, so it was at least tolerable. Besides, I had no idea where my sunglasses had gotten to and didn't have the energy to go looking. I sat down at the top of the concrete stairs leading up to the back door and set my tea on the first step down. Tommy settled himself beside me, his mug cupped in both hands. I drew a bent cigarette out of my pack, tucked it between my lips and lit it with the ease of long practice. I drew the smoke into my lungs, relishing the cool tingle of the menthol.

"Do you mind?" Tommy asked, tilting his head toward the pack.

"You smoke?"

"I quit at the academy – calisthenics were killing me. But I think I deserve a hit about now."

I shrugged, shook a cigarette to the top of the pack, and offered it to Tommy. "I've always been an enabler, you know."

He drew the cigarette out and leaned over as I struck the Zippo again, held it out towards him. He let the tip touch the flame, puffed the cigarette to life, and took a long, almost sensuous drag. He released the smoke through his nose with a sigh, rolling his eyes in melodramatic ecstasy. "Oh, fuck *me*, that's good."

"Don't go backsliding on me, O'Connor," I said with a tiny grin. "The big 'C' don't mean shit to me these days, but I don't want to be responsible for *your* early demise, too."

"One-time thing, I swear."

The tea was still boiling hot so we both just let it sit. It wasn't exactly the ideal drink for the weather, either, although it was considerably cooler this afternoon than it had been the last few weeks. St. Louis could be weird like that. It could be hotter than hell for a month, and then out of the blue you'd get a whole week where the temperature never got above seventy-five. It wasn't quite that cool at the moment, but it was hell of a lot better than it had been.

I glanced over at the garage with a guilty twist in my belly. "You see the car?" Tommy nodded.

I winced. "So exactly how pissed are you?"

He shrugged noncommittally. "Shit happens."

"I really am sorry about that."

"Don't be," he said, taking another drag from his cigarette and flicking ash from the tip. "It's just a car. It can be fixed. Doesn't seem all that important right now."

"Get an estimate. I'll pay for the damages."

He shook his head. "I'll show it to Dad. I doubt he'll want to trust her to a body shop."

"Well, whatever it costs, I'll pay." I reached down and took a sip of my tea, scalded my tongue badly. Fortunately, that sort of thing healed within a minute or so with my batteries fully charged. The sudden recollection of where that charge had come from was like a punch in the gut. "Have you given much thought to exactly how utterly *fucked* we are at the moment?"

Tommy set his mug down and slipped down a step so he could lean back on his elbow and turn towards me. "Well, on the plus side of things, there are actually a *few* bright spots. First, we can take *you* off the threat list for a while." He met my gaze for a moment, I'm sure taking note of the deep crimson color of my eyes. I hadn't had the heart to look at them yet, knowing what that change had cost. "Second, not only did you manage to take down one of the wights, but a *big* son of a bitch, at that. *And* we identified the 'leader of the pack', so to speak." He was sensitive enough to just leave that sitting there instead of delving into the details.

"Last but not least," he continued, "just before the callout to the bottling plant, Mike and I were briefed on an interview conducted with the family of the third revenant victim we found – Connie Walden. They led the detectives to a coworker who ID'd a boyfriend – one her family didn't even *know* about. Turns out he was among the missing persons reports in my dining room – guy named Justin Hoefler."

"Rap sheet?"

Tommy nodded. "Minor stuff for the most part. Petty theft, misdemeanor assault, drunk and disorderly. But he had a restraining order taken out against him four years ago by an ex. Apparently, he'd made some pretty serious threats after their breakup. I suspect that's why Walden kept her relationship with him a secret from her folks."

"Sounds like a peach," I muttered, the cigarette still hanging from my lips.

He turned a wry look my way, soldiered on. "If Hoefler *is* our guy – and at this point I think we have to assume he is – then all the wight-victim pairs were either dating couples or at least in a sexual relationship of some kind. If we were looking for a regular serial killer here, that would be the one thread that connects all our victims, and we'd probably chalk it up as being the most likely motivation behind their being targeted. Seeing the couples together or even witnessing public displays of affection is what catches the eye of our killer in the first place."

I frowned. "Is that really a thing?"

"Very much so," Tommy said. "Some serial killers lack the ability to make connections with other people or form any sort of lasting relationships. Sometimes they target people they perceive as having spurned their affections, and sometimes they just lash out at anybody who has what they can't find. You've heard of the Zodiac killer, right? And the Son of Sam?"

"Of course."

"Well, of the seven confirmed victims of the Zodiac killer, six were couples out together in remote areas: lovers' lanes, secluded beaches, places like that. And there may be dozens of other victims, murdered under similar circumstances, but the police couldn't definitively tie them to the Zodiac."

I raised my eyebrows. "You *gotta* stop binging true crime documentaries, Tommy."

He ignored me. "And six of the eight Son of Sam shootings were couples in parked cars or out for a walk. Then there's the Monster of Florence, the Night Stalker, the Golden–"

"Okay," I said, raising a hand to stop the dissertation. "So, we chase *that* angle – something about seeing couples together is what drew Leesy to them. That's where we'll pick things up." I took another sip of my tea. "But we need to *keep* working the vehicles belonging to either the victim or the revenant. That approach got us the closest we've been to Kennedy so far, even if it went sideways in the worst way imaginable."

"My thoughts exactly," Tommy said with a small smile. I think he was getting a kick out of watching me flex my amateur investigative skills.

I sighed. "Okay – I guess that wraps up the plus side of the ledger. What's the minus side look like?"

Tommy looked down at his mug, his face darkening. "Well, obviously, our biggest loss was Mike. And we missed out on what might have been our best chance to catch them all together in one place." He shook his head bitterly. "Should've gone in with the whole fucking SWAT team instead of six sitting ducks."

"I doubt it would have made any difference, Tommy," I said. "In all likelihood, all it would have done is up the body count. Mike made a mistake, but it wasn't going in without more cops."

He turned on me, eyes flashing. "*Mistake*?"

"Tommy, Mike was a great cop. And I loved him more than anything in this world. But he fucked up *big-time* that night." It broke my heart to say it out loud, but Tommy needed to hear it.

"How do you figure?" he asked, his voice becoming defensive.

"Mike knew what you were up against, and he led you in there anyway. He should *never* have tried to keep me out of it. Hell, *I* should have been the one to go in. *Alone.*"

"Cherry, he was trying to keep you safe!"

I nodded firmly. "*Exactly.* And now he's dead – along with two other cops. And if you try the same ignorant shit, it's going to get *you* killed, too. Tommy, you saw what I did to Lagorio. I'm just as strong as these people are, and I can handle myself against any of them. Mike still sees –" My voice caught again, and I covered the momentary lapse of control by taking another puff on my cigarette. "Mike could never see me as anything but the weak, vulnerable teenage girl I was the day I died. But I'm just as much of a monster as any of them."

"Cherry, you're not–"

"I am. In *every* way that counts in a fight. I'm the same kind of… *thing* the rest of them are. They can kill with a touch, but that shit won't work on me. And I can take a punch – the kind of punch that turns people's skulls into mush – and I can come up swinging. I could have slipped in there completely unseen and at least gotten the lay of the land before your people went in. And, goddammit, Mike *should* have known better."

Tommy seemed to calm down as he processed the facts I laid out before him. He didn't like the perceived slight at Mike, but he was at least willing to consider the source. Nobody loved Mike more than me, but I was only too familiar with the blind spot he suffered from where I was concerned.

"Unfortunately," he said after a beat. "Our vehicle approach is going to get exponentially more difficult now. We seized Lagorio's dually pickup and what was left of Carter's Cutlass, so we can't use those two rather unique vehicles to track down potential wights anymore. And Hoefler, our most likely candidate as wight number three, drove a goddamned white Honda Accord. Fucking fleet car. We BOLO'd it, but there's only about ten *thousand* of those in the Metro area, so that's gonna be fun."

I took one last drag on the cigarette as I let that settle in.

"And – to top it all off – I'm officially *off* the case, at least for as long as it matters." He sighed heavily. "Our resources are pretty limited at the moment."

"Well," I said, stubbing out the cigarette on the concrete, "what resources we *do* have are sitting in your dining room right now. Feel like doing some more digging?"

He sighed again and, after one last long drag on his own cigarette, dropped the butt into his untouched cup of tea. "Not really. But if we're going to find the people who killed Mike in the next five days, we'd better get back to work...."

Sixteen

TOMMY MADE A CALL TO a friend of his in the records section – one who wouldn't report him to the higher-ups for continuing an investigation while supposedly on leave – and asked them to email over scanned copies of some of the cold-case stuff on my sister. Stirring up that particular pot made me more than a little nervous, but we couldn't afford to miss even the slightest detail at this point.

While he was on the phone, I made three piles on the table – the known wights on one side, their victims on the other, and in the middle was the stack of people who had gone missing during the time frame in question. Tommy told me five of those had been resolved since they were filed, so we tossed them aside, leaving about three dozen open cases.

I pulled Benny Evans' file from the victim stack. Tommy and I poured over every statement and report in it, trying to identify who he might have been with the night he disappeared. Unfortunately, *his* car was accounted for – he'd never claimed it from the parking garage where he'd left it – so it seemed he hadn't been the one driving the night he was taken. He worked for one of the big financial companies downtown and had been one of the last of our victims to go missing, vanishing just a week or so before the full moon and three days before Karen Wagner. His coworkers said he had left work early that night, probably heading for a bar to get wasted. Several of them had expressed concerns that Benny may be developing a drinking problem, but nobody was exactly sure why.

"All right," I said, placing my hand on top of the middle pile. "We're going to have to cut some corners and make some educated guesses if we're going to narrow the field quickly here."

"Agreed," Tommy said.

"Now, with the exception of Karen, all of our victims and the wights we've associated with them were taken from *inside* the City – inside the *Fourth District*, in fact. I'd suggest we set aside all the files that *aren't* from inside the Fourth. Or at most, the Fourth and the districts that immediately surround it."

Tommy shook his head. "That only knocks out the First. Since the Department was reorganized in 2014, we're down from nine districts to six. And only the First isn't contiguous with the Fourth."

"Shit," I cursed under my breath. "Well, we can set aside the ones *outside* the City, at least. Might as well leave the First in, I guess."

Tommy sorted through the middle stack for a moment, setting most of the files aside and creating two new piles. "Okay," he said finally. "These are what's left. There are three from the Fourth, and seven more from the rest. Only two are from the First, so we'll leave them in like you suggested."

He laid each of the three from the Fourth District open in front of us. There were two females, Miranda Perez and Natalie Morris, and one male, Robert Zuckerberg. We took turns reading through each of their case files in detail.

"All right, my turn" Tommy said, holding up one of the folders. "Let's take another leap and assume your sister wanted younger, stronger types. Natalie Morris is sixty-three and needs regular insulin to survive. From the date she went missing until the full moon on the first of August was a space of nearly three weeks. There's no way she could have survived that long without her meds."

I shook my head. "I'll grant you the age thing might be a *little* useful, but remember -Morris could have been the revenant, not the victim. Leesy didn't *need* her alive."

Tommy sighed, nodded. "Yeah, but given her age and condition, would you agree we can still set her aside? At least for now? Especially since she was reported missing almost *two* full weeks before Benny."

"Fine. For now. But we can't discount her altogether. Whatever infirmities a person had in life, they won't wake up from a resurrection ritual with the same issues. Under the right set of circumstances, death can do a body good."

Tommy shot me a look, tossed Morris' folder on the discard pile.

I rubbed my eyes, feeling the pieces start to fall into place in my head. "I think you're dead-on about the couples angle, Tommy. But maybe…. what if the motive isn't jealously or anger at the relationship itself? Maybe it's purely a matter of convenience."

He mulled that over for a moment. "Two birds with one stone?"

I nodded. "Leesy isn't very big. Even as a wight, she'd have a tough time hauling unconscious people around all over the place." I shook my head, certain we were on the scent now. "Tommy, she was picking them off in *pairs*. Probably already *in* their cars. She could kill them quiet – out of sight – and then just drive them to wherever she had set things up in advance."

Tommy pursed his lips thoughtfully and nodded. "I'd say that fits the evidence pretty damned well. Dovetails nicely with everything we know so far. But the question still remains: who the fuck was in a car with Benny Evans the night he disappeared?"

I lifted the two remaining folders in the middle pile, one in each hand, glancing at the names on the tabs. "Looks like we're down to a man and a woman, so I guess the question before the group is: was Benny Evans gay or straight?"

Tommy grabbed a yellow form from the file, held it up. "Says here Benny came out to his family just before Christmas 2020. He was in a relationship with someone who had just proposed to him – a guy named Daniel Marlowe from St. Charles. But they separated – amicably, it seems – a few months ago. Missing persons had already followed up before Benny's body was found and cleared Marlowe as a suspect. He was in Seattle on business for two weeks, including the morning Benny failed to show up at his office."

I tapped another folder. "And Zuckerberg?"

Tommy flipped it open, leafed through a few pages. He looked up at me with a grin. "Also gay. No serious relationships as far as anybody knew.

He was last seen at a bar down on the Landing called… the Cobblestone Lounge. The night *before* Evans was reported missing."

Wanda had been passing through the dining room on her way to the kitchen, stopped in her tracks. "The Cobblestone? What about it?"

I glanced up at her in surprise. "We think it might be where one of our potential resurrection subjects went missing from. Why?"

"My cousin Edouard is the manager there. The two of us, we moved up here together when we were jus' teenagers. That *vye moun fou* go get himself into some kinda trouble again?"

"No, not at all," said Tommy. "But do you think he'd be willing to talk to us if we dropped in unannounced?"

She waved a hand. "No need to worry about 'unannounced'. I'll give him a call right now and tell him you're coming. *And* I'll tell him he better tell you everything he knows or I'm gonna come down there and *mete pye m nan bourik li*."

"Thanks, Momma," I said with a grin. I started gathering up all the missing persons files from the shortlist. "All right, you heard the woman, O'Connor. Go put on some cop-looking clothes while I get properly dressed. Time to get moving."

Tommy slid back his seat, headed for the stairs. "All right, but if we're gonna be partners now, there is one condition I'm gonna have to insist on."

"And that is?"

He managed a grin. "*I'm* driving…"

# # #

We left Dogtown and headed east towards Laclede's Landing and the Cobblestone Lounge, which was on Second Street between Morgan and Lucas. The name of the club was appropriate – the roads out in front of the buildings, some of which dated back to the mid-19th Century, were mostly constructed of large hand-cut, hand-laid red granite cobblestones. Over the years, these stones had settled and shifted until driving over them in any sort of vehicle, let alone one with as low a profile and as stiff a suspension as Tommy's Mustang, was a first-class kidney-buster. And navigating them in high heels was an ER visit waiting to happen. But they weren't about to be swapped out or paved over anytime soon. After all, this was the birthplace of St. Louis, where Pierre Laclede had founded the first settlement in 1764 and named it after King Louis the Ninth of France. It deserved a little respect.

Nowadays, the Landing was one of the City's true nightlife hotspots, home to a wide variety of bars, restaurants, nightclubs and even a big-time casino. You never knew what you were going to see strolling along its dimly lit streets after dark. Bachelorette parties on a bar crawl, drunken sports fans fresh from a Blues or Cardinals game – even families on vacation trying to navigate the rough roads and sidewalks with baby strollers and catching rides on the horse-drawn carriages that moved through the neighborhood day and night.

For me, it had the added benefit of being one of the few places in town where somebody who looked like I did would barely warrant a second glance from passers-by. I used to love going down there as a kid, and found it was even more fun as I had grown older – I had snatched more than a few unsavory types from its shadowy streets and alleys over the years. Unfortunately, the Landing attracted that sort occasionally as well, but I tried to do my part to keep those historic old streets safe for the good people of St. Louis.

Friday night was always a busy time down on the Landing, but the Cardinals were in the middle of a six-game road trip and City SC was in Florida, so it wasn't too hard to find a parking spot in one of the surface lots down the street from the Cobblestone Lounge. After having to put a shoulder to his door to get it open and listening to the mournful screech of the hinges as he closed it again, Tommy couldn't resist shooting me another evil glare. It was one of several I'd gotten during the drive over, each one coming as we both felt the clutch slip as he shifted gears or the transmission refused to engage smoothly. It was becoming apparent that the damage I had done was more than just cosmetic, but Tommy wasn't as angry with me as he was feeling sorry for his poor, mistreated baby. Or so I hoped.

He had chosen something halfway between his civilian clothes and regular duty suit, sticking with jeans but swapping out his t-shirt for a polo and a sport coat. He wore his shield on his belt where it was clearly visible, and I could tell by the fall of his jacket that his Beretta was in its usual spot under his left arm. I was still in my same old hunting clothes – Wanda had been kind enough to stitch up the huge gash in the left shoulder of my shirt and cloak and run all my clothes through the wash again, so I finally had on clean underwear again. My mother would have been so proud.

We crossed Second Street and passed under the maroon awning that hung over a small outdoor seating area surrounding the entrance to the Cobblestone Lounge. A rainbow flag fluttered in the light breeze from a pole that stood out next to a second-story window, one of dozens that still flew from businesses and restaurants around the City since Pride Week at the end of June. The Cobblestone Lounge flew theirs year-round, and it was a popular spot for people of all orientations to meet up and mingle.

As we stepped through the front door, there was a pretty good crowd gathered inside. We walked up to the bar and waited patiently until the good-looking, well-built young man serving drinks worked his way down to our end.

"What can I get you folks?" he asked, smiling amiably.

Tommy flashed his ID, made sure his shield was noticed. "I'm Detective Thomas O'Connor, St. Louis Metro Homicide. This is my associate, Miss Chandra."

I smiled and nodded, while simultaneously kicking Tommy sharply in the shin underneath the bar rail.

The young man nodded, seeming not to notice Tommy's wince and sideways glare. "Something I can help you with?"

"We'd like to speak with the night manager, Edouard Quebodeaux. We have a few questions regarding a missing persons case."

"Sure thing," the bartender said, tossing his bar towel over his shoulder. "Eddie's in the back. I'll go get him."

The bartender turned and disappeared into the kitchen.

"What the hell was the kick for?" Tommy hissed at me under his breath.

I realized I didn't have a really good answer for that – just seemed like the right thing to do at the time. "General principles."

"You want to start going by *Cherry Bomb* out on the street, I'll accommodate you."

"No," I said, sighing. "Sorry. I guess it just reminded me too much of Mike."

Before he could respond, a tall, lean man in linen slacks and a garishly colored Hawaiian print shirt came out from the back. He smiled brightly as he approached. "Detective O'Conner?" he said, extending a hand to Tommy, who returned his greeting. He reached over and took my own hand, pressing a kiss to the back of my glove while staring straight into my eyes. I had a feeling I wasn't the first grave wight *he'd* come across, either. "And Mademoiselle.... *Chandra*, was it?"

I gave him a small, knowing smile but just nodded. "Wanda told me you were coming," he drawled. "But she certainly was stingy on the details." His eyes still hadn't left mine. His attention might have made me uncomfortable under normal circumstances, but I could see much of Wanda in him, from his tawny skin to his warm, liquid brown eyes to the subtle Creole lilt to his speech. I'd have guessed him to be in his mid-fifties, but with some folks you never can tell. If he and Wanda were teenagers together, he had to be quite a bit older than that.

Tommy seemed unsettled by Edouard's fixation on me, and he quickly moved to get down to business. "Mr. Quebodeaux–"

"Just Eddie, please," the older man said, finally turning to look at Tommy.

"Okay. Eddie. We're here following up on a missing persons case – a man who was last seen here in late July. Robert Zuckerberg?" He held out the photo of Zuckerberg from the files he had placed in front of him on the bar.

Eddie glanced at the picture, but only for a second. "Yeah, that's Bob. Regular customer around here – works in sales over at the Convention Center. Usually comes in here at least once or twice a week, mostly on the weekends. But I already told all this to the detectives who were here a few weeks ago."

"Yes, I know," Tommy said with a nod. "We're actually more interested in who else he might have been hanging around with that night." He reached into his folders again and came out with a slab shot of Benny Evans. "Do you recognize this man?"

Eddie took the photo from Tommy, reached into his shirt pocket to retrieve a small pair of wire-rimmed glasses, which he perched on the end of his nose. He gave the photo a good look, then nodded. "*O wi*, he's a regular here, too. Though not as much as Bob was. Ben-something, right?"

"Evans," Tommy said, his voice tightening as he sensed a break coming our way. "Benny Evans."

"You know, now that you mention it, I'm pretty sure he was here that same night that Bob went missing."

"Robert Zuckerberg and this man were here *together* on the night they both disappeared?" I asked.

"Well," Edouard said with a shrug. "Never said *that*. They were both *here*, but I never said they were *together*. Bob sat in his usual booth over there by the stage with some of his friends. This *jenn gason* here, he was sitting at the end of the bar talking with a woman most of the night."

Tommy frowned. "A woman?"

"*O wi. Yon bél fanm,* that one. Just gorgeous – Latina lady with big dark eyes, long black hair. Never seen *her* in here before."

In a flash of insight, I realized that Edouard was giving us a pretty good general description of one other candidate in our files. I dug down to the bottom of Tommy's pile, came out with a photo of Miranda Perez. "This her?"

Again, Edouard peered down his nose through his cheaters again. He nodded confidently. "That's her, all right. Never caught her name, but I ain't likely to forget this one anytime soon."

"I don't suppose you overheard any part of their conversation?" Tommy asked.

Edouard managed to look mildly offended. "Son, I don't make it my business to go buttin' my nose into other folks' private talks. I got no time for eavesdropping on my customers when I got a business to run. But from the way Benny was acting, I'd guess he was pretty shook up about something. Seemed on the verge of tears more'n a few times."

The breakup with his fiancée. "Did they leave together?" I asked, certain I already knew the answer.

"Oh, well, Benny had himself worked up pretty good, and he was in no shape to be driving. I asked *jén dam sa* myself if she was planning on getting him home or if I needed to call him a cab. She said she'd see him home safe."

Tommy reached out and shook Edouard's hand. "Thanks, Eddie. You've been a big help."

"My pleasure, detective," Eddie said with a smile. He glanced at me. "You make sure you tell Wanda that for me, okay? I don't need her comin' down here to rip the seat outta my trousers thinkin' I was anything less than hospitable to you folks."

I grinned, shaking Edouard's hand as well. "I'll make sure she knows. And thanks again, Eddie."

Tommy gathered up the files and we headed back out the front door and into the night.

The air was even cooler now, and thick with the musty smell of mildew and river water. But the excitement over our new discovery made everything seem lighter and brighter somehow.

We reached Tommy's car and as soon as we slid inside, I turned to Tommy with a satisfied smile. "So, it looks like our fourth and final mystery guest is Miranda Perez, huh?"

Tommy nodded. "Looks that way. I'm still not sure I buy the fact that Zuckerberg's disappearance from the same spot on the same night is just a coincidence, but I think it's safe to assume at this point that Perez is almost certainly our only unidentified wight."

"Does it say in her file what kind of car she drives?"

Tommy flipped it open, scanning each sheet until he found what he was looking for. He grinned. "Well, this ought to be a little easier to find than a goddamned white Accord."

"What is it?"

He flashed a picture towards me. "How about a hundred-fifty-thousand-dollar Audi R8?"

I returned his grin. "Can't be too many of those zipping around town. What does this chick do for a living, anyway?"

"Sports therapy and rehabilitation specialist."

"Must be big money in that."

"Huge. You should see her client list."

"Major league, huh?"

"Literally. Put it this way: if she really is out of the picture, the major sports teams in this town might go straight down the crapper for the next few seasons."

I shook my head, my grin fading away quickly. "Well, then, I'll add that to the long list of reasons I'm going to kick my sister's ass when I find her…"

Seventeen

WE MADE IT BACK TO Tommy's house around ten-thirty that night. On the way back, Tommy called his buddy again and asked him to update the old BOLO on Perez's Audi. We found Wanda asleep in Tommy's overstuffed recliner with HGTV blaring on the television. I roused her gently, and she joined us in the dining room where I brought her up to speed on our new discoveries.

"Momma," I said, sliding into one of the chairs around the table. "Back at my apartment you mentioned there were some poisons that might work to take down a grave wight?"

She nodded. "There aren't many, but I seem to remember two or three."

"Such as?"

"Well, let's jus' have a look," she said, heading back towards the living room. She was gone for a moment and when she returned, she was carrying a heavy, leather-bound tome that looked remarkably similar to the partial one I had taken from Reginald Hargrove's basement years ago. I guess it must have been tucked into the enormous shoulder bag she had brought along from home. Wanda set the book reverently in the center of the dining room table and carefully began turning pages.

"Momma, where on Earth did this come from?" I asked.

"When your friend Thomas here called me after he got home from the factory the other night and found you in the state you were in, I dug this out of an old steamer trunk full of stuff they sent me after my *maman* passed years ago.

167

There's no title here, but she called it *le Livre des Morts Vivants*. Everything I ever learned about grave wights came straight outta this book. Figured there might be somethin' in here we could use to help bring you around."

"Well, *'le livre'* is just a book, right?" Tommy asked from across the table. "And – if my high school French is still worth a damn – *'le Mort Vivant'* means 'the living dead', right?"

Wanda nodded. "*O wi*. This old book is chock-full of grave wight lore, and even contains detailed descriptions of the actual rituals for bringing the dead back to life."

I stared at Tommy for a moment, a slight smile tugging at my lips. "You took *French?*"

He shrugged. "I thought it might get me laid."

"Not so much?"

"Not so much."

I chuckled and rolled my eyes before leaning in close to peer over Wanda's shoulder. I frowned deeply – I couldn't read a word of it. Hargrove's book had been written in an antiquated form of English. And though this book had been put down with an elegant, graceful hand, I couldn't make heads or tails of it.

"But that's not exactly French, is it Wanda?" Tommy asked, frowning deeply.

"That, *Cher*, is *Kouri-Vini* – the *true* Louisiana Creole. Not too many folks this far up the river can even speak it, let alone read or write it. I can puzzle out most of what's written here, but even *I* struggle with some of the phrasing. Growin' up, my family spoke their own mishmash dialect – somethin' 'bout halfway between Louisiana and Haitian Creole, so there's a fair amount of this I have to make some educated guesses at," she said with a droll little smile as she continued to leaf through the thin, brittle pages. "This book has been passed down through the women in my family for I can't tell you how many generations. When I was little, my ol' *bonne-maman* told me it was copied into *Kouri-Vini* from an even older book that had come over on a ship from Spain way back in the 1780's. Supposedly, there's only a handful of these left in the whole world, and most of those kept under lock and key."

"Why's that?" Tommy asked.

"Because, *jenn gason*, the magic set down in these pages is counted among the very blackest of the dark arts," Wanda said with great solemnity. She turned to glance at me for a moment. "I mean no offense by what I'm about to say, *cher* – you know I love you to pieces. But bringing back to this world that which has moved on to the next is considered to be among the foulest and most profane violations of the natural order of things that man has ever attempted."

I scoffed. "No offense taken, Momma. I couldn't agree more."

Tommy seemed on the verge of saying something several times, but in the end, he held his peace. I think he *had* taken offense to Wanda referring to my existence as a sacrilege or some sort of abomination. But he hadn't seen what I'd seen over the years, hadn't done the things I'd done to survive. And while I did my best to use my abilities in service of what Mike and I considered to be the greater good, I had never completely accepted his fervent belief that the world was a better place for my presence in it. I just couldn't.

"The Church and the old-time practitioners never did see eye to eye on *much*, but the one thing they always could agree on was that whenever one of these books surfaced, it needed to be destroyed straight away. To make sure it didn't end up fallin' into the wrong hands," Wanda said. "The lure of bringing back lost loved ones is jus' too strong. And grievin' folk, well, they're just not known for makin' the best decisions. But the *cost...*" She shook her head, a pained expression on her face. "*Bondye mwen*, the cost is jus' *too* high."

I shook my head. "I'll go you one worse, Tommy. Imagine for a minute the absolute devastation that a book like this would have wrought in the hands of Adolph Hitler. Or Genghis Khan. Armies of nearly immortal undead under the absolute control of one person. An army that kills without weapons or remorse, moving across the globe like a plague of locusts."

Tommy paled, swallowed hard. "I always heard Hitler and his inner circle were fanatically obsessed with the occult. At least that's what *Raider of the Lost Ark* told me."

I nodded grimly. "And I'll bet this is one of the reasons why. A book like this in the hands of someone *truly* evil? It could bring on an apocalypse."

After a few minutes of browsing, Wanda turned up a full-page, hand-colored illustration that showed a pale woman in a long white dress with eyes the color of fresh blood. "Ah-ha!" she said at last. "*O wi*, here it is, *cher*: wightsbane."

"*Wightsbane*?"

"That's as good a translation as I can give you. Looks like jus' powdered mandrake root mixed with Abramelin oil to me. But it's supposed to do the trick."

Tommy frowned. "Is that something we can buy locally?"

Wanda nodded. "There's still a few shops left around town that sell stuff like that. Most of the folks workin' there got just about enough *real* power to turn food into shit, but there's a fair-sized Wicca community hereabouts. I guess they must sell enough to keep the doors open, at least."

"And this is the most powerful one of the bunch?" I asked.

"That's the one that's supposed to work the fastest. If you put even a drop or two in a glass of water, I'd wager that'd probably be more than enough to take one down."

"Okay, hang on," Tommy said, holding up his hands. "Let's assume for one second this stuff actually works. How in Christ's name are we supposed to get them to *drink* it?"

Wanda shook her head. "No need for all that," she snapped. "And you blaspheme like that in front of me again, *jenn gason*, I'm gonna put you straight over my knee, *konprann?*" I stifled a grin as she flipped to the next page of the book. "Look, there's instructions right here for workin' up a thick paste of this stuff and spreading it over stakes and spears and knives and whatnot. Might not kill as fast as drinkin' it – maybe not even at all. But it's supposed to stop the wound from healing up. Makes 'em take the hit like us regular folk do."

I turned that over in my mind for a few moments before finally glancing up at Tommy. "What do you carry, O'Connor? Beretta 92?"

He nodded, his face showing just a touch of surprise. "You know guns?"

"Cop's kid, remember? Dad started taking me to the shooting range with him when I was ten." I smiled wanly at the memory. "I think it was his way of apologizing for my little sister being born. Like he wanted to reassure me he'd still have time for us to spend together on our own, even though the new baby was getting all the attention at home."

He reached into his holster and drew out his sidearm. He dropped the magazine, racked the slide to eject the round in the chamber, and offered it to me grip first. "That's the same nine-millimeter 92D they issued me at the Academy."

I took the gun from him, reached over to pick up the ejected cartridge. I held the round up to the light, examined the base of the cartridge. "Winchesters."

"Yeah – Rangers. Hundred forty-seven grain jacketed hollow points. The Union and a lot of the newer guys have been pushing for the Department to move up to the .40 Smith and Wesson for years. But that old nine has always worked fine for me."

"What if we were to pack this wightsbane shit into a hollow-point bullet and seal it over?"

Tommy looked at me for a second before a grin spread across his face. "Yeah, I see where you're going with this. Roy Scheider in *Jaws 2*...." He reached over and took the round from my hand, peering at the tip. "So, if this wightsbane stuff really works, then I'm back on the front lines again, right?"

"Not so fast, hotshot. We'll need to test them out first, but maybe – *maybe* – we can at least give you a fighting chance against one of these assholes."

"How do you propose we test them out?"

I shook my head. "Not *we*, Tommy. *Me*."

His face flushed red. "Cherry, you can't go in alone against four of these guys. They'll mop the floor with you."

"And you can't go in at *all* until we know for sure these wightsbane rounds will put one of these fuckers down for the count. That's the same thinking that got Mike killed, Tommy. You can't see them, you can't sense them, and they can kill you with the touch of a hand."

Tommy's features hardened. "The full moon is Wednesday, Cherry. We're not going to have time for a dry run here. Not unless you've got a spare wight tied up in a basement somewhere we can use for target practice."

I said nothing, but I wasn't ready to give in just yet.

"Look," Tommy said, "I've been thinking about this a lot since that night at the factory, and you just said it yourself – they can kill with a *touch*.

But those leather gloves of yours have worked well enough for years to keep you from accidentally taking someone out with a brush of the hand, right?"

I glanced at Momma Wanda, who nodded cautiously. "Yeah."

Tommy plowed on. "Well, the way I understand it, a wight's ability to take a life depends on *direct* skin-to-skin contact."

"More or less. So what?"

He grinned. "*So…* what if we make that impossible?"

I folded my arms across my chest. "And how *exactly* do you plan to do that?"

He crossed the room, ducking through a small door that appeared to lead down to the basement. He was gone a minute or two, and when he returned, he had a bundle of heavy clothing draped over one arm and a pair of bulky leather boots dangling from the other. "*Voila!*" he said with a grin.

Wanda rolled her eyes as I walked over to him and pulled a stiff black leather jacket from his arms, holding it up to for closer inspection. The material was unusually thick and heavy, and appeared to have some sort of light armor plating inserted beneath the surface of the chest, back, and shoulders.

"What the hell is this?"

"Motorcycle racing leathers."

I shot him a skeptical look. "You ride?"

He nodded. "I used to do track days when I was younger. I gave it up the third time I broke my collar bone. But this stuff will stand up to a hundred mile per hour skid on your ass across asphalt pavement."

My first instinct was to dismiss it out of hand. But the closer I looked at the jacket and pants, the more I started to believe he might be onto something. I had to admit, if I ran into somebody wearing that getup during a hunt, it *would* be pretty tough to take them down quickly before they had a chance to fight back. Not impossible, but *tough.* "Well, it'd be better if it was all one piece, but with the boots and gloves, they *would* have a hard time getting at you from the neck down. You got a plan for the head and neck?"

"My regular helmet and visor will cover most of it – I'll lose some peripheral vision and my hearing won't be the best, but if I can't see them or hear them anyway until they attack, what difference does it make?" He fingered the collar of the jacket. "These zip up pretty high. Maybe we can just use a bandana or balaclava to cover the gap."

I sighed heavily, finally shook my head. "No, Tommy. It's too dangerous. They can still get at you, even in that outfit."

He glared at me, the frustration in his eyes slipping towards anger. "And if one of them is carrying a blade, they can lop your damned head off. Look, neither of us is going to be *completely* safe going into this."

"I won't have you putting your life on the line for me."

He rolled his eyes. "Dammit, Cherry, I put my life on the line every time I walk out that fucking door. Most of the time, it's for people whose names I'll never even *know*. That's my *job*."

"I understand that, Tommy. Better than most. But there's one big difference between those people you risk your life for and *me*."

"And what's that?"

"I'm already dead…"

#   #   #

We all turned in around midnight – Wanda was planning on returning home, but I begged her to stay for her own safety. I insisted she take the guest room I'd been staying in while I slept on the couch in the living room. Tommy gallantly offered me his own bed, but I refused. I could sleep anywhere – even on a twelve-inch-wide concrete ledge under a bridge over the Mississippi River – and Tommy's couch was still more comfortable than my bed back at the apartment. And with the shit we'd been through lately, where I lay my head would be pretty far down on the list of things keeping me awake.

I did eventually drift off sometime around two a.m., but was wide awake before five-thirty, my body sensing the coming dawn long before the sun appeared on the horizon. I switched on the morning news and watched at a volume only I could hear until Tommy came down an hour or so later, looking a little better than he had the day before. The dark circles under his eyes were still there, but they didn't seem as pronounced. And subtle changes in his body language suggested that finally having the beginnings of a semi-workable plan for taking down the people who killed Mike had him itching for a little payback.

"Morning," I said as he reached the bottom of the stairs. "Sleep well?"

"All right, I guess," he said, stifling a yawn. "Woke up a few times with some bad dreams, but all in all I'm feeling a little better this morning." He glanced at the television. "News still all over what happened at the bottling plant?"

"Yeah, but the Department is doing a pretty good job of stonewalling them, though. They've identified Mike and the other two officers by name but won't divulge details. They're just taking refuge behind the old "can't jeopardize an ongoing investigation" line."

Tommy dropped into his recliner. "Well, the good news is, from what I heard during my debrief, nobody saw any of what went on between you and Lagorio. Bad news is there'll be trace evidence of your presence all over that place. Add to that the fact that we have two dead cops with no identifiable cause of death and a suspect with his head hacked off – the PR folks are going to have a bitch of a time spinning this as just a run-of-the-mill bust gone wrong."

"What kind of trace evidence are we talking about?"

"The worst of it will be tissue left behind on the shattered glass from the Cutlass, and on the hole the knife punched in its side. There are probably shoeprints and fibers, too. But they'd have to arrest you to have anything to match it to."

"Well, *that's* not going to happen." I considered the rest for a second. "DNA?"

"They'll probably get some. But a cold-case file from 1997 is old enough that there's a chance your DNA isn't even *in* CODIS – especially considering you were the victim and not some unknown assailant. Plus, they'd have to arrest you and have just cause to subpoena a sample."

"Honestly, I don't think my DNA would be the first thing they'd notice if I got arrested. Besides, I'd never let them take me 'alive'. They'd have to knock me down with a head shot, and then it's just a matter of sneaking out of the morgue when I wake up again."

Tommy grimaced. "Well, let's try to avoid that problem altogether, shall we?" He raised himself out of the chair again with a weary groan. "Coffee?"

"Please."

"Black, no sugar, right?" he called over his shoulder as he headed for the kitchen.

I smiled for no reason I could explain. "You got it."

\#   \#   \#

Wanda came down a short time later as Tommy was getting ready to put together a quick breakfast. He made egg sandwiches for the two of them and, while they ate, I made notes on a little yellow legal pad.

"What are you writing there?" Tommy asked around a mouthful.

"Shopping list," I said. "You and I have to run out and get the supplies we need to work up the wightsbane stuff. Plus, I've got one other item on my list – *that* one we may have a little trouble finding."

"What's that?"

"A sword."

Tommy and Wanda both stopped chewing and stared at me for a moment. "A *sword*?" Tommy asked, eyes wide.

"Yup. If we're going toe-to-toe with these bastards, I need something besides that big-ass Bowie knife to separate heads from shoulders."

Tommy grimaced but nodded. "There's a pawn shop in South City that has all kinds of swords for sale. Mike and I were in there a few months ago following up a lead – a CI told us drive-by shooters had been trading in handguns for replacements. This one guy had a whole wall of swords – mostly cheap replica shit, but he had one or two that were legit."

"Well, that'll be the first stop on our agenda." I glanced at Wanda. "Are you planning on heading home today?"

"*O wi*, but just for a bit. I need to collect some fresh clothes, and I've got a little shopping of my own to do."

I handed her my list. "Before you go, we'll need the names of the places where we can get our wightsbane ingredients and a list of *exactly* what to buy. And I know it's an imposition, but *please* be back before nightfall," I said, placing my hand over hers. Mike's life force was still surging through my system, so I didn't have to reign the hunger in too hard. "I've already lost too many people I care about, Momma. I can't handle any more."

She smiled, her warm brown eyes shining with unshed tears. "Don't you go worrying about me, *tifi*. I have been taking care of myself since long before even *you* were born, *cher*."

#   #   #

Tommy's pawn shop did not disappoint. They must have had twenty or thirty swords of varying lengths and styles hanging on the wall, ranging from real World War Two Japanese *katanas* to dull knockoff replicas of Jon Snow's sword from *Game of Thrones*. It seemed the owner was an amateur collector himself and knew more about long blades than one might expect from the proprietor of a downtown Midwestern pawn shop.

After carefully examining a few of the pieces he recommended, I ended up settling on a shorter style Japanese blade he called a *wakizashi*. The sword was flexible high-carbon steel along the backbone with a harder, clay-tempered edge, and measured just over twenty inches to the hilt – perfect for close quarters. The blade was well-balanced and felt comfortable in my hand. Price was a little steep – we couldn't talk him down below three hundred dollars – but Tommy was happy to front me the money until I could pay him back.

With that item checked off the list, we headed out towards the Delmar Loop to the first of the specialty shops Wanda had suggested. We were able to get the Abramelin oil we needed at the first stop, but the only type of powdered mandrake they had on the shelf was what Wanda had referred to as "false" or "English" mandrake. While this variety was apparently toxic to the living, she had been explicit in her instructions to purchase only the 'true' mandrake, *Mandragora officinarum* – whatever the hell that meant. It seems many American practitioners make do with mayapple or other substitutes, but Wanda wasn't sure anything but the true form would work as well – if it worked at *all* – and we just couldn't take the risk.

Three more shops, three more strikeouts, and most of the afternoon had gone by before we finally found the real deal in the last shop on Wanda's list. Like the sword, it was startlingly expensive, but we had no choice but to pay what they were asking.

We returned to the house a little after three, and immediately set up shop on the breakfast bar to start working up what we hoped would be genuine magic bullets. Wanda had left very specific instructions on how to prepare the mixture in both a liquid and a thicker, more paste-like form.

Tommy sniffed at first completed batch of the mixture dubiously. "You really think this is going to *do* anything?"

I glanced at him for a moment, then reached out and picked up a box cutter from the counter. "Only one way to find out..."

"Cherry, I don't –"

Before he could interfere, I dipped the tip of the blade in the muddy gold liquid and drug it gently across the smooth, pale skin of my inner forearm.

Ho-ly SHIT!!!!

The searing pain that accompanied the passage of the blade across my skin was shocking. I hadn't even broken the skin, but the thin pink line of the scratch quickly turned into a nasty, mottled brown streak a half an inch wide, and a faint wisp of smoke issued from the wound. As the room filled with a stench like burnt hair, I leaped to my feet and darted to the sink, turning the faucet on full blast and submerging my forearm in the cool water. The pain abated a bit, fading even further as I gingerly scrubbed the skin with dish soap and a scouring pad.

Tommy rushed to my side, taking hold of my arm. "Goddammit, Cherry. What the *fuck* did you do that for?"

I shook my head, releasing a breath as the pain slowly faded. "We had to know if this was going to work."

We both examined the skin under the bright lights over the sink. The wound had begun to blister and peel, but I could already feel the faint tingle of the healing process beginning to take hold beneath.

Tommy released my wrist and gave me a gentle slap on the back of the head. "No more experiments, you dufus."

I nodded, watching in fascination as the wound began to fade. "But now we know."

Tommy walked away, shaking his head and muttering under his breath. He crossed through the dining room and ducked into the basement, returning with three full boxes of ammunition and one partial. He set them down on the counter with a thud and returned to his seat with an annoyed glare. I joined him, still rubbing my forearm, and got to work without a word.

Once we had the wightsbane mixed up to a consistency something like wall spackle, we sat in Tommy's kitchen with white plastic knives for the next three hours and carefully scraped a tiny dollop of the stuff into the open end of each round, packing it in tight. After that was done, I grabbed the candles I had purchased at the first shop we went to from the bag – black, of course, just to creep Tommy out a little more – and lit one with my Zippo. I let the wick burn down to the wax and, as it began to run, held the candle over each bullet and let a single drop fall onto the tip.

I did a pretty good job overall – I only missed on half a dozen or so – and when the wax cooled and hardened, we went back with the box cutter and trimmed it flush with the nose of the bullet and removed any overspill along the sides. Tommy was concerned that either loose wightsbane goop or excess wax could cause a round to fail to feed properly or get hung up as it was ejected. Either scenario would likely end very badly, so we used rubbing alcohol and vinegar to make certain the outsides of the cartridges were spotlessly clean.

When we finished, Tommy went out to his car for a minute and came back with a handful of spare magazines and a metal case about the length of my arm.

"What've you got there?"

Instead of answering, he just set the case on the counter and flipped it open. Inside was a short-barreled black rifle with a thumbhole grip and a heavy shoulder stock. "The Beretta Cx4 Storm semi-automatic carbine. It uses the exact same nine-millimeter ammo and magazines as my 92, but it gives you a little better range and handling." He lifted the rifle from the case and handed it to me.

"I've never seen one of these before," I said, racking the charging handle to make sure the chamber was empty before shouldering the rifle and testing the weight and balance.

"I'm not surprised. The Department issued these as standard equipment for years as a trunk gun, for when we needed something with a bit more range and accuracy than a handgun. But they didn't come along until well after your dad's time on the force."

"So, you're going in with this?"

"Yup. And," he said, reaching into the small of his back, "I've got a little toy surprise for you, too." He came out with another semi-automatic pistol, this one much smaller than his own sidearm. The whole gun was less than six inches long, and probably not even a full inch wide. "Smith and Wesson, compact nine-millimeter. My personal backup piece."

I set the carbine aside and took the little pistol from him, hefted it. "Damn. It's crazy light."

"Yes, ma'am. That's what you call 'Tactical Tupperware'. But that little firecracker carries just as much wallop as those other two at close range, so when you pull the trigger, hang on tight. Mags are smaller – max loadout is eight with one in the pipe – but it'll fit your hands a lot better than that big Beretta of mine. And all these rounds we prepped will fit it just fine."

I turned the gun over in my hands. It felt perfect. With this in one hand and my shiny new *wakizashi* in the other, I felt like I could handle just about anything Leesy and her goons could throw at us. "Thanks, Tommy."

"My pleasure," he said with a smile. "You ready to start loading up some magazines?"

"Hell yes, I am."

It took over an hour, but by the time we were finished, we had seven fourteen-round Beretta magazines and four seven-round mags for the little Smith and Wesson, all fully loaded with wightsbane bullets. Tommy suggested we pick up another box or two of ammo, but I figured if nearly a hundred and seventy-five rounds wasn't enough, our chances of getting out of this fight alive weren't going to be improved by just slinging more lead around.

Tommy came up with a little pack of fluorescent orange target dots and stuck one on the bottom of each mag. "Don't want to accidentally get these mixed up with my duty rounds. Whether I end up shooting wights with plain old JHP's or shooting regular bad guys with poisoned ones – I'm gonna venture a guess and say either one would land me in some pretty serious shit."

"Well," I said, surveying our little arsenal with satisfaction. "I think there's just a couple more things we still need before we can put all this firepower to good use."

Tommy nodded firmly with a grim smile and a fierce glint in his dark blue eyes. "A confirmed target and a clear line of fire."

"Damn straight…"

Eighteen

WANDA RAN RIGHT UP AGAINST the curfew I had asked her to observe, returning to the house around seven-thirty loaded up with department store shopping bags and dragging a small carry-on-type wheeled suitcase. Tommy hopped off the couch to help relieve her of her burden, hauling all of it upstairs to the room she was staying in.

"Come along, *cher*," she said as soon as Tommy returned to the living room. "I have a few things I want you to see."

She took my arm and hauled me out of the recliner, pulling me along behind her until we reached the upstairs guest room. Tommy had placed her suitcase in the corner and lined up the dozen or so shopping bags along the top of the dresser nearby. Wanda immediately started rooting through them, pulling items out one at a time and transferring them to the bed.

As I realized what she had been doing all afternoon, my eyes began to well up with tears for what seemed like the hundredth time in the last few days. Lying on the bed was a simple knee-length black dress, black stockings with subtle lace embellishments, and a pair of beautiful black leather pumps with much shorter heels than I was accustomed to wearing. There were matching black silk gloves, a tiny clutch purse, and the *coup de grâce* – a little black pillbox hat with a fishnet veil that would cover most of my face.

"Oh, Momma," I said, my throat tightening around the words. "You shouldn't have done all this. I can't–"

"Nonsense, child," she said, resting her hand against my cheek. "Your young man was absolutely right. You are–"

"Momma, he's not my–"

"Oh *hush!* Now, you are going to attend your uncle's funeral and sit there with your head held high and be the daughter you always were to him. There's no reason in the world for you to be ashamed of yourself. Tommy tells me Michael didn't have any other kin left to stand for him. I know he would have been proud to have you there to represent him as his family."

I reached down and lifted the hem of the dress, fingering the luxurious material gently. Without a doubt, this would be the finest clothing I had owned since long before I died. It had to have cost Wanda a small fortune. "I don't even know what to say. I just… thank you *so* much."

Momma pulled me into yet another crushing embrace. "You don't need to say a thing, *cher*. It's my privilege. It's clear your uncle was a wonderful man – you won't find many like him anywhere in this whole wide world. This is the least I can do to honor his memory and everything he did for you." She released me from her embrace and turned back towards the bed. "Well, don't jus' stand there gawk', *tifi*. Start tryin' everything on."

I grinned and quickly stripped down. Wanda had stopped by Victoria's Secret as well, because she had a new black bra and matching panties for me as well. "Momma," I asked as I slipped into the new undergarments. "How on earth did you know what sizes to buy?"

She looked at me with a teasing smile. "*Cher*, I have seen you butt naked about as many times over the last five years as *you* have. I have helped you get dressed every single night. *And*, I have been a club mother for somethin' jus' this side of forever. Do you honestly think I wouldn't know the exact size of every single thing you wear?"

I smiled and shook my head as I continued to dress. "You know, I think I'm just not used to having so many people involved in my day-to-day life. I spend so much time in the shadows, it never really occurred to me that anybody else actually cared whether I live or die. Or die and… Oh, dammit, you know what I mean."

"*Mwen fé*, I surely do."

Getting into most of the clothes was easy enough, but I struggled a bit with the dress. Wanda had to help me get my arms through the sleeves and shimmy the silk fabric down over my hips. She did up the zipper in back and then walked me over towards the mirror hanging on the back of the door.

The woman staring back at me in the reflection might have been the spitting image of my mother at the same age I was when I died – the way she had looked in the photos I had seen of her with my dad when they were newlyweds. Besides my eyes, of course, and the fact that I was a few dozen shades paler, but with the same high cheekbones, the same strong chin and defined jawline, the same shade of bright red hair. I was thunderstruck for a moment, unable to move or speak.

"*Bon seyé, cher*, you sure do clean up good," Wanda said softly, a proud smile lighting her dark features and glittering in her warm brown eyes. She reached over and picked up the pillbox hat, settling it gently on top of my head at a stylish angle. "I swear, you are a *vision* in that outfit."

I smiled reservedly. "Thank you, Momma. It looks… it's just so *beautiful*."

She took me by the arm again and started leading me into the hall. "*O wi*, that it is. And I'm certain your young man will think so, too."

I rolled my eyes but followed her without resistance. "Momma, for the last time, Tommy is not 'my young man'. We're friends and we're partners – at least until he decides to ditch me, arrest me, or shoot me when this is all over. And that's *all* it's ever going to be."

She turned and smiled at me briefly as we reached the top of the stairs. "Umm hmm…" she said, her voice tinged with amusement. "Well, we'll just see about that once he gets a look at you like this…"

We reached the bottom of the stairs and Wanda guided me out to stand in the middle of the living room like it was some kind of debutante ball. Tommy looked up at me from his spot on the couch and rose quickly to his feet. His mouth opened and closed a few times, but nothing came out. I suddenly felt terribly foolish and self-conscious in that fancy getup, and if I could have blushed my face would have been flaming red at that moment. "Not a word, O'Connor," I snapped, jabbing a finger in his direction. "Just remember, this was *your* stupid-assed idea."

He took a few steps towards me, pausing a short distance away. He stared, and after a moment he spread his hands wide and shook his head slowly. "I wouldn't even know what to say, Cherry. You look–"

"Ridiculous."

"– *breathtaking*."

I stood there for a moment, not completely sure if he was making fun of me or not. But the astonished look in his eyes was hard to mistake. He had sincerely meant every word he had just said.

"I… thank you, Tommy," I said gratefully. I tugged at the hem of the dress. "You don't think I'll attract too much attention in public like this, do you?"

He grinned, raised an eyebrow. "Oh, you'll attract attention, all right. Just not the way you think. If we were going to anything but a funeral, you'd be fighting off the guys all night."

"Yeah, right," I said with a sneer. "Well, at least I've got experience with *that*."

"You know," he said, his grin widening as he closed the distance between us again. "We're still going to introduce you as Mike's foster daughter so you can stand at the ceremony. But I think I'm gonna go ahead tell everybody there you're my girlfriend, too. It'll keep the wolves at bay and give my already studly reputation in the ranks quite a boost."

I glared at him through narrowed eyes before lashing out to punch him in the upper arm again, making sure to aim for the same spot I'd caught him in a week or so ago. But again, he just winced, rubbed his arm, and smiled even more…

# # #

Sunday was excruciating. We had everything prepped and ready to go on a moment's notice, but there were no new developments and no sign of any of the missing vehicles or their owners anywhere in the whole Major Case Squad jurisdiction. Tommy kept in constant contact with the lead officers on the missing persons cases, even hinting that he had turned up some sketchy information that suggested Miranda Perez may have been involved with the suspects responsible for the deaths of Mike and the others at the bottling plant. He was hoping to get her case moved a little higher up the ladder, as cop killers tend to warrant special attention from rank-and-file police officers.

But Leesy had obviously been deliberate and methodical in her efforts to cover her tracks.

Clever, conniving little shit, my sister. Always was.

The security cameras outside the Cobblestone had picked Perez up leaving the bar and, although the images of the man she was with were too grainy and out-of-focus to positively identify him, Tommy and I were now certain it was Benny Evans. We hadn't passed that information on to missing persons just yet – if *we* didn't find Perez first, the City would be holding memorial services for a lot more dead cops.

Trying to direct an excess of nervous energy towards a useful purpose, I ended up spending most of the day in Tommy's dusty unfinished basement, doing my best to practice with my new sword. I had never really *handled* a long blade before, let alone tried to fight somebody with one.

My early efforts were not encouraging. I think I was way more of a danger to myself than anybody else at that point, and that's before we smeared poison all over the blade. Poison that was supposed to kill things like me pretty effectively and, at minimum, hurt like a motherfucker.

Tommy wandered down once after I had been out of sight for a while, just to see what I was up to. He was intrigued enough to sit down on the stairs to watch. His presence didn't help. All he managed to do was make me feel even more awkward and uncomfortable and clumsy. And when an attempt at a fierce downward-slicing stroke bounced off a floor joist with a resounding *clang* and damn near came back and hit me in the face, an outburst of poorly stifled snickering nearly got him beheaded.

"Oh, fuck you, Tommy! Don't you have anything better to do?" I snarled, checking the edge of the blade for damage under the light of a bare bulb suspended from the ceiling.

"Absolutely *not*," he said, still grinning. "This is the single most entertaining thing I've seen like… *ever.*"

"Well, piss off upstairs, why don't you? This isn't as easy as it looks."

"I have no doubt." He rose from his seat in the peanut gallery. "Look, put that thing down before you hurt yourself–" I glared crimson daggers at him. "– *or* me, and wait right there for a second, okay? I think I have an idea."

"First time for everything, I guess," I scoffed, my pride still smarting after almost cutting my nose off in front of him a moment ago.

Tommy kept on grinning as he hustled upstairs. He left me cooling my heels for a couple of minutes while I listened to the floorboards creak and pop as he crossed overhead several times. When he returned, his arms were loaded down with his laptop and half a dozen Blu-Ray cases.

"What's all that shit?"

He set the laptop down on a workbench against the wall and tapped out a quick staccato pattern on the keyboard. A new image came up and he waved me over. As I bent down to peer at the screen, I spent another moment seriously resisting the urge to try out the *wakizashi* on Tommy's exposed neck. "*YouTube*?" I asked incredulously. "Are you insane?"

"Well, admittedly, you don't really strike me as the type who spends a lot of time on the internet."

I shrugged. "You'd be surprised. Tracking down potential targets could be a full-time job if Mike was giving me jack shit. But I don't usually waste my time watching videos of guys punching each other in the nuts or cats playing the piano, either."

"Wow. You really *are* that old, huh?"

"Tommy…."

"Look, that's *not* the only stuff that's available out there, Cherry."

I folded my arms and stared at him, lips twisted into a patronizing sneer.

"I'm dead serious. This is pretty much how everybody learns to do *everything* these days. You won't *believe* the kind of instructional videos you can find on here." He scrolled down until he found one that looked promising. "See, right here: Samurai sword training at Myung Song Kim Martial Arts. And look, there's a whole series of them."

I leaned in close again. He had my attention now – *some* legit training was better than none, I guess. But I eyed the pile of movies warily. "What's the rest of this crap?"

"Oh," he said, reaching down and flashing the front cover of each Blu-Ray towards me in turn, his grin widening with every new selection. "We've got… *Seven Samurai, Yojimbo, The Hidden Fortress* – did you know, this one is actually the original source material for *Star Wars?* – *Harakiri, 13 Assassins*, and… *Lone Wolf and Cub: Sword of Vengeance*. I figure if YouTube can't help, maybe Japanese cinema will save the day. Those are some pretty bad-ass movies, lady – you could learn a thing or two."

I sighed and rolled my eyes, but his enthusiasm was infectious. I tried and failed to suppress a chuckle and a rueful grin. "Jesus, Tommy, if we're pinning what little hope we have on YouTube videos and samurai movies, we are well and truly fucked after all."

# # #

The rest of the day passed at a glacial pace. Tommy was constantly on the phone with his friends at the Department, getting ready for tomorrow's service. Wanda passed the time watching TV shows about people who go around town fixing up overpriced houses to sell to obnoxiously unreasonable buyers. I mostly just sat on my ass and fumed between workouts. I was getting a little better with each practice session, but one day of training does not a fearsome samurai make – even with the help of an overly enthusiastic YouTube sensei.

Afternoon passed into evening, and while Wanda and Tommy picked at a light supper, I sat on the back porch and chain smoked until long after the sun had gone down. I think Tommy and I were both dreading turning in for the night, knowing what awaited us with the coming of the first light. Wanda headed to bed around ten-thirty, but Tommy and I sat at the breakfast bar sipping good Irish whiskey and trading stories about our time with Mike until well after two in the morning. Between us we polished off an entire bottle of Red Breast, with Tommy pouring two-finger rounds at a steady, deliberate pace. And we drank a toast to Mike with each and every one until the last of the bottle was gone.

It was odd – every story Tommy told, it seemed as though I already knew it by heart, only I saw them all from Mike's point-of-view. Sharing our memories seemed to draw Mike's own to the surface from wherever I kept them safe and sound – crisp, vivid images of my mom and dad, of Tommy and the other men he'd known and served alongside over the years, and – most bittersweet of all – his loving memories of me. Mike had never been the type to wear his heart on his sleeve, and I had never realized the true depth of his fatherly love and affection for me. It made me feel insensitive and self-absorbed. *How could I have been so blind?*

Downing his final dram in a single go, Tommy finally slid sideways out of his chair and muttered a slurred good night, resting his hand fondly on my shoulder for a moment as he passed before tottering off towards the stairs. I sat in the kitchen for another hour before finally changing into Tommy's yellow t-shirt again – yeah, he wasn't getting *that* back anytime soon – and went to lie down on the couch. I tried to force myself to get at least a few hours of sleep, but it would not come.

In the end, I just stared at the ceiling and wept silent tears until the morning sun returned, marking the beginning of what would surely be one of the most difficult days of my life.

#   #   #

Monday morning dawned hazy and humid and still, with the promise of brutally hot temperatures later in the day. Tommy came downstairs a few minutes after six, already decked out in his best uniform, but now with a black mourning band wrapped across his shield. He would be one of six pallbearers for Mike's casket, hand-picked detectives and police officers who had served closely with him over the years. Mikey had been well-known and respected across the Department, and when word got out that he didn't have any family left to serve in that capacity, offers had flooded in from every district and division, from men and women who had known him – some only by reputation – and wanted to honor his service and sacrifice. So many had come in that most of the offers had to be gratefully and graciously declined.

I sat up on the couch, kicking the thin blanket aside. "You're up early."

"I have to leave now, Cherry," Tommy said, grabbing his uniform hat from the hall tree by the front door as he reached the bottom step. "I'm supposed to be at headquarters by seven to begin the preparations. Procession steps off at ten, so you and Wanda should be there by eight-thirty or nine at the latest. You can use my parking pass to access the employee lot. When the procession starts, you'll both be with me and the other pallbearers in the first limousine behind the hearses."

I felt a thrill of real fear go through me. *Limousine?* "Big crowd, huh?"

He nodded. "There are officers coming in from all over the country just to stand along the route, and probably a few thousand citizens, too." Tommy glanced down at my trembling hands, then reached out and pulled me into a strong embrace. "It's going to be all right, Cherry. It'll be a hell of a long day, but we'll get through it together. I'll be right beside you when I'm not directly involved in the service, and Wanda will be with you the whole time."

I nodded, shoving back the tears that welled up suddenly. "I know. This is just a lot to handle. After what happened with my dad and–"

"It's gonna be tough," he said quietly, releasing me but still holding me by both shoulders. "But you're not alone this time. Your friends will be there for you." His smile was sad and thin, and once again I saw the pain and exhaustion he was trying so hard to hide. He let out a ragged sigh. "And you'll be there for *them*."

This time *I* hugged *him*, held him tightly for a beat before pulling back. He smiled and started backing away. "See you shortly." He tucked his hat under his arm, spun on a heel, and headed for the back door.

When he was gone, I trudged upstairs to find Wanda showered and puttering about in a fluffy pink bathrobe. I quickly got in and out of the shower myself and dressed in my new clothes. Wanda did my hair up in a demure, elegant style that was so different from my usual look that I hardly recognized myself in the mirror. I started to apply my makeup, but my hands were shaking so badly she finally took pity on me and stepped in. Years of working in the clubs had blessed her with a skill set that would rival any makeup artist in Hollywood, and by the time she was done, I had to admit that she had almost managed to make me look human. If not for the color of my eyes, even *I* might have been fooled. And given that much of the service would be held outdoors, my eyes would be hidden behind dark glasses nearly the entire time.

We made it out the door by eight, but – as Tommy had warned – ran straight into a terrible traffic snarl. What should have taken fifteen minutes took nearly an hour, and by the time we finally pulled into the lot at Police Headquarters, we just managed to catch Tommy coming out the front door of the building. He took a moment to introduce me to the Chief of Police and the Executive Officer of the Homicide Division. As planned, he used the name Chandra Barrow – Tommy thought of that one, 'barrow' meaning 'grave" and all – and each expressed their sincere condolences for my loss. I don't know how well each had known Mike – both were relatively new hires – but nobody questioned my introduction as his foster daughter.

The procession itself was a wonder to behold. There were so many patrol cars and motorcycles in line in front of and behind the hearses and limousines, I wondered briefly who was left to keep watch over the rest of the City. Immediately in front of the hearses rode three mounted officers on chestnut horses, with a fourth snow-white horse trailing riderless behind on a lead rein. It was a moving, heartbreaking sight to see.

At ten o'clock sharp, the mournful wail of the bagpipes began, drummers took up the beat, and the whole procession began to move. I stared out the window at the mass of people lining the sidewalks three and four deep and watching from open windows above. I saw officers dressed in a myriad of uniforms from police departments all over the country, each of them standing at full attention and saluting as the hearses passed by.

By the time we reached the Cathedral Basilica, my brain had long since slipped into a sort of self-defense mode – I remember bits and pieces of the ride and making my way up to the church, but most of it was a grey blur. As we took our places on the Cathedral steps, the bagpipers began to play a familiar air – one I knew only too well: "Minstrel Boy". The bitter memories of my father's service – some of which I had watched from an alley half a mile away – came rushing forward and I actually wavered a bit, leaning on Wanda for support. She reached over and wrapped an arm around my shoulders, making sure I stayed upright. I watched as Tommy and the others lifted Mike's flag-draped casket from the rails in the rear of the lead hearse. They passed by us and headed into the church, as more officers stationed outside guided us to our seats in the front pew.

I have very few clear memories of the next few hours – a lot of words like duty and dedication and selflessness and sacrifice. But that's all they were to me, and I'm sure to most of the other survivors: just *words*.

The most striking part of the ceremony came at the end. Over speakers positioned around the interior of the church, the voice of the Department's radio dispatcher read out the traditional Last Call, and the already quiet assembly fell into an absolute silence as her words echoed throughout the Cathedral:

"Metro Dispatch, calling Two Five Nine Four… Metro Dispatch calling Two Five Nine Four. All units, no response from Two Five Nine Four. All units, Sergeant Michael Benjamin, Badge Number Two Five Nine Four, is out of service. End of watch, August twenty-second, 2023. Sergeant Benjamin, your forty years of dedication, service, and devotion to the citizens of St. Louis will never be forgotten. Rest easy, Sergeant Benjamin. We'll take it from here."

Out of service… End of watch… Tears began coursing down my cheeks harder than they had since I woke up in Tommy's guestroom two days after the massacre.

The procedure was repeated two more times for Officers Haller and Kasun before – mercifully – the memorial wound to a close. But there was one last moment that will be forever etched into my memory: as Mike's partner, Tommy was permitted the chance to honor him with a personal salute, as I knew Mike had done for my father. And in a formal, military manner, Tommy approached the dais, drew himself to full attention, and saluted Mike's flag-draped casket. Most of the people there probably couldn't tell, but my eyes were sharp enough to see the subtle, ragged shudder of his breathing, the trembling in his arms and shoulders as he held the salute. Tommy was barely holding it together, and my heart broke for him.

The pallbearers took their places again and began to march the caskets back out of the church as the bagpiper struck up "Minstrel Boy" again. The whole process reversed itself, and soon the procession was moving again. Mike was an Army vet, so he was to be laid to rest at Jefferson Barracks National Cemetery with full honors. The service there was almost more than I could bear. Through the bagpiper playing "Going Home", the three-round rifle volley, the bugle weeping out "Taps" over the rolling green hills – right up until the Chief approached to hand me the folded flag from Mike's casket, I was an absolute wreck. With his official duties complete, Tommy was able to stay beside me throughout the service, my gloved hand held tightly in his. He and Wanda sat on either side of me, and I leaned heavily against them just to keep from sliding out of my seat.

Finally, the slow, mournful tones of "Amazing Grace" began to fill the air, first from the piper alone before being taken up by the military band assembled behind the crowd of mourners. As the song neared its final stanzas, the piper began slowly walking away from the graveside, the music gently fading away as he passed over the hill, as though he was actually escorting Mike's spirit as it rose gently into the hazy morning sky.

With the graveside service concluded, I stood and did my duty as dozens of Mike's fellow officers stopped by to offer their condolences. All I could think of was getting back to the limo and away from the throngs of people. The assembly eventually dispersed, and Tommy took my hand again and led me back toward where the vehicles waited, with Wanda following a step or two behind.

As Tommy reached up to open the door of the limo, I felt a chill ripple up my spine and caught a brief flash of movement out of the corner of my eye. I stopped in my tracks and stared intensely at the spot where I had seen the strange motion. Normally, I would have dismissed it as nothing but a trick of the light – the sun wreaking havoc on my overly sensitive eyes.

No, I knew exactly what I had seen: my sister Annaliese, dressed in a flowing white gown, dancing in the shade of a lone fir tree a hundred yards or so away. I opened myself to the power, trying to pinpoint her presence, but by the time I was actively looking for her, she was gone. It was her though – I was absolutely certain of that - and for me to have seen her at all, she must have dropped her camouflage glamour for an instant, making sure I had seen her face.

And she was *laughing*…

Nineteen

AFTER THE SERVICE, MANY OF the City's off-duty officers, particularly those who had served alongside Mike in the Fourth District as well as the old Sixth, gathered at O'Connor's Pub. Wanda had elected to return to Tommy's house, and he'd loaned her the little Smith and Wesson pistol, loaded up with wightsbane rounds.

Tommy's dad was milling through the crowd, greeting old friends, and introducing himself to younger officers while Tommy's grandfather and brothers kept the drinks flowing non-stop. For his part, Tommy was never more than arm's reach away from me, even when his dad and brothers came around. He introduced me to each of them in turn, and they were all cut from the same cloth: tall, broad-shouldered, with Tommy's dishwater blond hair and strikingly dark, sapphire-blue eyes. His youngest brother was probably in his mid-twenties and came off as an incorrigible flirt. He complimented the unique color of my eyes, affected a ridiculously exaggerated Irish accent, and was on the verge of waxing poetic when Tommy collared him from behind and frog-marched him back towards the bar.

"You'll have to ignore Colin," Tommy said wearily as he returned to the high-top table where I sat. "Dad won't fess up to it, but I'm fairly certain he was dropped on his head as a child."

"Oh, I don't know," I said, taking a sip from my whiskey glass and glancing solicitously back toward the bar. The setup was just too good to let Tommy slide, and I flashed him a wicked smile. "Clearly, *he* inherited the looks in the family. Your older brother Brady seems to have gotten the brains and the business savvy. So, what does that leave for you?"

Tommy grabbed his tumbler from the table and threw back the contents in a single go. "Abnormally oversized anatomical features," he said, without missing a beat.

I actually laughed out loud at that. "Yeah, I noticed that. So where exactly *do* you buy those clown shoes you wear?"

He stared me down through narrowed eyes, just barely able to stifle a grin. "Remind me again why I'm helping you."

"My sparkling charisma, vulnerability, and chaste, ladylike demeanor?"

"No, that's definitely not it," he said, laughing. He stared at me for a second, undoubtedly noting the weariness that infused my every movement. "It's getting late – you want to get out of here?"

I sighed. "Desperately. Mike's gone and I can't stomach any more of people's pity. There's only forty-eight hours left in the lunar cycle, at which point Kennedy is dead and we'll have at least one more grave wight to deal with. It's time to get back to work."

"I agree. No Irish goodbyes, though – let's make proper apologies to Dad and the boys and get the fuck out of here."

While Tommy spoke to his family, I stood nearby, eavesdropping on two of the off-duty officers sitting at the bar. They were chatting about the Boston Marathon bombing case. The tenth anniversary had been earlier this year, and it had been all over the news cycle again. I knew the basic chain of events – how those assholes had tried to flee town by carjacking some guy in a Mercedes SUV. But what caught my ear was the officers ridiculing the bombers for stealing a Mercedes equipped with GPS tracking and recovery assistance built in. The carjacking victim had managed to escape, made a call to 911, and the cops were on the bombers in minutes.

Son of a bitch! If Mercedes made that feature available in a vehicle that cost half of what Miranda Perez's Audi supercar went for….

I reached over and grabbed Tommy by the sleeve. "Tommy, has anybody looked into whether or not Miranda Perez had any sort of GPS recovery system in that fancy sports car of hers?"

He looked at me for a moment, shrugged. "Yeah, I'm sure they did.

I think it's pretty standard procedure to track cell phones and GPS tagged vehicles in missing persons cases."

"You're certain?"

"No," he said, heading for the door. "But let's find out."

We reached the car, and as Tommy guided the Mustang through the narrow Dogtown streets the few short blocks back to his house, he made a call to headquarters to touch base with Missing Persons. He finally hung up and turned to me with a sigh. "Seems Audi didn't offer GPS recovery on that year and model. We recovered her abandoned cell phone in a vacant lot in Hamilton Heights, but that was as far as they got."

I wasn't ready to give up yet. "Tommy, that car costs more than most people's houses. Even if the dealer didn't offer a tracker, that doesn't mean she didn't have an aftermarket one installed."

Tommy nodded. "Yup, and you and I are going to pay a visit to Miranda Perez's insurance agent in the morning and find out what kind of discounts she was getting on her premiums."

#   #   #

We found Wanda sacked out in the recliner once again, Tommy's little nine-millimeter resting on a TV tray beside her. I snuck up and moved it safely out of reach before waking her and helping her upstairs to her room. Once I had her settled, I changed out of my fancy clothes and back into my now beloved, comfy yellow t-shirt, when I realized I hadn't heard Tommy come upstairs. I went looking and found him seated at the breakfast bar with only a small light on over the stove. A six pack of Guinness bottles sat on the table in front of him, two dead soldiers already standing watch.

After a moment, he noticed me watching from the darkened doorway to the dining room. "Buy you a beer?" he asked, his voice gruff with suppressed emotion.

"Abso-fucking-lutely" I answered quietly, sliding onto the bar-height chair beside him. The beer wouldn't do much to settle my nerves, but the company just might.

He popped the top off a fresh bottle with his keychain and handed it to me.

"Hell of a day," I said, taking a big swig of the beer.

Tommy just nodded, turning his own bottle round and round in his hands.

"You holding up?" I asked, eyeing him carefully. It felt odd to be asking the question, since I felt like my own sanity was still hanging by a thread.

"Yeah. I'll survive. It's just… I feel *strange*, you know."

"I do. Obviously, I wasn't involved in Dad's funeral at all, but I remember my mom's well enough. In the lead up, everybody's so busy making arrangements and running around like idiots that you don't have time to really sit and just think about stuff. It's when the visitations and the memorial services and the potluck suppers are all over and everybody's gone home that you find yourself sitting alone saying… '*Okay, now what?*'"

"Yeah, I'd say that pretty well sums it," he muttered, sipping at his beer. "I mean, the idea of moving on without Mike doesn't even seem real to me yet. And who knows when – or even *if* – they'll clear me to come back. I guess I'll get a new partner. All of Mike's open cases will probably transfer to me. And sooner or later, they'll have to promote somebody to–"

"Hey," I said gently, reaching out to carefully take his hand in both of my own cool, gloveless ones. "Just let that stuff lay for now. It'll be waiting for you when you get back. Right now, we need to stay focused on the task at hand – finding the people who took Mike away from us and making them pay, right?"

"Right," he said, managing a passably confident nod. He suddenly looked up at me, his eyes seeming almost pitch black in the dim light. "Cherry, have you *really* thought about what it is you're setting out to do here? I mean, this is your *sister* we're talking about. You've been praying for some sign of her to turn up for years, and now here we are loading up poisoned bullets to take her out."

I was silent for a long moment. When I finally spoke, I found myself doing something I rarely did in everyday circumstances: choosing my words very, very carefully. "Tommy, taking out Lagorio the other night came way too easily for me. It *should* have been harder. Given a different set of circumstances and a slightly more intelligent murderer, I could very well have been in exactly his position when I was resurrected. Looking at his dossier, he didn't seem like a bad guy in life. Bit of a meathead, maybe, but by no means *evil*."

Tommy nodded. "For once, the old Nuremburg defense actually has merit: he probably *was* just following orders."

I nodded. "Orders he didn't have the option or ability to disregard or disobey, no matter what he felt about their morality. I don't think he *wanted* to be a cop killer. I don't think he *wanted* to stomp on me until my insides rattled like a bag of antlers. But Leesy – my *sister* – *ordered* him to do it. By my count, she's directly or indirectly responsible for the deaths of at least *fifteen* people in just the last two months. That we *know* of. And sure, maybe Carter and Hoefler aren't the biggest losses to society, but none of them asked for what happened to them."

He shook his head wearily. "But we can't let them keep on killing like this, either. I know. It's just…" He gave my hand a squeeze. The power that flowed between us was minimal – not much more than a tickle – but I could still feel the warm, gossamer strands of his soul drifting back and forth, swaying like the branches of a willow tree in a gentle spring breeze. "It's just the whole night, while I was spending time with my brothers, all I could think was: *Could* you *do it? If it was one of them? Could you look down the barrel of a gun at one of their faces and pull the trigger?*"

"And what did you come up with?"

He looked down, his mouth a thin line. "Not a goddamned thing."

I nodded once again. "Me neither. Tommy, I fully expect she's going to make us hack and blast our way through a bunch of people who have no control over their actions just to *get* to her. And God only knows what we'll find when we do."

He lifted his chin, met my gaze. "You really think she's lost it? That she's beyond saving?"

I didn't know how to respond to that, ended up just shrugging. "I think some part of me is still holding out hope for her. That somehow, we can bring her back from all the death and destruction she's caused. But *realistically?*" I shook my head. "Look, I don't know what happened to her after that bastard Hargrove sold her off. God only knows what sort of hell she's been living through all these years, what kind of torture or torment she might have endured. It's possible that somebody has abused her to the point that everything human left inside of her – of the little girl she used to be – is just... *gone*." I sighed heavily. "But I do know this: she killed Mike in cold blood, with her eyes wide open and a smile on her face. And if she's crossed some line, become some... rabid dog *monster*... then it's my responsibility to stop her. And I'll have to learn to live with that. If I can."

He glanced up at me again with a look in his eyes that said he *really* didn't want to say what he was about to say, but he was going to say it anyway. "And what if *she's* just following orders, too?"

"Then someday I'm gonna find out who put her up to this," I said, my temper flaring suddenly and violently. "Because if that's the case and I'm forced to put her down anyway, I will spend the rest of my existence hunting them to the ends of the earth. And there won't be a hole deep enough or a shadow dark enough in this miserable fucking world to hide them from me."

We sat there in silence until all the beer was gone and exhaustion finally began to overtake us. I headed for the couch and Tommy started to climb the stairs, every step seeming to tax the last of the energy reserves in his body.

He was almost to the top when I spoke again. "I saw her today, you know."

He froze, ducking down to stick his head through the gap between the ceiling and the baluster rail. I could see his eyes wide and shining in the darkness. "What?"

"I said, I saw her."

"You actually *saw* Annaliese?"

I nodded, although I knew he couldn't see me as clearly as I could see him. "At the cemetery, just as we were leaving Mike's service. She must have been there the whole time, just watching us." My voice broke, and tears began to spill from my eyes again. "She was *laughing* at us, Tommy... she was laughing at *me*. Now, does that sound like somebody who's not in control of their own actions to you?"

He sighed heavily. "No, I can't say it does. And you're sure it was her?"

"As sure as I'm seeing you now."

Tommy was silent again for a moment, before turning and heading back upstairs again. "Goodnight, Cherry," was all he could think of to say.

I couldn't come up with anything better.

\#   \#   \#

Surprisingly, I had very little difficulty falling asleep that night. I just huddled under the blanket, turned my face into the back of the couch, and pretty much passed out cold. Even grave wights have their limits, I guess. I slept a little fitfully, disturbed by dreams in which Leesy skipped among the grave markers in a cemetery, dragging a stuffed toucan and twirling the hem of a white nightgown covered in neon-pink vomit like a ball gown.

I awoke again to the smell of fresh coffee brewing, and I could tell by the sound of the footfalls in the kitchen that it was Wanda and not Tommy who was already up and around. I glanced at the grandfather clock that stood near the base of the stairs. It was already after eight-thirty in the morning. *Jesus* – I hadn't slept in this late in forever, even after working a nine to three shift at the club.

I climbed off the couch and padded into the kitchen. Wanda turned and smiled broadly as I entered. "Morning, my little Cherry Bomb. You finally seen fit to rise up off that couch and start your day, I see."

"I'm rising, but I ain't shining. Tommy still asleep?"

"Far as I know. I heard him get up out of bed once around three-thirty and head to the restroom in a hurry. I'm afraid he might have been sick."

"That wouldn't surprise me. Alcohol and grief are a terrible mixture."

She nodded. "Your young man seems the strong, capable sort, though. He'll be all right."

At this point I knew she was just screwing with me, but I took the bait anyway. "For the last time, Momma, Tommy is–"

"Tommy is what?"

I spun about as the 'young man' in question came trudging into the kitchen from the dining room. "Looking like he's been in a dryer with rocks, that's what," I said, shaking my head in dismay. "You look like boiled shit."

"Good," he muttered. "The way I feel, I was afraid it might be worse."

Tommy's hair was a rumpled mess, and he was dressed in yet another concert t-shirt – *Styx* this time, of all god-awful things – and just blue-plaid boxer shorts below the waist. Clearly, casual dress was to be the order of the day. I just hoped to God those drawers of his had a button fly. I didn't feel like seeing any more of him this morning than I already had.

Wanda turned away from whatever she was doing at the sink and pointed toward the opposite side of the kitchen with a long-bladed knife. "There's coffee in the pot, and I'll have something cooked up for our breakfast here in a bit, *cher*."

Tommy shuffled over towards the pot and filled two mugs, handing me one before turning to the fridge for his precious French vanilla creamer. Seemed like a bad idea to me, hung-over as he probably was, but he was a big boy. I wasn't gonna tell him what to do.

I slid into the closest chair, sipping at the strong black brew as Tommy made his way over to sit down. "So," I said. "We gonna pay a visit to Miranda Perez's insurance agent this morning?"

He nodded, stifling a huge yawn. "Yeah. I seriously doubt they'll give out information like that over the phone. I'll probably have to bluster a bit even after I show them a badge. We don't have time to screw with a warrant, though, and I don't want to go stepping on toes over at Missing Persons. We may still need their help."

I glanced at the clock on the wall behind me, did a quick computation in my head. "The full moon is in just about… thirty-six hours. The first midnight falls a few hours after that. Assuming Kennedy *is* still alive, they probably have her trussed up somewhere waiting for a new revenant to awake." I paused, my chest tightening at the thought of losing another friend. "If she's not, then they probably already have her tucked into a power circle with some other poor bastard staked out nearby. Either way, we need to find them fast before somebody else dies."

"Then I guess we better move our asses, then. Out the door in an hour?"

I nodded and rose from my seat, heading straight for the stairs, coffee mug in hand. "I'll shower while you eat. Don't fuck around – the fuse is getting too damned short…"

# # #

Fifty-five minutes later, Tommy and I were backing out of his garage and heading for Perez's insurance agent's office in Clayton, the address of which we'd found in her missing persons file. We pulled up outside the tall, glass-facade tower a few minutes before ten. We had to wait around a couple of minutes for the office to open, but soon we were seated across a small desk from a short, heavy-set man in an ill-fitting, blue pinstripe suit.

As expected, he wanted to drag his feet, but Tommy made it clear that if we were going to find Perez alive – which *we* both knew wasn't going to happen – we had to move quickly. Any delay on the agent's part could mean life or death for Miss Perez. The man hemmed and hawed for a few minutes, but finally gave us what we wanted: Miranda Perez had, indeed, installed an after-market GPS locator and stolen vehicle recovery system in her car, receiving a hefty discount on her premiums in return. The document the agent showed us verifying the installation indicated it had been done by a local shop in Tower Grove South called – believe it or not – Grand Theft Not-O.

Good grief...

We thanked the agent for his help and promised to keep his role in voluntarily turning over the information as quiet as possible. In truth, the man had nothing to fear – Miranda Perez's kidnapping and murder was *never* going to trial – but we couldn't just come right out and say that. We just thanked him again and headed back to the car.

Tommy did a quick Google search on his phone and turned up the address for the custom shop that had done the work. He popped the worn clutch and tore away from the curb, swinging out onto the interstate a few minutes later and heading east back towards downtown. We exited again at Grand – Tommy shot me an evil glare as we passed the section of guardrail there streaked with Dark Highland Green paint – and made our way south towards Tower Grove Park. The shop wasn't far from the intersection of Grand and Chippewa, and we arrived there shortly after eleven.

I realized as we walked up to the front door of the shop that I was becoming obsessed with the clock, pulling my phone out every couple of minutes to check the time. For all I knew, Kennedy was already dead, but I had this inexplicable conviction she was still alive, and that her life was slipping through our hands like grains of sand with every passing moment.

The guy at Grand Theft Not-O was much more accommodating than the insurance agent had been – apparently, he wasn't as concerned with protecting his client's privacy. I guess when you looked at it from his perspective, telling the cops where to find a stolen car was just part of the job. It's not like we were stalking the poor woman – we just wanted to get the damned car back. The fact that the sign out front said they guaranteed one hundred percent of the vehicle's original retail value if their system failed to lead to its recovery probably helped grease the wheels as well. A hundred and fifty grand will loosen a lot of people's tongues.

The shop's owner, a tall, thickly built bald man who introduced himself as Buster Williams, motioned for the two of us to follow him behind the counter. In back, out of sight of the general public, was a surprisingly high-tech setup. A dozen workstations filled a spacious open office area, and the sounds of people working and the whine of power tools was clearly audible through the thin wall between the workspace and the installation garage on the other side.

Buster sat down behind one of the terminals and shuffled the mouse around to bring the machine out of its electronic slumber. "Okay," he said, navigating through a series of screens before finding the one he wanted. "You said the name was Perez, right?"

"That's right," Tommy said, leaning down to look over Buster's shoulder. I hung back, since I had no trouble reading the screen clearly from halfway across the room. "Miranda Perez. The car is a 2019 Audi R8."

Buster nodded. "Oh, yeah. I remember it well. Very nicely tricked out, that one." He chuckled to himself. "And the car wasn't too shabby either."

Tommy glanced back at me, knowing my eyes were rolling behind my sunglasses. He just grinned sheepishly.

"Yeah, here it is," Buster said. He scribbled a ten-digit number down on a sheet of paper next to the terminal, then began working his way through screens again. Eventually he arrived at the right one and, glancing back and forth between the paper and the screen, entered the ID code into the system. After only a moment's hesitation, the screen shifted and brought up what looked to be a very close cousin of Google Earth.

As we watched intently, the screen went from showing the whole blue-green globe of the earth to a parachutist's view that seemed to be plummeting straight toward the central part of the country. It kept falling, the level of detail improving as it went, until the familiar, gentle curves of the Mississippi and Missouri Rivers surrounding the City came into view. The image fell further and further until it finally settled in what looked to be a largely residential area about a mile and a half due north of Forest Park. It was probably less than three miles away from Tommy's own house in Dogtown.

Tommy leaned in close to the screen. "That's the old Hempstead Elementary School. The district shut it down years ago."

"How accurate is that trace?" I asked.

Buster turned to look at me over his shoulder. "Those coordinates are good to within about ten meters. That's where your Audi is, all right – probably parked right behind that school building, on the side away from the road."

Tommy stared straight at me. "Missing Persons said they tracked Perez's cell phone to an empty lot in Hamilton Heights."

I nodded, pointing at the screen. "Yup. And Hempstead is smack in the *middle* of Hamilton Heights. Hamilton Avenue and Minerva, to be exact."

Tommy turned back towards the shop owner. "Can you get us a printout of that?" he asked.

"Yeah, sure thing." Buster tapped out a few more keys and a printer at the end of the table churned noisily for a moment before spitting out a color image of the whole site with the car's exact location marked with a yellow push-pin symbol.

Tommy snatched it up, gave it a quick once-over, and started heading for the front door. "Thank you, Mr. Williams. You've been extremely helpful." He snagged my hand as he passed and started dragging me back towards the car.

"Hey, no problem, officer," Buster called after us. "Just make sure she knows how you found it, okay? Pretty lady like that, maybe I can get her to do a little testimonial in one of my commercials."

Sorry, pal. That ain't gonna happen, I thought as we blasted out the main entrance and back into the light and heat of the midday sun again.

Twenty

WHAT FOLLOWED NEXT WAS BASICALLY the car ride from hell. Tommy and I got into it like I'd never gotten into it with *anybody* before – not Mike, not Dad, not Leesy, *nobody* – and the stupidest part was I knew I was wrong before the shouting even started.

Things started going south when I noticed Tommy was taking the I-64 exit for Hampton Avenue instead of continuing to Skinker Boulevard. Only Skinker would take us anywhere near Hempstead School – Hampton was on the way *back* to Tommy's house.

"Where the *hell* are you going?" I asked, turning to face Tommy straight on.

"Home." He refused to look at me. "I'm taking you home."

"The *fuck* you are," I shouted. "We have to go scout this place out, and you're not going up there alone."

"Yes, I am," he said, still staring straight ahead. "Cherry, you need to stop and think–"

"Tommy, I am seriously not having this discussion *again* with you right now. You are not doing this by yourself." From that point on, the details of the fight get a little fuzzy. There was a lot of screaming, a fair amount of pounding my fists on the dashboard, and enough F-bombs to make Quentin Tarantino blush.

Tommy weathered it for a while, but eventually he'd had enough. "*Goddammit*, Charlotte!" he roared, his voice filled with an anger and an annoyance I'd not heard from him before. And the sound of him using my real name struck me nearly as hard. He slammed on the brakes and swung the car hard up against the nearest convenient stretch of curb. "Will you please just shut the *fuck* up for once and listen to what somebody else has to say?"

To say he knocked me back on my heels with that little outburst would have been a colossal understatement. I was absolutely stunned, unable to do anything but gape at him in shock and surprise. I eventually managed to close my mouth after a moment, folding my arms defensively across my chest.

"Now, answer me this," he said angrily. "Can you tell when a human being is nearby?"

I hesitated before answering. "Sometimes."

"*Sometimes.*" He shook his head and rolled his eyes. "Okay, well, can you sense when a *particular* human being is nearby? As in, pick *one* out from the crowd?"

I was already starting to see where he was going with this, and the fact that I wasn't going to win this argument was becoming all too clear. "No."

"But you can sure as hell sense when another *wight* is nearby, now, can't you?"

I remained determinedly sullen. "Yes," I snapped, resigning myself to childish, one-word responses for the duration.

"And do you think it's even remotely possible that you are the *only* wight in the entire universe who has been blessed with this amazing ability?"

"No."

"And you haven't got the *foggiest* idea how far out that ability might reach, do you?"

"No."

"Or how long after a feeding you'll start showing up on their radar again, right?"

I just stared back at him, grinding my teeth.

He sighed heavily. "Cherry, you can't go anywhere near that school until it's for real. If they sense you nearby and find out you've discovered their... I don't know, their *secret lair* or whatever, then they are going to rabbit. Kennedy is as good as dead, and the cycle of hiding and killing and resurrection rituals will start all over again. Christ, we'll be *swimming* in corpses for another whole month. You want that on your conscience?"

"Of course not."

"Then let me do my fucking job, okay?" He reached out and gripped my upper arm tightly. "You're *not* responsible for me, Cherry. Any more than you were responsible for Mike. We are police officers. We go to work every day knowing we might not be coming home. And while you are not sworn to protect *me*, I *am* sworn to protect the people of this City. And I'm not going to let your thoughtless, prideful, hard-headed *jack-assery* put their lives at risk."

I said nothing for a long time. When I finally spoke, my voice was quiet and properly subdued. "What's your plan?"

He sighed again, releasing my arm and guiding the car back out onto the road again. "After I drop you off, I'm going to put on something forgettable with a ball cap and sunglasses and I'm just going to go for a walk. I'm going to park a couple of streets away from the school and I'm going to take a nice long walk around the block. I'll confirm that Perez's car is there, maybe get the lay of the land, and I'll get the *hell* out of Dodge. And then, when I get back, we'll figure out how and when we're going to move in."

Now it was my turn to sigh heavily. I couldn't argue with anything he had said, and his plan was the best chance we had of keeping them all bunched together. "Fine. Do it your way," I said, the bitterness slowly fading from my voice. "But I swear to God, O'Connor, if you get yourself killed, I am going to bring you back myself just to spend the rest of eternity kicking the living shit out of you."

He laughed out loud at that. "Well, at least if there's a funeral, you've already got a dress."

#   #   #

The wait for Tommy to return from his reconnaissance mission was excruciating. I don't know exactly how long it takes for someone to walk around a city block, but he had been gone for hours and I was left climbing the walls. Wanda did her best to reassure me, but I just had to suffer through the all-too-familiar feeling of waiting for someone I cared about to come walking through the door again, safe and sound.

I did have one minor brainstorm while he was gone, an idea that might help us overcome some of the problems we were certain to have with wights we couldn't see when we entered the school. I raided Tommy's refrigerator and poked around in his garage for a while before I found what I was looking for, then I gathered everything up and carried it back into the kitchen to start work.

And so it was that when Tommy finally did come walking through the back door, he found the breakfast bar piled high with red plastic gas cans, short lengths of cotton clothesline, a drill, and every pickle, jelly, jam, and condiment jar I could dig out of the fridge.

"Jesus H. Christ, Cherry," he said, his face a mask of shock and disbelief. "What in the name of God are you *doing* in here?"

"*Gade bouch ou, jenn gason!*" trickled in softly from somewhere in the living room.

I didn't need to speak Creole to figure that one out. I grinned. "Call it my own personal take on the *Anarchist Cookbook*," I said, continuing to sort through my materials. "So did you find the Audi?"

He stared around in mild disbelief but nodded. "Not only the Audi, but what looks to be Justin Hoefler's white Honda Accord, too. They're both parked on the backside of the old gymnasium and covered with tarps and old pallets."

"Excellent – then we've got them all together in one place after all."

"Looks like." He glared at me and waved his hand at the mess I'd made of his little kitchen. "Cherry, do I even want to *ask*?"

I just grinned wickedly. "Well, we know that, like me, Carter has fed this lunar cycle. And Lagorio is dead – as in *permanently* dead. So that leaves Hoefler and Perez and probably Annaliese still with the ability to use the concealment glamour against us."

He wandered around to the kitchen sink and stared into the side with the garbage disposal, where a vile, foul-smelling mix of miscellaneous foodstuffs was still waiting to be washed away. He spotted one particular bottle among the clutter and picked it up, wincing as he read the label. "And this relates to you dumping out my brand new thirty-five-dollar jar of Charroux mustard *how* exactly?"

I grimaced slightly – *Who the hell pays thirty-five bucks for mustard?* – but soldiered on. "I took each of these little jars and washed them out. Then I drilled a hole through the lid and I'm getting ready to pull a piece of cotton clothesline through each one. Then I'll fill the jars with gasoline, seal them up tight, and – *BAM!* – pocket-sized Molotov cocktails."

Tommy just shook his head at me as he rolled his erstwhile mustard jar around in his hand. "How exactly do you plan to deploy these? Effectively, I mean."

"Well, my ability to sense a wight has *some* directionality. It's rough at best, but at the first hint of a tingle, we toss one of these in the general direction and light the bastards up. I figure all we have to do is splatter a little on them and we'll either set them on fire, or they'll be so preoccupied with not being incinerated that they'll forget all about maintaining the glamour. And that's when we take them out."

He thought about it carefully for a long moment, then gave me a small smile. "You know, I think this might actually work. Although next time, maybe wait for me to get home to help you pick out the jars. Some of this shit is *really* hard to come by."

"Sorry, O'Connor," I said mockingly. "I wasn't aware you were a gourmet mustard connoisseur."

He grinned widely. "Hey, wait until you try that stuff on an honest-to-goodness Busch Stadium hotdog. It's worth sneaking it in just for the experience."

"Afraid I'm past the hotdog-eating phase of my existence, Tommy-boy."

"Your loss," he said as he tossed the little bottle he was holding into the air towards me. "And besides, I think I've got a much better name for your little guerilla weapons than just plain old Molotov cocktails."

"And what's that?"

He flashed that shit-eating grin of his. "Cherry bombs…"

# # #

Tommy pitched in to help me finish assembling the makeshift firebombs, and we retired to the dining room for the rest of the evening to discuss what he'd seen in detail. I was a little pissed when he revealed how close he had risked getting to the building to verify the presence of the vehicles concealed under the tarps, but it was no good bitching now. He'd made it back alive, so it was hard to be *too* pissed.

A quick internet search showed that Hempstead School had been placed on the National Register of Historic Places before being shut down by the St. Louis Public School District for budgetary reasons in 2003. It was built way back in 1907, and from the outside looked as much like a church or small cathedral as it did an elementary school. But the big bonus of turning up the historic landmark application was that it included a complete set of floor plans detailing the interior layout.

Unfortunately, the building had been largely gutted in 2014 by a fire that was believed to have been caused by lightning. That, in turn, threw the accuracy and reliability of our maps into question, since we had no idea how much of the interior had survived the four-alarm blaze. Whole sections of flooring could be missing, corridors could be blocked with fallen debris – who knew? The one thing we were able to determine with any degree of certainty was that the gymnasium addition seemed to have been undamaged by the fire, and right now that seemed like the most likely spot for our quarry to have gone to ground.

Between the two of us, we poured over the plans and identified the most likely ambush spots and the areas where we would be the most exposed and vulnerable as we made our way into the school. Tommy had briefly argued that we should saddle up immediately and move in tonight, but I convinced him otherwise. We had to have all of them together at one time – if even one wight slipped away, we were screwed, and we'd be collecting bodies all across St. Louis from now until the next full moon. And next time, we would certainly have a much harder time tracking them down without the vehicles to locate them.

I figured the best chance we had to catch them all in the same place at the same time was just before midnight on Wednesday – a little over twenty-four hours from now – when all of them would probably be gathered to witness the resurrection I was sure Leesy had planned.

So, we would sit tight and wait. We would take our time, take every precaution, and do everything we possibly could to bring this whole bloody mess to an end without losing any more lives in the process.

And I was also absolutely certain of just one other thing: sometime before midnight tomorrow, I would find myself face-to-face with my little sister for the first time in over twenty-six years. And I had some questions that she was going to answer to my satisfaction. And if I didn't like the answers I got, then by *God* there was going to be hell to pay…

# # #

I awoke Wednesday morning to heavy grey-black clouds, intermittent flashes of intense lightning, and an ominous rolling thunder so powerful that it shook Tommy's house to its foundations. A steady rain was pouring outside, and it seemed as if the skies themselves were dreading the coming of the full moon. Tonight would be the second full moon of August – a Blue Moon – and the almanac said it was a supermoon at that. Massive in the night sky, the power it exuded was immense, and its transit had been like the scrape of fingernails on a blackboard inside my skull. It had kept me awake and writhing on the couch the entire night. It had dropped below the horizon shortly after dawn and was on the other side of the world now, but I could still feel its inexorable pull, as if through the very bones of the earth itself. I was finally able to sleep then, but I knew it would rise again shortly after dark, reaching its true peak just before nine-thirty that night.

In total, I probably managed to get maybe three or four hours of fitful sleep, and Tommy slept in much later than he was used to again. His body seemed to instinctively know we would need the extra rest. It was nearly ten before we joined Wanda in the kitchen and briefed her on the basic details of our plans for the night. She was shaken, to say the least, but she knew that what we were preparing for was something that had to be done. And she also knew there wasn't a soul in the world with any hope of success besides the two of us.

She finally just kissed each of us on the forehead, whispered a brief prayer, and hurried out of the kitchen before her emotional control gave way.

Oddly – incongruously – Tommy asked me what I was planning to wear that night. After gaping at him blankly for a moment, I said I hadn't given it much thought and would probably just wear the same clothes I always wore on a hunt. But he wasn't pleased with that at all. The cloak was unnecessary, he said. Worse, it could get hung up on any debris and would be a hindrance to my range of motion. And he felt like the heels of my boots would be a menace in the unsure footing of a burned-out building. Generally, he was going to insist on something a little more tactical in nature.

And so shortly after noon, I found myself standing in the middle of a store out near the Galleria that specialized in survivalist-type paraphernalia. Tommy paid for everything, and soon I was decked out in black leather tactical boots, black cargo pants with a stiff belt designed to support a heavy holster, and a lightweight black compression top that molded itself to my every contour like it was painted on. I had to admit, the freedom of movement was reassuring, and it made me feel just a tiny bit invincible, like some kind of black-ops mercenary out of a Tom Clancy novel.

We returned to the house and began to check out our gear, cleaning and testing and making sure that everything was in perfect working order. Tommy outfitted me with a paddle holster for the little nine-millimeter pistol, and we fiddled with a spare rifle sling until it held the *wakizashi* in place diagonally across my back at exactly the right angle.

Tommy waited to dress until well after dark – the leathers were just too hot and uncomfortable to sit around in. But as night fell, he began collecting his gear as well. He would drive over in just the pants and boots and a black t-shirt, donning the heavy leather jacket when we arrived. He had picked out a thick black neoprene balaclava at the outfitter's shop earlier in the day, allowing him the option of leaving the helmet behind. We both agreed that what limited extra protection it would have provided wasn't worth compromising his mobility or peripheral vision. Besides, if they were close enough to club him over the head, they were close enough to shove a knife into his chest.

The only exposed skin on his body would be a tiny gap at his collar and a small area around his eyes, and he would have a much better chance of seeing or hearing an attack coming if his head wasn't enclosed in the bulky, restrictive helmet. I desperately wanted him to wear a bulletproof vest as well, but not only would it not fit comfortably under the leathers, he could barely twist his torso around with it on.

Ten o'clock finally arrived – the time we had agreed upon for our departure – and we gathered our gear and headed for the garage in virtual silence. We loaded most of the stuff into the trunk and got underway. Tommy wound his way through light traffic onto the interstate, turning north onto Skinker until it reached Page, before finally cutting the engine and coasting to a stop near the intersection of Page and Hamilton. We would not risk getting any closer.

A steady rain began to fall as we stepped out of the Mustang. Tommy double checked the Beretta in his holster, then retrieved the carbine from the trunk. "You ready for this?" he asked, his voice a harsh whisper.

"Fuck no. You?"

"Fuck no. But what the hell," he said, jacking back the charging handle on the Storm's receiver. "Six weeks ago, I'd have called this make-believe horseshit – bunch of mumbo-jumbo to shake up the yokels. And now here I am, half of a crack assault team getting ready to ambush a lair of the undead. How's that for a movie plot, huh?"

I grinned in spite of it all. *Crack assault team?* "Sounds like one I'd pay to see."

I couldn't see much of his face beneath the balaclava, but I could tell from the gleam in his eyes that some part of him was having way too much fun. "Saddle up, sister," he drawled with a bad John Wayne twang. "Time to lock and load."

I rolled my eyes, but the smile never left my face. "You've been waiting a long time to say something like that, haven't you?"

He chuckled softly. "Are you kidding? I've been waiting my whole *life* for that."

I reached into a box in the trunk and retrieved our makeshift firebombs stuffed into a heavyweight plastic bag. I handed three to Tommy with an orange Bic lighter and stuffed three more into the leg pockets of my cargo pants. The gas-soaked wicks bled onto the fabric a bit, but smelling like a filling station was the least of my worries at the moment. I made sure my fully fueled Zippo was in my right front pocket where it belonged and then held my fist out to Tommy. "Dirty deeds…."

Tommy bumped my fist with his own. "Done dirt cheap."

I smiled grimly and motioned for us to move out.

Twenty-One

WE ARRIVED AT THE FRONT of the old school building, a dramatic triple marble arch structure that faced out onto Minerva Avenue. A quick check showed the main doors were still boarded up tight – they must have been using one of the two alternate entrances to go in and out. Those entrances were smaller, and the quarters would be tighter if it came to a fight, but our options were limited. The east entrance was closest to the gym, so we checked that one first. Sure enough, we found the plywood had only been propped up to *look* like it was still sealed, and we carefully moved the board aside and slipped inside the narrow entryway.

Before I even crossed the threshold, I felt the familiar tingle of power that confirmed we were in the right place. But the feeling was still sweeping and unfocused, with no single point that stood out from the ambient background energy that seemed to fill every nook and cranny of the place. Reaching up to activate an LED light set on a picatinny rail under the barrel of the Storm, Tommy pressed the carbine tight against his shoulder, sweeping the beam of light back and forth across the gloom and up the short, narrow stairwell that led to the main floor.

As we approached the stairs, a quick glance ahead showed that while the fire damage was severe, the floors themselves seemed stable enough. Lightning crashed and rippled across the sky through gaping holes in the ceiling high overhead and rain dripped steadily in the silent halls, but we didn't seem to be in immediate danger of having the ground open up beneath our feet and plunging into the sub-basement. I slipped the *wakizashi* from its scabbard, holding it out in front of me as we made our way slowly up the stairs that led from the small entry foyer to the first-floor landing.

I turned to Tommy, whispered harshly in his ear. "You stay glued to me, got it? Back-to-back the whole time. I don't want to feel your body pull away from mine for one second, you understand?"

"Jesus, Cherry," he said, the smirk I knew was on his face instantly recognizable in his voice. "Keep it in your pants, ya hussy. This is hardly the time to start getting frisky...."

I didn't even dignify that with a response.

"Spidey-Senses tingling yet?"

I shook my head. "Nothing. At least nothing close. Come on. Let's move."

We had just started to move away from the upper landing when I felt a sudden surge of energy and, with a loud thump, a bulky figure dropped from a beam overhead and landed in the narrow hallway twenty feet in front of us: *Carter.*

"Oh, lordy, lordy – if it isn't the Cherry Bomb herself," he said as he looked me up and down with ruby red eyes. "That was one hell of a show you put on the other night."

"Glad you enjoyed it," I snarled, pointing the tip of the sword straight at him.

"Hell, yeah, I did. I mean, *damn* girl, you got one fine set of–"

A single shot rang out, and Lester Carter's head burst like a water balloon. I watched in stunned silence as he dropped to his knees and then pitched forward onto what was left of the lower half of his face. His body twitched for just a few seconds and then lay still.

I slowly rounded on Tommy, who was just lowering the still-smoking barrel of the Storm towards the floor. "What the fuck was *that*, O'Connor?"

I could see him shrug. "You wanted to chat him up first? Besides, what can I say? I can't stand a man who doesn't know how to talk to a lady."

"Two seconds ago, I was a cheap hussy."

"Hey, I never said *cheap.*"

I smiled but shook my head. "That was way too easy. They knew he had no chance against us without the glamour. Leesy just wants to see what we brought to the party."

We cautiously approached Carter's body. Tommy nudged his shoulder with the toe of his boot. "I'd call that a successful test of the wightsbane rounds, though."

I nodded, kneeling next to the body for a moment. The edges of the wound were smouldering faintly, but there was no sign of tissue regeneration yet. "That it was. Come on," I said, motioning towards the corridor to our left. "Let's keep moving."

The gymnasium was through two sets of double doors and down a corridor to the left. Beyond the glass windows of the distant entryway, through a spider web of cracks and soot, I could see the soft, flickering glow of candlelight. I felt another strong crackle of power pass close by, to the right and behind this time. There was nothing but a food prep area that way, and we were standing in the only way in or out.

"Tommy," I hissed. "Cherry bomb."

He retrieved one from a pocket, held it up to the light from his rifle. The lighter I had given him finally caught on the third strike – the rain dripping through the roof was falling even heavier now – and he lit the fuse on what had once been his precious jar of imported mustard. I figured if it was gone, he might as well be the one to use it. "Where?"

I pointed down the corridor to the right into the kitchen area. Tommy gave it a hard underarm heave and it landed in the middle of the white tile floor. Instantly, the room filled with a blinding flash of light as the bottle burst and the flames spread across the floor. A banshee shriek echoed through the enclosed space, and a heartbeat later, Justin Hoefler appeared out of nowhere just a few yards away from us, fire licking at the sleeve of his shirt and one trouser leg. He was completely out of his mind, his eyes faded to pure, featureless white orbs. He ignored the flames and charged straight at us.

If he thought he was going to run me down to get to Tommy, he miscalculated badly. I took a step back, braced myself, and held the blade of the sword straight out in front of my body. Hoefler ran right into it. It punched through his sternum and came out through his spine. The effect of the poison-covered blade was immediate – his whole body froze, and the wound began bubbling with a foul-smelling black ooze.

I kicked out to drive Hoefler back and ripped the blade out of his chest. He staggered but stayed on his feet. *"Tommy, down!"* I shouted. I felt him slide to the floor behind me, clearing the way for me to take up a batter's stance – my samurai skills were clearly still a work in progress – aim, and swing for the fences. The blade passed through Hoefler's neck with barely a drop in forward momentum, and his head rolled from his shoulders and bounced across the floor. His body toppled straight back like a statue falling over, hit the ground, and lay still.

I stood there stunned for a long moment, and I could hear Tommy's rapid breathing at my back. He slowly rose to stand beside me again. "You okay?" he asked shakily.

I nodded, still trying to find my voice. I stepped forward and stamped out the flames flickering along the edges of Hoefler's clothing. We didn't need him going up like Karen Wagner just yet. As far as I knew, the corridor we were standing in was the only way in or out of the gymnasium, and I didn't feel like having our only escape route cut off by a fire burning at a few thousand degrees.

"Two down," Tommy whispered, his breath coming in short, shallow gasps. I think he was almost as scared as I was – it was just harder for him to hide.

"Two to go," I responded. I reached into another pocket and came out with a rag that I had smeared with the wightsbane mixture. After rubbing it along the sword to freshen the coating of poison, I gestured with the tip of my blade towards the soft light at the end of the corridor leading to the gym. "That way."

The next few yards were probably the most dangerous part of our journey. The corridor that led to the gym was narrow, windowless, and cramped. And undoubtedly Miranda Perez was waiting for us somewhere not far away. We'd been damned lucky so far. I was starting to wonder when the other shoe was going to drop.

We were halfway down the corridor when, without warning – no tingle, no prickle, no *nothing* – Miranda Perez dropped down from where she had been hiding among the exposed utility conduits overhead. She landed right on top of us, her feet striking my sword hand and sending the *wakizashi* clattering down the hallway out of reach. I went down hard, crashing into Tommy and causing his head to ricochet off the nearby brick wall.

He dropped straight to the ground, his eyes glassy and unfocused. As I hit the floor, I rolled over and looked up at Perez standing over his body, ready to pounce. I suddenly realized how she had managed to get so close without setting off my alarms. Though her eyes were the blank expanses of a grave wight under a master's control, I felt nothing from her. She had fed – and very recently – deliberately sacrificing the glamour for stealth. Like Karen, I had felt nothing though we had passed within a few feet of where she was hiding.

When she realized I was getting up, she shifted her attention to me and charged. I had only just cleared the pistol from its holster when she lashed out with one foot and swatted it out of my hand. It bounced off the wall next to Tommy and then she was on me, kicking and stomping like a crazed animal. She grazed the line of my jaw with a spinning roundhouse kick that would almost certainly have shattered the bones underneath into powder if it had connected. While she was still off-balance, I dropped to one knee and drove a punch into the area above her groin that was intended to drive straight through to the other side.

She crumpled up and fell to her knees. I crawled towards where the sword lay, my outstretched hand just brushing the pommel before she latched onto my left leg with both hands and dragged me back. I quickly rolled over onto my back and, taking careful aim, kicked straight out into the middle of her face, smearing that pert little nose of hers sideway across her cheek with the heel of my boot.

I pulled myself clear of her and finally got my hands around the grip of the sword. I scrambled to my feet and turned back towards Perez. She was on her knees staring up at me, a feral snarl further marring her battered features. I pointed the *wakizashi* straight forward and lunged, driving the blade though the middle of her forehead. She fell forward and began flopping and thrashing wildly, so much so that I lost my grip on the blade, which seemed firmly lodged in her skull. The seizure went on for what seemed like an eternity before she finally lay still, her head propped up at an odd angle by the handle of the sword.

I ran to Tommy's side. He was just getting to his feet. "You okay?" I asked, steadying him as he swayed.

He nodded, reaching up to pull the balaclava off. He gingerly probed the back of his head, and when his fingers came away, I could smell blood on them. "Guess I should have worn the helmet after all…."

"How bad is that?" I asked.

"Just a split, but I'm a bleeder so it looks worse than it is. She rang my bell pretty good, but I'm all right."

I glanced over my shoulder towards the gym. "You wanna sit this round out?"

He stared me straight in the eyes before bending down and retrieving the Storm from where it had fallen to the floor. "Cherry, if you think there is *any* fucking way I'm letting you walk in there alone, *you're* the one who needs their head looked at."

I grinned. "Well, all right then." I turned and walked over to where Perez was still lying face down. I kicked her over partially onto her back, put my boot on her throat, and yanked the sword out of her skull with a wet squelch. I turned and faced O'Connor, who handed me the pistol he had recovered. "Come on, Tommy. Let's finish this…"

#   #   #

Annaliese sat at half-court of the old gymnasium – crisscross-applesauce as we used to say when we were kids. Her eyes were closed, and she was dressed in the same pristine, flowing white satin dress that I had seen her in at the cemetery. Now that I had the chance to really look at it, it *was* strangely reminiscent of the nightgown she had worn the night we were taken by Reginald Hargrove. Minus the neon vomit, of course. I wondered briefly if the resemblance was deliberate, an attempt to stay my hand if and when it came to blows.

Candles burned in a dozen places around the gym, filling the space with a shifting, ethereal glow that caused shadows to dance like black spirits moving all around the room. At the far end under an old basketball goal,

I could see a man's body lying spread-eagled on the floor, surrounded by a circle of power painted in what my nose told me was human blood. It was already crackling with pent-up energy collected over the past several hours as the full moon made its slow pass overhead. With midnight fast approaching, the power had reached such intensity that the prickling of my skin was almost painful and the hair on the back of my neck was standing on end. About halfway between Leesy and the prone figure on the floor, I could see a petite, slender woman securely tied to a heavy chair: *Kennedy.* She appeared to be out cold.

But Kennedy wasn't alone. Another still form was lying on the floor of the gym, splayed out at the base of the wall nearest Annaliese. The barely detectable scent of perfume reached through the miasma of blood and corruption to seize my heart in an icy grip: *Oscar de la Renta....*

Fighting a rising panic, I slipped quickly into the room, Tommy just a few steps behind. He slid to my right, keeping the carbine trained on my sister. As soon as we moved in, Leesy's eyes snapped open. In the dim candlelight, I could see they were vacant white marbles – no irises at all.

"Tommy," I whispered harshly, jerking my chin towards the inert figure on the floor against the wall. "Don't do anything sudden. She's got Momma, too."

I heard his sharp intake of breath, could hear the tightness in his voice. "*Fuck....* Cherry, is she – "

"I don't know. But don't let Annaliese anywhere near her."

Annaliese's icy gaze focused on me, and her mouth split into a wide, feral smile. "Jesus, Char, I thought you'd never get here. Midnight's coming and I was afraid you'd miss the show." She turned and glanced back towards where the ritual tableau had been laid out. "Won't be long now, and the very last of your friends will be dead because you failed them."

She's in her right mind, or close enough. How is that even possible? She should be a raving maniac by now.... "What the *fuck* are you doing here?" I snapped, staring at her down the length of my blade.

She lifted her chin, sniffed the air. "Wightsbane?" She shook her head, clicking her tongue. "That's hardly fair play, sis."

"Was it fair play when you snatched innocent people off the street and turned them into monsters?"

"And look how you butchered those same citizens out there in the corridors. Shameful, really. Don't you consider yourself to be the 'good guy' in all this?"

"I asked you a question – why are you *here?*"

She ignored me, turned to look at Tommy. "And who is this? A gentleman suitor, perhaps?" Her voice sounded like we were back sitting around the little table in her bedroom, having a goddamned tea party.

I glanced over at my partner for a split second. "Him?" I scoffed derisively. "Are you *nuts?* He's expendable – hired help."

She laughed, a high-pitched girlish giggle that was terrifying in its innocence. "You're still such a terrible liar, Charlotte. You wouldn't let just anyone come along on this suicide mission. He's somebody you trust to cover your back, who knows who and what you are. He clearly means *something* to you." She giggled again, the sound sending shivers up my back.

My head was starting to spin. Too much was happening, and my exhausted brain was struggling just to keep up. "How the hell are you still *talking* to me like this? Shouldn't you be pure revenant by now?"

She smiled coyly. "Still wallowing in ignorance, I see," she said, shaking her head. "There's so much you don't know, Charlotte. So much you could have learned from a true Master – someone who can delay the onset of the madness with a single word. Not forever, of course, but long enough to be useful at times."

"*Your* master??"

"Mirsad. The man Hargrove enslaved me to in exchange for the knowledge he needed to bring *your* sorry ass back from the grave." She shook her head again, turned her attention back to Tommy. "You know, I took the old broad over there because I thought *she* was the last person left you still cared about, and I *wanted* you to watch her die. But it seems I've missed one, haven't I? So now after I've fed on her, I guess I'll just gut him like I did Mike and scatter his innards around like confetti!"

Momma's still alive.... A wave of relief ran through me, but it was short-lived. I did my best to keep her attention. "You really think he means *anything* to me?"

"I know he does."

With a lightning-fast movement, I reached up with my right hand and seized Tommy by the neck with an iron grip, my fingers wrapping around the bare skin above his collar. As I lifted him off the floor, he instantly went rigid, and I held him there for a long moment before tossing his inert form across the gymnasium. He skidded across the worn hardwood floor, sliding through the dust and debris before eventually coming to a stop against the far wall almost thirty feet away.

"Still think so?" I asked, staring straight into her featureless eyes.

Annaliese watched impassively for a moment before slowly rising from the floor. I thought she would move towards where Tommy's body lay, but instead she moved to my left and began to circle me, slowly spiraling in to close the distance between us. I moved with her, trying to insert my body between her and the others.

Lowering the sword, I quickly raised the little pistol and drew a bead on her chest. "What the *hell* is wrong with you, Leesy?"

Her eyes widened with a dreadful fury. "Don't call me that!" she shrieked, her voice suddenly ragged and torn.

"I've *always* called you that. After Mom died, you wouldn't let us call you anything else. So, what *am* I supposed to call you now?"

"Doesn't really matter. This conversation won't last long."

I shook my head in confusion, unable to reconcile the sweet, precocious little girl I had known with the cold-blooded murderer who was circling me now like a shark, moving almost imperceptibly closer with each step. "What the hell are you trying to prove here? Was there a point to all of this – the killing, the games?"

"You used to like playing games when we were little. But then you *changed*," she said softly. She giggled again. "Then again, haven't we all?"

"What do you mean, I *changed?*"

"You used to be *happy* spending time with me. We ran around outside and swam in the neighbor's pool and played Barbies in your bedroom. But then all that went away. Mom was gone, and the only thing that mattered in your life was *you*. You and those vapid whores you used to hang out with."

"I grew up, Leesy. I grew older. I couldn't help the fact that we were born so many years apart."

Her face twisted and changed, becoming something even less human than it had seemed only a moment ago. "And you never *tried*."

"That's not true. You were–"

"I was *nothing* to you. I was *less* than nothing to you. I was a burden. One you couldn't be bothered with anymore. I needed you, Charlotte. I needed you to listen. I needed you to care." Her face twisted into a mask of rage. "I needed you to save me from that bastard Hargrove. From Mirsad. To keep me from being taken and tortured and broken for *years*, Charlotte. *Years!*"

Her ranting was becoming unfocused now and time was growing short. "Why did you come back here?"

"The Master sent me, of course."

"So, you're just following orders, huh?"

"*Orders?*" She giggled maniacally. "When Mirsad decided you needed to be dealt with, I *begged* him to let me come. To let *me* be the one to do it. And he was only too happy to oblige. I think he found it rather… *poetic*."

"You *asked* him to come for me?"

"Of course, I did," she snarled furiously. "Don't let these pretty eyes fool you, Char. I'm not under anyone's *control* right now but my own. And if you were going down, sis, then by *God* I was going to be there to twist the knife."

"But what does Mirsad want with me? Fuck, how does he even know I *exist?*"

"Don't flatter yourself – Mirsad knows many secrets people think belong to them alone. Sad truth is, this isn't even about you, really. Not particularly"

"So why–"

"The only thing special about you, Charlotte, is that you aren't under *anyone's* control. And the idea of a grave wight roaming free without a Master's guiding hand – it's just not something Mirsad is comfortable with. The danger a creature like you poses to our… *way of life* is far too high. Someone so reckless and idiotic simply cannot be permitted to jeopardize everything we've built." She scoffed derisively. "You're just not worth it."

I had no idea what she was talking about. She was talking as if there were grave wights everywhere, some sort of thriving sub-culture of the undead. How could I not know that? How could I have spent the last quarter-century as one of them, and had never even so much as crossed paths with another being like me? That just wasn't possible. *Was it?*

"Why didn't you just destroy me then? I'd have *never* seen it coming. Why did you have to hurt all these other people? *Innocent* people."

She laughed maniacally, her blank eyes glittering in the shifting light. "Mirsad just wants you taken down. But I wanted you taken *apart*. Gutted and stripped of everything you loved. When I was done, I wanted you begging me to finish you off. You're already dead, sis. I wanted *more*."

I choked down a sob, dragging my sleeve across my eyes. "And what happens *after*?" I cried, trying to keep my voice from trembling. "Once you've restored balance to your little world?"

"Then I'll return to him. As I must. I intended to take the others back with me as well, but you went and royally screwed *that* plan all to hell."

My voice was becoming far more ragged and broken than I wanted or expected it to be. "You don't have to do this, Annaliese. It doesn't have to be this way. I can help you —"

"Little late, sis. I needed your help thirty years ago. Now, the only thing I want from you is your *life*. Or what's left of it anyway." As she spat the last words at me, I noticed for the first time that she was keeping one hand low to the side, and every now and then the candlelight would glint off a thin folding blade nearly the length of her forearm.

I swallowed hard. I knew that knife — I had seen it in Mike's mind. "That's quite a toy you've got there," I said, jerking my chin towards the blade at her side. "That's the same one you used to kill Uncle Mike, right?"

She slowly raised it up, turning it over in her hand and admiring the gleam of the candlelight off the etched steel, grinning like the Cheshire Cat. "Recognize it, do you? Oh man, that was my *pièce de résistance*, don't you think? Setting it up so that *you* were the one to actually end 'Uncle' Mike's life? God, that was delicious." She held the knife up in front of her. "It really is beautiful, isn't it? It's called a *navaja*. It was a gift from Mirsad when he sent me on my way."

The blade itself was thin and relatively short, probably less than six inches long, and turned up at the tip a bit like a hunting knife. But the handle was what made the weapon unique. It was round and long – at least as long as the blade – and curved gently near the middle. The pommel bent yet again near the end and was adorned with a flourish of intricate metalwork, like the tail of a rattlesnake. "I've never seen anything like it."

"I'm not surprised," she said, still maintaining that innocent, childish tone even as she tested the edge of the blade with her thumb. "It's a traditional fighting knife among the Roma in the south of Spain. This particular one is over two hundred years old. They used to call them *santólios*, after the oils they used to administer Last Rites. Care to venture a guess as to why?"

"Not really."

"Because if you found yourself up against a *navaja* in a fight, you always ended up needing a priest." She looked up at me, just a few feet away now, vacant eyes seeming to shine with a cold light of their own. "How about you, Charlotte? Been to church lately?"

She moved fast – much faster than I expected. And for the briefest instant – staring down the barrel of the little pistol at my erstwhile baby sister – I froze. Then she was on me before I could react, leaping into the air and driving both feet straight into my chest. I went down hard, and the back of my head slammed into the ground with enough force to leave me wobbly and disoriented for a split second. The pistol and the sword clattered away, and she pressed her advantage.

She rushed at me as I regained my feet, the razor-sharp blade whispering through the air in a scythe-like sweep. I jumped back, the tip of the knife ripping open the front of my shirt just below my ribcage. My boots came down on the blade of the *wakizashi*, and I fell to the ground again, groping for the handle of the sword. But she kept coming, and that moment of inattention as I scrambled for a weapon was all she needed.

She jumped straight up into the air and landed on my chest with both knees, driving me hard into the ground, my ribs crunching under the impact. She slid back, straddling my legs as she drove the knife so deep into my lower belly, I felt it punch out though my back and into the wooden floor beneath me. Then, with an excruciating slowness, she began to move the blade diagonally across my body, tearing a gap that ran from my left hip to my navel, the exposed tip digging a splintered furrow in the gymnasium floor.

She stared down at me, eyes wide and wild, a manic grin twisting her lips. "And now I want *you* to feel what it's like to be torn open – to have everything inside you ripped out," she snarled, her face a contorted mask of revenant fury. "The way I felt when you abandoned me. When you abandoned Dad. When you let both of us *die*."

An anguished cry escaped my lips. The pain was almost unbearable. "I didn't *let* any of that happen," I shrieked. "I wasn't even–"

She suddenly paused. "Oh, Jesus Christ, Charlotte," she said, her voice dripping with contempt. "Just shut the fuck up and take it like a grown-up, would you?"

She ripped the blade out of my belly and raised it high overhead, clearly intent on driving it down through my skull. I knew a moment after she pulled it back out, my mind would be gone, leaving me helpless and confused while she slowly sawed my head from my neck.

Just as the blade reached its apex, the silence in the gym was shattered by a single gunshot, the sound deafening in the enclosed, echoing space. Leesy's head snapped back, and when she brought it forward again, I could see a neat hole in the middle of her forehead. The entire back of her skull had exploded, sending a gout of clear fluid and brain matter raining down across my legs. Both arms dropped to her side, the *navaja* bouncing across the floor. Her eyes were open but completely vacant – I saw absolutely nothing of her consciousness remaining there.

I glanced to the right, saw Tommy down on one knee, a small revolver in his hand. I quickly scuttled out from beneath what had once been my baby sister, her mindless body still on its knees, swaying slowly from side to side.

Tommy moved up alongside me, helped me get at least up onto my elbows. "You all right?"

I winced and managed to nod hesitantly. I could see the tear in my lower abdomen, the shiny grayish-pink mass of my intestines bulging through the gap in the flesh. "Yeah, I think so," I said through gritted teeth. "For somebody who just came within a few seconds of being gutted like a catfish."

Tommy examined the wound. I was afraid he'd get sick or lose it, but he surprised me by barely reacting at all. I guess he'd seen worse. We both had. "She didn't poison the blade, did she?" he asked.

I shook my head. "Doesn't feel like it. I think she planned to finish me off slowly once I couldn't fight back anymore."

"Just don't move, okay? We've got to find something to bind this up so you don't dump your guts in the floorboard of my car." He glanced back towards where Leesy still knelt, her mouth open, eyes vacant and glassy. "I'm sorry, Cherry. I didn't want to shoot, but–"

"No," I said quickly. "You did what you had to do. Another second and *I'd* be the one with a hole through my head."

He showed me the revolver he held. It was the smallest handgun I had ever seen. "Five-shot Ruger LCR. Backup for my backup – I grabbed it on our way out the door. The rounds are just plain hollow points – no wightsbane." He tilted his head towards Leesy. "Which means that headshot will heal. We can take her with us, try to –"

"No, Tommy," I muttered, shaking my head as I stared at her in dismay. "*Whoever* that is, it's not my Leesy anymore. My sister died a very long time ago. And as long as Mirsad is alive, she can never be herself again. Hell, even if she *was* freed, she would never be able to live with the things she's done. *I* couldn't. I wouldn't want to try."

He grasped my hand. "I'm sorry."

"Me, too," I said, my eyes suddenly stinging. I shook it off, looked him up and down briefly. "*You* all right?"

He nodded. "A little battered, but the body armor helped. That was quick thinking, tossing me aside like that and focusing her attention solely on you."

I managed a weak smile. "Is that what I did? I thought I was just getting you the hell out of my way before you fucked something up and got me killed. *Again.*" I turned to look up at him. "So, you got the message when I latched on?"

He nodded. "Stay still. Stay down. Stay quiet. Only act if there's no other choice."

"I wasn't entirely sure that would work, you know. I can *read* people with a touch, but I've never tried *sending* a message before."

"Well, it came through loud and clear. Although I'd appreciate it if next time you included a warning about throwing me halfway across a gymnasium before you actually go and *do* it."

I managed a pained grin. "I'll try to keep that in mind."

He turned towards Leesy again. "So, what do we do now? Patrol units will be here any minute. Somebody had to have heard those shots fired, even with the thunderstorm for cover."

I fixed his gaze with mine, my eyes starting to fill with tears I had no hope of holding back. I finally forced myself to glance back at Annaliese. "She's not going anywhere," I said, my voice breaking. "Go find me something to bind this wound up with."

He rose and darted back the way we came at nearly a dead run. He was gone for longer than I expected, and when he returned, he appeared carrying what looked to be Justin Hoefler's scorched trousers. He dropped to one knee and started to help wrap them around my midsection. "Sorry about this – I couldn't find anything else that would be long enough to cover you."

Once we had the legs of the pants wrapped twice around my belly and double knotted, I motioned for Tommy to help me to my feet. He seemed unsure, but I nodded firmly. He reached down and took hold under both of my arms, gently lifting me up until I was standing beside him, leaning against him for support. As I steadied myself, he handed me the pistol I had lost in the fight, and I slid it back into the holster at my side.

I reached into the right-side pocket of my cargo pants, came out with a single glass jar of gasoline that had somehow survived the attack unbroken. I held it in my hand – staring down at it vacantly, swirling the contents around, testing the heft – before with an almost lazy flick of the wrist, I tossed it high into the air and watched as it came crashing down onto the ground where Annaliese knelt, the contents splattering all over the floor and soaking the front of her white satin gown.

I stood there for another long moment, tears pouring down my cheeks, my body wracked with quiet sobs. Finally, I reached into another pocket, drew out a crumpled pack of cigarettes and my Zippo. I tucked one between my lips and lit it with hands that shook terribly, snapping the lighter closed. I took one long drag, held it for a long moment, and released the smoke into the still, stifling air. I limped two steps towards Leesy and, taking the smoldering cigarette between my thumb and middle finger, I flicked it into the puddle of fluid that surrounded her.

Instantly, her entire body was engulfed in flames. There was no thrashing about, no screaming – just an incredible blast of intense heat that sent both Tommy and me staggering several steps back away from the inferno. I stood and watched my sister's body burn for a moment before finding my voice. "Gather up what's left of the others," I said softly, a whisper barely audible over the roar of the flames. "We'll throw them on the pyre, too."

Tommy hesitated, looking around the room. "A fire that intense is going to bring this whole building down."

"I know. And by the time it burns out, there won't be a goddamned thing left for the CSU guys to find. Just make sure you recover the brass from the shots you fired."

I limped over and bent down carefully, retrieving Leesy's blade from where it had fallen and handing it to Tommy. "Check on Momma and cut Kennedy loose."

He rushed to Wanda's side, checked her pulse before smiling at me. She was starting to come around, muttering under her breath in a constant stream of Creole curses. Tommy patted her cheek before hurrying over to Kennedy, cutting the ropes that bound her to the chair and setting her free. He carried her out the nearby fire exit, then returned to do as I'd asked. He headed down the hall again, returning first with Miranda Perez tossed over his shoulder. He lowered her down until she was cradled in his arms and, moving as close to the flames as he dared, he tossed her body into the blaze. The second trip, he came back dragging Hoefler's headless corpse with one hand, the lower half having been stripped to the underwear to fashion my bandage. Hoefler's head dangled from his other hand. These, too, were consigned to the flames. He finally entered the gym with Lester Carter across his shoulders in a fireman's carry. But by now the exhaustion was clearly taking hold, and he barely managed to avoid falling backward into the fire himself as he let the body drop.

The blaze burned with a sun-like intensity now and began spreading rapidly across the old hardwood floor. He supported me as we hobbled over towards the door where he had taken Kennedy. Wanda was on her feet already and was tottering towards the exit herself.

"You okay, Momma?" I asked, grimacing in pain.

She nodded, smiling weakly. "I'd say I've been worse, but that would be a bald-faced lie. I'll make it – don't you worry yourself over me, *cher.*"

Tommy reached the door first and had just pushed it open when out of the corner of my eye, I caught a flash of movement. We all turned toward the back wall of the gym where the body still lying in the power circle – in the light of the blaze I recognized it now as Robert Zuckerberg – was slowly sitting up, eyes white as snow, an unearthly howl rising in his throat. *Midnight... motherfucker!* In a flash, the revenant rose to his feet and shot towards Tommy at incredible speed.

Without a second thought, I reached down to my hip, drew out the pistol, and fired one round that entered Zuckerberg's right eye socket and exited behind his left ear. His momentum carried him several steps forward, but he quickly fell forward onto his face and skidded to a stop at our feet.

For a moment, nobody moved or spoke. Then, without a word, Tommy leaned me against the door frame, took Zuckerberg by his outstretched hand, and wearily dragged his body into the rapidly widening circle of flame. He watched for a moment to make sure it caught fire, then returned to my side, pausing to pick up the spent casing from where it landed on the floor.

We staggered outside and Tommy knelt down, lifting Kennedy into his arms once again from where he had gently laid her in the weeds. Leaning against each other for support, the three of us began limping across the parking lot as fast as we could under the circumstances. He managed not to drop Kennedy, and with Wanda's help I managed not to drop my intestines. With the sound of fire engines approaching in the distance, gradually overriding the occasional crash of lightning and the deep bass rumble of thunder, we slowly made our way through a driving rain back to the car and began the short drive back to Tommy's house.

Epilogue

EVEN WITH THE RAIN, THE fire department was unable to bring the fire at the old elementary school under control until almost dawn, by which time the gymnasium addition had collapsed in upon itself and most of what had survived the last fire had been destroyed. Somehow, the outer brick walls still managed to stay standing, and in the weeks that followed calls would come from the surrounding community once again to save the historic landmark. But I held out little hope that would happen. In fact, I found myself praying that it wouldn't. As beautiful and historic as the old building was, I wanted nothing more than to see it razed, its very foundations ripped from the earth, and the ground salted as a ward against the return of the evil that had dwelt there, if only for a very short time.

After the events at the school, no more bodies turned up with strange burns or under inexplicable circumstance, so it seemed we truly had destroyed the noxious weed that had sprouted in the City of St Louis in the blistering hot summer of 2023 – root, leaf, and stem. Nothing in the way of incriminating evidence was ever recovered from the school building and – as it had in 2014 – the fire was written off to a lightning strike. I found it hard to believe that the fire marshal found nothing amiss in a blaze that had burned so hot and fast that it had carved a hollow in the earth in the center of the old gymnasium five feet deep and twenty feet wide, but if he ever suspected anything, not a word of it was ever spoken to the press.

Kennedy had gone home to Chicago with Wanda's help and some

money I had given her, her memories scrambled through the use of my powers just enough so that she remembered little, if anything, of the time she had spent in Leesy's tender loving care, or even of me. I silently wished her the best and prayed that the memories of whatever she endured over those dark days never found their way to the surface again, even in the worst of her nightmares.

In the meantime, I returned home and, eventually, to The Daily Grind when it finally re-opened. The drive-through was finished, although the Village was still dragging their feet on issuing the special-use permit. But Vic would get his way eventually – the owner of a club that brings as much money into a community as The Daily Grind almost always wins out in the end.

The crowds were slow coming back – not surprising given what had happened there just a few weeks ago. But each night that passed saw a few more people come through the door, and every weekend the crowd grew just a little bit larger, a little less reserved. Soon things would be back to normal. Or so I hoped.

I hunted a lot that first month, walking the most dangerous streets in town wearing very little in the way of clothing, until eventually I was jumped in an alley behind a grocery store ten days before the next full moon. I left the would-be rapist tucked underneath a dumpster and made my way back home to my apartment, the hunger sated again for another cycle.

Tommy and I saw little of each other for quite some time after the events at the school – hardly talked at all. We agreed it was probably better to lay low for a while. More than a month passed, and the first hints of an early autumn had begun to add a welcome chill to the air each night as I left the club and made my way on foot to the Metrolink station.

But one Saturday, just after midnight, I was leaving the club early – the customers were still finding their way back, and tips had been hard to come by. I was almost halfway across the lot when I heard the familiar cackle and gurgle of a Mustang firing up. I stood and watched as the car eased away from where it was tucked against the security fence and headed my way.

As it drew closer, I noticed there was no sign of the damage I had inflicted with the guardrail at the Grand Avenue exit. Tommy's precious Bullitt was as pretty as a picture once again.

The car drew up alongside me and – without the power windows Mike's Tahoe had – Tommy leaned across the passenger seat to throw open the door. "Give you a lift?"

I leaned down, eyed him with amusement across the interior. "Well, hello, stranger. Where the fuck have *you* been? Haven't heard from you in weeks."

He nodded. "It's been busy."

"So you're back to work?"

"Yeah, they didn't really drag that out too much. I was back on duty the week after the school, and they let me sit for the exam not too long after that."

"*Exam?*"

He pulled aside his jacket, showed me the shiny new Detective Sergeant's badge clipped to his belt.

"Nice," I said. "Congratulations. I'd say it's definitely well-deserved, even if you and I are the only people who know why."

He shrugged. "I had one hell of a teacher."

"Yeah," I said with a rueful smile. "We both did."

He grinned. "Come on. Get in. There's something I need to talk to you about."

I rolled my eyes but slid into the passenger seat anyway. I noticed Jerry watching me from the entrance to the club and shot him a friendly wave to let him know everything was okay. For his part, Tommy popped the clutch and tore out of the lot, slinging gravel the whole way.

"Hey, O'Connor?" I asked, as he turned onto the main road.

"Yeah?"

"You didn't by chance happen to say… *wander* into the club at some point tonight while I was performing, did you?"

He shook his head firmly. "Oooooh no – absolutely not."

I grinned. "Good. Because – just for the record – if I ever catch you in there while I'm working, I will straight up *end* you. *Capisce?*"

"*Capisce*," he said in his best Corleone accent.

As he merged out onto the interstate, he reached into the back seat and handed me a heavy, oversized manila envelope.

"What the hell is all this?" I asked.

"Take a peek."

I fiddled with the little metal tabs until I got the flap to open, then drew out the massive stack of papers inside. "You want to give me the bullet points or are you gonna make me read the whole fucking thing?"

"Those, Charlotte Baum, are the papers officially establishing the Charles Andrew Baum Memorial Trust."

"The *what?*"

He grinned. "I got a call from Mike's attorney a week ago. Turns out his will directed all of his retirement savings, his house, and the benefits from a pretty hefty life insurance policy towards the establishment of a memorial trust in your father's name."

I frowned, shook my head. "Why?"

"Well, mostly so he could leave everything he had to *you.*"

Now I was more confused than ever. "Tommy, 'Charlotte Baum' has been legally dead for decades. She can't *inherit* anything – she doesn't exist."

"No, but Thomas Liam O'Connor does. Mike named me the executor of his estate and sole trustee for the memorial fund. He must have made the final changes just before he died, once he'd seen enough to know I wouldn't leave you twisting in the wind."

"Which means what?"

"Which means that I now have sole control over Mike's entire estate. And that gives *me* the right to give it all to you. All in exact accordance with the detailed instructions Mike left behind."

For a long time, I could not speak. Unexpected and uncontrollable tears began spilling down my cheeks, and I couldn't seem to find my voice.

"Of course," Tommy continued, "everything will *legally* remain the property of the trust and under my control – you being deceased and all – but you can stay in the house free and clear for as long as you…. *keep going.* There was enough money there to establish an annuity that will pay the taxes, the utilities – everything. It's all yours." He wagged his head. "Minus a small executor's fee. I was entitled to take quite a bit more – five percent of the estate – but I only accepted enough to fix the damage to the car."

I laughed around my tears, a sob escaping my throat. "I suppose that's the least I owe you." I turned to stare at him. "Tommy, I don't know what to say. I just… thank you."

He shook his head. "Don't thank me. Mike set this up ages ago. If anything was ever to happen to him, he wanted to make sure you were taken care of."

By now we had crossed over the Musial Bridge into Missouri and made the wide turn onto Cass Avenue to head for my apartment. We rode the rest of the way in silence. I just cradled the papers to my chest and missed my Uncle Mikey terribly.

Finally, Tommy pulled up alongside the curb in front of my apartment. I turned and looked him in the eyes and smiled. On an impulse, I leaned over and kissed him quickly on the cheek. A tiny crackle of power passed between us and, as I pulled back, he stared at me, his gaze locked with mine. "Your eyes," he said softly. "Dark pink?"

I nodded. "Still looking for this month's lucky customer. But it's early. Something will turn up."

He paused for a moment. Something was obviously troubling him, but it took him a while to find the words. "Cherry," he said quietly. "You told me a while back that the only thing keeping you anchored to this world – keeping you from taking the easy way out – was Mike." He stared down at his hands for a long moment. "Well… Mike's gone. And this thing with your sister is settled. And –"

I touched his arm and smiled wanly. "I appreciate your concern, but there's no need to start worrying about me now, Tommy." I sighed, looked away for a moment. "It's true – there was a time when I had very little left to hang onto, to keep pushing me out of bed each day. To keep me from finally letting myself rest in peace." I glanced up, meeting his eyes again. "But things have changed. I have friends – *family* even, of a sort. And I meant what I said to you before – this Mirsad character made me what I am. And then he made me kill my sister. So… I still have a job to do – one that doesn't involve poles and pasties. That's about as much as anybody can hope for these days."

I smiled again and turned away, opening the door and stepping out into the cool evening air. I closed the door behind me, leaned back through the open window, and gave him a wink.

"See ya around, *Sarge*." I patted the windowsill and started to turn away.

"Hey, Cherry," Tommy called suddenly. I dropped down into the window opening again, watched as he reached into the back seat once more and came out with still another envelope. He stared at it uncertainly for a moment, then handed it over.

"What's this now?" I asked. This envelope was sealed. "The pink slip to your Bullitt?"

He tilted his head to the side, grinned. "Not likely. Just… you know, take a look at it tonight and give me a call tomorrow. Okay?"

I was more than a little bemused, but I nodded. "I will." I pulled back again, waved. "Good night, Tommy O'Connor."

He grinned. "Good night, Cherry Bomb." He turned away, shifted the car into first gear, and peeled away from the curb, leaving a long double streak of black burnt rubber behind.

I watched him go until the triple taillights faded out of sight, then turned and headed for the front door of my apartment. I climbed the stairs in the dark, feeling that now-familiar weariness beginning to spread throughout my body.

I fiddled with the keys for a moment before managing to get the apartment door open. Once inside, I tossed the pile of papers on the table and, leaning down into the fridge, snagged the last bottle of Guinness I had left. I popped the top off, took a long pull, flipped on the kitchen light, and dropped into a chair at the table.

I leafed through the documents from Mike's attorney for a while. Most of it went right over my head and the whole thing was still just a little too raw to muddle through without breaking down again. And the whole time I sat there, Tommy's sealed envelope beckoned silently.

Eventually curiosity got the best of me. I picked it up, slid a finger inside the flap, and ripped it open. Inside was a black and white copy of a police report. The name said Harold Turner, and a quick scan of his record showed him to be a repeat child sex offender. The file had a handwritten yellow Post-It note stuck to it that said Turner had been released from a mental health facility in Creve Coeur three days ago over the vehement protests of his parole office, the district attorney, and the families of his victims. His psych profile suggested a high likelihood of recidivism, but apparently his supervising physician had certified him as 'rehabilitated' – a dubious prospect at best and undoubtedly the result of a very large cash payment from Harold's wealthy family.

Huh, I thought, a cold smile tugging at the corner of my mouth. *The man of my dreams...*

I tossed the envelope aside to study the file in depth, and it landed on the table with a surprisingly heavy thump. Frowning, I snagged the envelope back, held open the top, and peeked inside.

A wide smile spread over my face as I reached in and pulled out the last thing left in Tommy's little care package.

A single Charm's Blow-Pop.

Cherry.

Of course...

Acknowledgements

THE BOOK YOU HOLD IN your hands is the culmination of a lifetime of wishes, hopes, and fifty years' worth of absent-minded daydreams. It would absolutely not have been possible without the unwavering love, support, and *infinite* patience of my beautiful wife and long-suffering partner for the last thirty-five years, Becky Wilburn.

Thank you to my beautiful children, Megan and Josh – I'm so proud of the incredible people you've become. You will always be my greatest creation.

Thanks, of course, to In Churl Yo and Jason Henderson of Castle Bridge Media who took a chance and gave me an opportunity I've been waiting my whole life for.

To my parents, Rich and Kathy, my eternal gratitude for fostering a love for reading and writing for as long as I can remember. And to my sister, Chris, who has always supported everything I've done.

A huge thank you to all my early readers, both for this book, the ones that preceded it, and the ones I haven't finished yet: Lance, Sam, Jamie T, Michelle, Dave, Mike, Jamie K, Angie, Stephenie, and of course Becky, Megan, and Josh.

Much appreciation to Amanda Rutter for her outstanding editing of the first draft of this book and for patiently listening to all my stupid questions and answering all my annoying emails for the past six years. This book would never have made it this far without you, and it certainly wouldn't have been the novel it ended up being.

Thanks to Christopher Morgan who provided invaluable advice and encouragement that helped me keep pushing to bring this book into being when it seemed on the verge of being shelved forever.

A special thank you to Bagpiper Dan Jackson at bagpiperdan.com for his unique insight and the detailed information that helped me (I hope) re-create an authentic St. Louis police department funeral service in all its somber beauty.

And finally, a huge thanks to you, the readers. As I grow older, I've really come to appreciate that time is an infinitely precious commodity, and I'm honored you chose to spend some of yours with this story.

CASTLE BRIDGE MEDIA RECOMMENDS...

If you liked this book, you might also enjoy reading the following titles from Castle Bridge Media available on Amazon or by order at your favorite book store:

Animal Charmer
By Rain Nox

Austinites
By In Churl Yo

Bloodsucker City
By Jim Towns

The Burning Gem
By Don Sawyer

THE CASTLE OF HORROR ANTHOLOGY SERIES
Volume 1
Volume 2: Holiday Horrors
Volume 3: Scary Summer Stories
Volume 4: Women Running From Houses
Volume 5: Thinly Veiled: The 70s
Volume 6: Femme Fatales*
Volume 7: Love Gone Wrong
Volume 8: Thinly Veiled: The 80s
Volume 9: Young Adult
Volume 10: Thinly Veiled: Saturday Mournings
Edited By Jason Henderson and In Churl Yo
*Edited By P.J. Hoover

Castle of Horror Podcast Book of Great Horror: Our Favorites, Top Tens and Bizarre Pleasures
Edited By Jason Henderson

Cherry Dark
By R.L. Wilburn

Dream State
By Martin Ott

Dominic
By Lee Guzman

FRENCH DECEPTION
A Forgery in Paris
By Janice Nagourney
A Forgery in Lyon
By Janice Nagourney

FuturePast Sci-Fi Anthology
Edited by In Churl Yo

GLAZIER'S GAP
Ghosts of the Forbidden
By Leanna Renee Hieber

Hellfall
By Jay Gould

Isonation
By In Churl Yo

JAYU CITY CHRONICLES
The Hermes Protocol
By Chris M. Arnone
Necropolis Alpha
By Chris M. Arnone

Junk Film: Why Bad Movies Matter
By Katharine Coldiron

MID-LIFE CRISIS THRILLERS
18 Miles From Town
By Jason Henderson
Lost Angel
By Sam Knight
Ties That Kill
By Deven Greene

Nightwalkers: Gothic Horror Movies
By Bruce Lanier Wright

THE PATH
The Blue-Spangled Blue
By David Bowles
The Deepest Green
By David Bowles

SURF MYSTIC
Night of the Book Man
By Peyton Douglas
Dark of the Curl
By Peyton Douglas

Yesterday's Tomorrows: The Golden Age of Science Fiction Movies
By Bruce Lanier Wright

Please remember to leave us your reviews on Amazon and Goodreads!

THANK YOU FOR SUPPORTING INDEPENDENT PUBLISHERS AND AUTHORS!

castlebridgemedia.com

www.ingramcontent.com/pod-product-compliance
Lightning Source LLC
Chambersburg PA
CBHW032033310726
48972CB00002B/649